W9-AWQ-497

# A SAMBA

*for*

# SHERLOCK

# A SAMBA

## *for*

# SHERLOCK

### JÔ SOARES

*Translated from the Portuguese*
*by Clifford E. Landers*

PANTHEON BOOKS *New York*

All rights reserved under International and Pan-American
Copyright Conventions. Published in the United States
by Pantheon Books, a division of Random House, Inc.,
New York, and simultaneously in Canada by Random House
of Canada Limited, Toronto. Originally published in
Brazil by Companhia das Letras, São Paulo, in 1995.
Copyright © 1995 by Jô Soares.

Library of Congress Cataloging-in-Publication Data

Soares, Jô.
[O Xangô de Baker Street. English]
A samba for Sherlock / Jô Soares: translated from the
Portuguese by Clifford E. Landers.
p.    cm.
ISBN 0-375-40065-6
1. Holmes, Sherlock (Fictitious character)—Fiction.
I. Title.
PQ9698.29.0177X3613    1997
869.3—dc21                                      97-2944
CIP

Random House Web Address: http://www.randomhouse.com

Book design by M. Kristen Bearse

Printed in the United States of America
First American Edition
2  4  6  8  9  7  5  3  1

*This book is dedicated to my friends Rubem Fonseca,*
*Fernando Morais, and Hilton Marques,*
*who had the patience and affection to read it before publication.*

*And to Flávia, who read it still earlier,*
*over my shoulder.*

We are all more or less mad.

BAUDELAIRE

Humor is not a mood
but a way of looking at the world.

WITTGENSTEIN

I am grateful for the valuable and dedicated collaboration of the research done by Ângela Marques da Costa and Lilia Schwarcz. I also wish to thank Ricardo and Paulo Santoro, Affonso Romano de Sant'Anna, Edinha Diniz, Antônio Houaiss, Massimo Ferrari, João Lara Mesquita, José Bonifácio de Oliveira Sobrinho, Eliana Caruso, Walter de Logumedê, Israel Klabin, Max Nunes, Júlio Medaglia, and Maria Emília Bender. Not to mention the team at DEDOC: Juraci, Duncan, Luís Arturo, Pepe, Bizuca, Zulmira, Eliseu, Ferrão, and Jorgel Miguel, who were of such help in my early-morning consultations.

# A SAMBA

*for*

# SHERLOCK

# I

At three A.M., a few Negro slaves could still be seen carrying barrels filled with trash and excrement from the
whorehouses on Regente Street. Everything was stacked at a
nearby spot, creating yet another of the dunghill embank-
ments that dotted the landscape of the city of Rio de Janeiro in
that month of May 1886. Some of the slaves competed to see
who could most quickly make the largest pile, and banderoles
were implanted atop the filth when they saw that no more or-
dure could be accommodated there. Then the populace waited
for the rains, the natural drainage that would carry everything
out to sea, washing the streets and contaminating the city.
Once the storms passed, small perfumed handkerchiefs raised
to the nose would allow the wealthy and the noble to pretend
that the precarious drainage supplied by the City Improve-
ments Company was comparable to the enviable network of
sewers in Paris.

At the corner where Regente crossed Hospício Street, a pale
figure dressed in black, a wide-brimmed hat pulled over his
eyes, waits motionless for the final customers to depart. Despite the heat, he is wearing a cape that covers him to his an-
kles. Under the cape, which accentuates his thinness, is an
indistinct object which might be a package or a cudgel. A

young woman, almost a girl, tipsy from wine, comes out of the third whorehouse. Her red skirt is open at the side up to the hip and her breasts are exposed, for her thin, cheap yellow blouse had not withstood the voracious attacks of her drunker clients. Completely intoxicated, she is barely aware of the exhibition of her breasts. She looks for a less filthy corner to vomit in, and then laughs at her concern: "Since it's vomit, why not look for the dirtiest place?" Deep down, it's a matter of pure superstition. Even though it's vomit, it's hers, and it displeases her to see the fruit of her nausea added to the feces of others. She turns into a dark alleyway and contests with some large rats for the dubious honor of occupying the territory. She leans against the fence behind one of the bordellos and, her chin inside the house's backyard, awaits the disgorgement. As if it were all merely a well-rehearsed scene from *Grand Guignol*, the man in black leaps upon her, a dagger in one hand, and lays open her neck with surgical precision. Through the open gullet surges a cascade of blood mixed with the first outpouring of vomit that was already making its way through her throat. Without haste, the man kneels beside the young whore. With the knife he slices a twelve-inch flap of skin from the left side of the woman's torso and carefully stores it in the pocket of his frock coat. Rising, he finally reveals the object concealed under his cape. Neither a package nor a cudgel: a violin. He rips out a string, the *mi,* or E, and, lifting the young woman's skirt, coils the string torn from the tuning peg into the curly hair of the cadaver's pubis. Satiated, he leaves calmly down Regente Street, playing one of Paganini's twenty-one *capricci* on the instrument's three remaining strings.

∼

The audience, applauding excitedly, sensed it was experiencing an historical moment in Brazilian theater. For months the entire city had prepared itself to receive her, and the Imperial Theater of São Pedro de Alcântara, on Constituição Square, in the Rossio district, had been remodeled in anticipation of her arrival. The dressing room had been redecorated by Madame Rosenvald, of the House of Parasites, on Ouvidor Street, and enlarged following instructions sent ahead by letter from the actress's secretary. There was now a new set of armchairs, a sofa, and a chaise longue in green velvet *capitoné*. A screen separated this part of the room, where she would receive her visitors, from the smaller area where the actress changed clothes. On the stage, the dazzling, the unique, the eternal Sarah Bernhardt acknowledged in French the Brazilian applause. The *première*, the day before, of *Fédora*, by Victorien Sardou, had been a colossal success; however, tonight's *Camille* had not been without incident. The actor Philippe Garnier, in the role of Armand Duval, had committed the imprudence of appearing smooth-shaven, without the lustrous mustache hitherto characteristic of Marguerite Gauthier's lover. From the upper gallery, a few students essayed a boo, hurling lit cigarette butts upon the elegant folk who jammed the *fauteuils* of the parterre. Artur Azevedo had risen from his seat and proffered a vehement defense of the play, saying that la Bernhardt "represented France itself." The author had met Sarah in Paris, and it was he who had given her the title "Divine." At the end of the play, four small boys in livery came onstage bearing flowers from the emperor. Picked from the gardens of the imperial palace, they were in extremely good taste, save, perhaps, the enormous hydrangeas that comprised the bouquet brought from Petrópolis. The young romantics who had occupied the front rows rained on the Divine One a shower of camellias, the symbol of abolitionism, grown in the slave district of Leblon, and at the same time a less than subtle allusion to the primary vehicle associated with the world's greatest actress.

*"C'est pardonnable et c'est charmant..."* said la Bernhardt sotto voce to her colleagues onstage, who were holding back smiles as they attempted to dodge the pelting flowers. The curtain at the São Pedro descended for the twenty-third time.

*"Ça suffit,"* said Sarah, "otherwise we'll be here thanking them longer than we were to present the play. Alexandre would never forgive us," she concluded, referring to Dumas *fils*, author of the text.

Sarah and her troupe had arrived in Rio on the *Cotopaxi*, a few days earlier, on a Thursday, the 27th of May 1886. Despite its being one of the most pleasant months of the year, she complained of the heat, but was enchanted by the reception at dockside and further yet when students unharnessed the animals from her carriage and insisted on taking the horses' place, pulling the vehicle about the quay. Later, en route to the hotel, she requested that the coachman raise the top so she might better observe the landscape and the people crowding the streets for a glimpse of the Frenchwoman, but the Brazilian interpreter accompanying her intervened.

"No, madame. In Brazil it's not considered chic to travel with the top raised."

"Why not?"

"I do not know, madame. I think it's to give the impression that it's not all that hot here."

Now, she couldn't wait to return to her dressing room and remove her character's heavy clothing. At forty-two, she still looked like a girl and her energy was almost that of an adolescent, but the tropics are the tropics. She did not have a chance to do as she desired. At the dressing room door, surrounded by his retinue, Pedro de Alcântara João Carlo Leopoldo Salvador Bibiano Francisco Xavier de Paula Leocádio Miguel Gabriel Rafael Gonzaga, Emperor Pedro II of Brazil, awaited her. The sovereign had seen her on one of his trips to Europe and was one of the most fervent supporters of Sarah Bernhardt's coming to Rio. He had journeyed from Petrópolis especially for the *première*.

*"Vive l'empereur!"* she shouted from a distance as soon as the myth saw His Majesty, and those who heard could not detect if there was a touch of irony in the exclamation. Dom Pedro II flushed with pleasure. It was the first time he had received the greeting in French.

*"Et vive la reine du talent!"* rejoined the emperor.

The flatterers who surrounded him commented amongst themselves, pretending to speak softly, as if for Dom Pedro not to hear:

"What wit! What a riposte!"

In the dressing room, they sat on the new furniture that decorated the small room. Everyone was impeccably attired, in uniforms and gala dress. One could have thought they were installed in some Paris salon if not for the circles of sweat under every armpit. Sarah asked her secretary, Maurice Grau, for champagne while she went behind the screen and, aided by her dresser, removed pounds of drenched skirts and petticoats.

"I hope Your Excellency enjoyed the play."

"How not? I merely regret that our stages are not yet at the level of European theaters."

"Oh, *vous savez.* . . . A stage is a stage. What matters is what is put on them. . . . "

"In that case, today we had the greatest, the most beautiful, the most illuminated stage in the world," replied the emperor gallantly. "I only lament the absence of a good friend and probably one of your greatest admirers, the baroness of Avaré, Maria Luísa Catarina de Albuquerque. She speaks French like us and acted as a schoolgirl. The nuns said she had great talent. In one Christmas play staged by the Carmelites, she made the students' parents weep with her interpretation of an angel of the Lord."

"And what has prevented such a gifted spectator from coming to the play?" asked Sarah, taking a sip of champagne to conceal the sarcasm of the question.

"It happens that the baroness possessed an extremely rare violin, a Stradivarius. Her violin was stolen a few days ago, and since then Dona Luísa has been unable to reconcile herself to the loss. No pumpkin candy or slave's song can draw her from her profound melancholia. Her Negroes have commented that their mistress has *banzô*."

Sarah smiled, not understanding half of what was said.

"*Banzô?! Qu'est-ce que c'est?*"

"That's what the slaves call melancholia, sadness, madame. They miss Mother Africa. Imagine, some of them even die of *saudades.* As a matter of fact, *saudades* is an untranslatable word. It would be more or less like *avoir le cafard.*"

"What about the police? What do they say?"

"Unfortunately, the baroness Maria Luísa does not wish to involve the authorities. The violin was a gift from me, and, despite our friendship being purely platonic, the empress would not look kindly upon the story were it to appear in the newspapers."

"Then perhaps I can help you and your baroness," she said. "It so happens, Your Excellency, that I am very good friends with the greatest detective in the world: Sherlock Holmes. Naturally, Your Majesty has heard of Sherlock Holmes."

"I must confess my ignorance, madame. This is the first time I have heard that name."

"That's why I'm constantly telling his friend, Dr. Watson, to shake off his sloth and narrate the fantastic adventures of Holmes. Perhaps one day the good doctor will take my advice. Sherlock Holmes is the world's first deductive detective. He once found the missing jewels of a Russian singer after examining the clothes she had worn at a banquet offered for the emperor."

"For me?!"

"No, Majesty, Napoleon III . . . "

"I don't know any detectives," replied Dom Pedro, skipping over the small error. "Even though I do enjoy reading mystery stories. I don't know if Madame is familiar with the prose of Edgar Allan Poe. Poe created a fascinating character, a detective named Auguste Dupin. He appears in 'Murders in the Rue Morgue' and later in other stories such as 'The Mystery of Marie Roget' and 'The Purloined Letter.' I was quite impressed, because Dupin even succeeds in guessing what a person is thinking, solely through the use of deduction."

"Then I am certain that this fictional character cannot hold a candle to Holmes. I think he would love to see Brazil and would be unable to refuse an invitation from Your Majesty. In a short time he would find your friend's violin," concluded Sarah Bernhardt, emerging in her splendor from behind the screen, wearing a magnificent white dress. "And now, if Your Majesty will permit, a dinner awaits me at the Grande Hotel.

I'm dying of hunger. I don't eat before a performance and I'm mad to finally try Brazilian cuisine, about which I hear so much."

Having spoken, the actress extended her hand to the emperor, who kissed it respectfully. Everyone left the dressing room enchanted by the Divine One's charm. In a small notebook, Dom Pedro discreetly wrote down the detective's name.

## 2

The Grande Hotel was in the Catete district, on Marquês de Abrantes Street. Situated at the top of a small hill completely covered with gardens and groves of trees, it was the beneficiary of breezes from the ocean that could be seen in the distance. It was known for its spacious rooms and excellent service. Trolleys, ascending and descending beyond the entrance gate, afforded the hotel a romantic touch. The enormous dining room was decorated in the most refined taste: lace tablecloths from Ceará, huge candlesticks in the center of the table, Limoges dishes, Baccarat crystal, and heavy Christofle silverware in vermeil. Standing in wait around the table were several journalists and a few names from the city's literary bohemians. Present were the journalist Pardal Mallet, editor of the *News Gazette,* and the amusing Guimarães Passos, poet and archivist of the Household of the Royal Palace, one of the best-paid public servants in the empire. Passos was wont to say that he was a public servant but a private poet; a vested defender of the empire, he spent sleepless nights in the city's bars heatedly debating with his republican friends. Besides these two, Múcio Prado, editor and social chronicler of the *Journal of Commerce;* Belmiro de Almeida, creator of the recently launched magazine *Rataplan;* Eduardo Joaquim Correa, of the humorous newspaper *The Meddler;* Angelo Agostini, of the *Illustrated Review,* who unceasingly published cartoons caricaturing the emperor; and the millionaire dandy Alberto Fazelli, the son of Italian immigrants, who fancied himself irresistible. Considered the most sought-after fop in the city, Alberto had decided that he would die old and a bachelor, preferably in Paris. His friends mocked him, saying it would be better to live in Paris and die here. With the journalists were the young book dealer Miguel Solera de Lara, owner of the Aphrodite's Retreat bookstore, one of the meeting places of the city's intellectuals; the marquis of Salles, with heavy rings under his eyes and always dressed in black, a kind of *enfant gâté* of the court, an assiduous reader of his near-namesake the Marquis de Sade; and the famous tailor Salomão Calif, who clothed half the elegant population of the city, not to mention the plantation owners from São Paulo who would travel to the capital just to make use of his magic scissors. Also present was the owner of the hotel, Aurélio Vidal, with his friends, who filled most of the room. Curiously, no actors had been invited, and not a single woman was to be seen, save the Negro slaves who, with the other servants, would serve the dinner. The windows were open, displaying an incomparable view of the bay. At that time of year, four Negroes with fans were sufficient to cool the setting. Suddenly, one of the Negro boys who carried bags from the receiving area came running in.

"Mista Aurélio! Mista Aurélio! The lady is arriving!"

Over the head of the panting Negro lad, every male eye in the room caught sight of the marvelous Frenchwoman dressed in white. The boy nearly died of fright and ran rapidly back to the receiving area. Sarah Bernhardt stepped aside and let him pass. There was a pause, a beat of silence, and suddenly the entire room burst into frenetic applause: *"Bravo! Bravo!"*

*"Messieurs,* please! The performance is over and I'm hungry."

Everyone laughed and approached to observe at close range that phenomenon who had elected to grace Brazil's shores with her presence. The actress entered the room accompanied by her son, Maurice Bernhardt, a strikingly handsome young man of twenty-two. Maurice's father was the Belgian prince Henri de Ligne, with whom the actress had fallen in love while still young. Sarah had registered the boy with only her own name, as the son of an unknown father. The story of that romance is worthy of a melodrama. The prince, madly in love, had decided to marry the actress, then beginning her career. Henri's uncle, General de Ligne, like Duval's father in *Camille,* sought her out in Paris, without the prince's knowledge. In a polite but objective conversation, he made the actress understand that if the marriage were to come about, the prince would be immediately disinherited by the royal family, losing both his position and his patrimony. Her heart in shreds, Sarah Bernhardt left the prince, alleging that her career was more important to her. Prince Henri de Ligne never learned the true motive behind that painful separation.

If that night Sarah truly expected to experience the food of the country, she was to be disappointed. The menu, prepared by a French chef brought in especially for the occasion, copied to the letter that of the restaurants of Paris. Roland Blanchard had come to Brazil to make his fortune and had lived in the Botafogo district for many years. Sometimes he cooked for the emperor, and he had published a book of tips and recipes in which, among other things, he taught that one should not put on the platter a spoon that had previously been in the mouth. He further explained that, if a person felt an irresistible urge to spit, it was better to do so onto the floor than into the plate. On the menu that night were game, salads, fish, ham, cheeses, various wines, and champagne. Not even rice had been included to Brazilianize, however lightly, the French recipes. Sarah sat to the right of Aurélio Vidal, who occupied the place at the head of the table, with the marquis of Salles beside her, and across from Guimarães Passos. Seated beside the latter, Alberto Fazelli made every effort to get as close as possible, with his elbow almost in his neighbor's plate. The journalists immediately began their questions, transforming the dinner into a collective interview:

"What do you eat when you wake up?"

"Do you drink between acts?"

"What superstitions do you have?"

"What do you think of Brazil?"

"What shoe size do you wear?"

"How much do you weigh fully dressed?"

"And undressed?"

"It is true you can only memorize your lines while having a hot footbath?"

"How old are you?"

"What do you think of Brazilian men?" Alberto Fazelli asked lasciviously; he was not a journalist but was nevertheless impertinent.

"For the moment, I think only that they ask too many questions," said Sarah, emptying a goblet of wine.

To change the subject, Guimarães Passos interrupted these high-level questions:

"I trust you will forgive my colleagues' enthusiasm. I only regret that some of my friends were unable to come to the dinner. I'm sure you would love to speak with Olavo Bilac, who is an extraordinary poet. A pity he has yet to publish a book."

"Olavo Bilac?"

"Yes."

"And why did he not come?"

"Unfortunately, my friend Olavo took it in his head to become a republican and is in hiding at the moment. He published a small tract against the monarchy and is being sought by Mello Pimenta, of our police. Mello swore that Bilac will spend a night in jail. Do you agree that it's too soon for changes in our politics?"

*"Je ne me mêle pas de ces affaires . . . "* said Sarah, smiling.

"What did she say?" Pardal Mallet asked eagerly, from the other end of the table.

Alberto Fazelli translated as he had heard:

"She understands Mello has had seven affairs."

Múcio Prado, of the *Journal of Commerce,* quickly corrected:

"It's not quite that, Albertinho. She merely said she doesn't involve herself in these matters." And, taking advantage of the misunderstanding, he interjected a question: "I know that you were with our emperor. What can you tell us about the meeting?"

"Only that the emperor is very nice and is worried," the *comédienne* disclosed in a soft voice to the journalist. "Just think, they stole a Stradivarius violin from a friend of his, a baroness, who is disconsolate. I even suggested that he invite an English detective whom I know well, Sherlock Holmes, to unravel the mystery."

Múcio saw immediately that he had a good item for his column: baroness, friend of the emperor; it could only be Maria Luísa Catarina de Albuquerque. Until then, the only Stradivarius which he knew of in Rio was the extremely valuable instrument belonging to the violinist José White, the excellent Cuban musician who was an habitué of the court. Obviously, this other violin must have been a secret gift from Dom Pedro. Around the table, few took any notice of the information, perhaps because they had not understood the actress's rapid, whispered French, but the journalist knew that the *potin* would cause a small scandal in the court.

The food was so good that, despite the Divine One's presence, everyone fell silent around the table. When they were about to resume their questions after dessert, Sarah rose rapidly: "Gentlemen, everything was delicious, but tomorrow I have a rehearsal. Please, don't get up." Before anyone could help her, she stood up nimbly, allowing her napkin to fall to the floor. She left the room, light as a feather despite a full stomach, heading toward the stairs that led to her quarters.

Alberto Fazelli picked up the napkin, sniffed the cloth as if it were the lace handkerchief of his beloved, and declared profoundly, "That is what is known as taking French leave."

～

Police Inspector Mello Pimenta had, at the moment, greater worries than chasing after Olavo Bilac. The statement that he would oblige the poet to spend a night in jail had been more of a letting off of steam than a declaration of intent. In reality, there was no reason to pursue the "subversive" Bilac. Especially now, given the murder that he had begun to investigate. Mello Pimenta was short and fat, sporting a huge black beard *à la* Balzac. He suffered greatly from the heat, but nevertheless he was always to be seen in a suit with waistcoat, a shirt with a starched collar and stiff cuffs, very snug at the neck. Curiously, Pimenta never sweated. The policeman's corpulent appearance had deceived many a malefactor who underestimated his quickness: Mello Pimenta could run like a gazelle. Beside him, wearing a medical apron covered with coagulated bloodstains, was Dr. Saraiva, the state coroner. Extremely thin, Saraiva had a goatee and long white hair, also stained, for the coroner had the habit of absentmindedly scratching his head as he meditated over the autopsy he was performing. Seeing them side by side, it was impossible not to think of Don Quixote and Sancho Panza, his faithful squire. The two would meet at the morgue of the Third Order of Penitents, on Carioca Square. The police used the locale whenever the official morgue of the Santa Casa da Misericórdia, on Moura Square, was overcrowded with cadavers. Lying on the cold stone table, the body of the murdered girl was open, offering itself in even more obscene form than when she had practiced the oldest profession. She had been found by a Portuguese broom vendor crying his wares in the early hours: "Broooooooms! Duuuusters!" As soon as he entered the still-dark alley of Regente Street and sighted that horror, the poor man had dropped everything on the ground and run away screaming, "Oh, Jesus! It's Dantas' inferno, it's Dantas' inferno!" thus transporting pell-mell the Italian masterpiece to Iberian lands.

With the skilled hand of a professional of many years' practice—Saraiva had begun his career as an army doctor in the

Paraguayan War; according to legend, he had performed the autopsy on the Paraguayan dictator Solano López—the professor had made the classic incision, in the shape of a Y, exposing the young prostitute's internal organs. To Pimenta the ritual seemed useless, for the cause of death could only be the slashed throat, cut so deeply that the head had nearly been severed from the body. But to Saraiva, procedure was procedure. In a monotonous voice as he dissected, he discoursed to the inspector.

"By the advanced stage of rigor mortis, death must have occurred early the morning of Wednesday, the twenty-sixth day of May 1886. The victim appears to be between fifteen and twenty-one years of age. The body was found totally cold and bloodless. Lips cyanotic, pupils round and regular, bilaterally dilated. Liver damage, probably owing to excessive ingestion of alcoholic beverages. If she had not died from the murderous attack, the victim would in all certainty have been a candidate for early cirrhosis. The cause of death is the wound to the neck, which dilacerated the larynx and pharynx in a horizontal cut initiated from left to right. The injury was caused by a sharp instrument. It is clear from the pressure involved that the aggressor possesses great physical strength. A rectangular flap of skin approximately twelve inches by four inches was skillfully excised from the left side of the victim's torso, beginning with the uppermost sternal rib. The victim—"

Impatiently, Mello Pimenta interrupted: "Saraiva, we know all that. There's no detail that might have gone unnoticed in the first examination?"

"Of course there is. I've left the best for last." So saying, he placed in the inspector's hands the coiled violin string that he had found in the young whore's pubic hair.

"What's this?"

"I don't know exactly. It appears to be a string from a mandolin or some other musical instrument."

"At least it's a clue. A mandolin string."

"Or a ukulele, I'm not sure. Beyond any doubt it's from a musical instrument."

"Could the killer be a musician?"

"He might be and he might not be. From the violence of the crime and the place where I found the string, what I do know is that he's rather crazy."

"Why? Where was the string?" asked Pimenta suspiciously.

"Mixed in with the girl's pubic hairs. Poor thing, they were still quite sparse. . . . "

With a certain repugnance, Pimenta wrapped the string in a handkerchief and cleaned his hands on his own lapels. "May I take it?"

"Certainly, it's yours. Do you want me to wrap it as a gift?" laughed Dr. Saraiva, in a clear demonstration of the morbid sense of humor so common to his profession.

## 3

At 221 B, Baker Street, Sherlock Holmes had just served tea for himself and Dr. Watson. The doctor appeared totally absorbed in his newspaper.

"Two cubes, Watson?"

"Eh? Yes, please. . . . Strange. . . . Very strange. . . . "

"May I ask what is so strange?" said Holmes, handing him the cup and settling into his favorite armchair.

"As I read this news item, I experienced a curious sensation of déjà vu."

"Elementary, my dear Watson," said Sherlock Holmes, speaking the phrase that so irritated his friend.

"How so?"

"You are reading yesterday's *Times.*"

As Watson drew in his jaw, which had dropped, the door opened and Mrs. Hudson, the housekeeper, came in with a telegram. She was very excited.

"Calm yourself, Mrs. Hudson. I presume it is a message from Inspector Lestrade," stated the detective.

"You presume wrong, Mr. Holmes—it's a telegram from Brazil. From the emperor himself!"

"From the emperor of Brazil? Whatever can he want with you?" asked Watson, intrigued.

"I'll only know after reading it," replied Holmes. "Thank you, Mrs. Hudson. I see that despite doctor's orders you continue secretly eating eggs for breakfast."

Startled, the poor woman stammered with embarrassment: "That's true, Mr. Holmes. I can't resist them. . . . How did you find out?"

"Very simple, Mrs. Hudson. In your haste to ingest them, you allowed a speck of yolk to fall onto your blouse, causing a yellow stain. Thus I deduced that you disobeyed the doctor's orders."

The housekeeper looked abashedly at the collar of her blouse. "Well, Mr. Holmes, the truth is that what you call a yellow stain is a gold brooch, which belonged to my mother. But the odd thing is that I actually did have an omelet earlier this morning."

"Obviously. My deductions are always correct. It's your brooch that's wrong. You may go."

Quite reluctantly, the inquisitive housekeeper left, closing the door. Watson thought once again how silly was that great man's vanity in his refusal to wear glasses. Holmes went to the writing desk and opened the telegram with a knife that had been hurled at him some years before, during the hunt for a criminal in Spitalfields.

"Interesting, Watson. The emperor of Brazil, Pedro II, is inviting us to the capital, Rio de Janeiro."

"What? The capital of Brazil isn't Buenos Aires?" said the astonished Watson.

"No, Watson. Buenos Aires is the capital of Argentina."

"And what does the emperor of Brazil want with you?"

"It seems someone has stolen a Stradivarius violin from a friend and Dom Pedro is asking me to conduct a confidential investigation."

"How did he find out about us?"

"Not about us, my dear Watson. About me. Luckily for the emperor, my good friend, the great Sarah Bernhardt, is on a tour there."

"Fantastic! Then they have theaters in those parts?"

"Of course, Watson. Brazil is a peculiar country. It's the only monarchy in the Americas. The emperor is said to be a highly cultured man."

"I'm curious to understand how you know so much about this unusual empire," grumbled Watson.

The detective's culture was quite paradoxical. Holmes was capable of knowing details about foreign countries, geology, music, botany, chemistry, and anatomy while nonetheless remaining astonishingly ignorant of the theory of Copernicus and the makeup of the solar system. For Watson it was difficult to assimilate the fact of such a civilized human being of the nineteenth century having no knowledge that the earth revolved around the sun. At times this bothered him somewhat. Sherlock magnanimously patted the doctor on the shoulder.

"Don't sulk, my friend. I learnt these facts by accident. Through a Scottish-American intermediary whom I met in France."

"Who?"

"His name is Alexander. You don't know him."

"Alexander?"

"Yes, Alexander Graham Bell, inventor of that modern wonder, the telephone."

"I didn't know you got along with Americans," said Watson ironically, with a touch of pique.

"I was introduced to him six years ago. Do you recall when I went to Paris? Bell was there to receive the Volta Prize, fifty thousand francs, for his invention."

"You don't mean to tell me that Bell knows the emperor of Brazil?" continued the still skeptical Watson.

"Not only does he know him, Dom Pedro was also the first to use the telephone publicly, at the Philadelphia Centennial Exposition. Bell told me about it, laughing heartily. Unwittingly, he played a joke on him. Do you know what the first phrase was that he had the monarch speak when he tried the apparatus?"

"I'm sure I haven't the faintest idea."

"'To be or not to be, that is the question. . . .' And then the emperor added in astonishment, 'Good Lord! The thing talks!'" concluded the detective, chuckling at the incident. Then, pensive, he relit his pipe. "Perhaps this is a good opportunity to become acquainted with the country. . . . After all, Dom Pedro is a monarch of the highest lineage: Bragança, Bourbon, Orléans, Hapsburg; almost enough to provoke envy in our beloved Queen Victoria," stated Holmes, half-closing his eyes and blowing a puff of smoke in Watson's face.

"Well then, we'd better get our bags together. When you half-close your eyes and blow smoke in my face, it's a sign you're thinking of travel."

"Let's not be precipitous, Watson. First, see in that *Times* from yesterday when the next steamer is leaving for Brazil."

Watson opened to the page with notices of ship departures.

"Here it is. We're in luck. The *Aquitania,* of the Cunard Lines, is leaving tomorrow for South America."

"Excellent. Ask Mrs. Hudson to take care of the reservations. What a coincidence, Watson: you were reading yesterday's newspaper and we're traveling tomorrow. I hope that's not a bad omen," reflected Sherlock Holmes, not making a great deal of sense.

"I didn't know you were superstitious, Holmes," said Watson, rising and finally smiling.

*"Yo no creo en brujas, pero que las hay, las hay."*

"What does that mean?"

"I haven't the slightest idea, but the Spanish always repeat the phrase when someone mentions superstition," answered Holmes, who had little patience with translating archaic Iberian sayings.

Watson left the room thinking that he'd never seen a longer telegram.

# 4

*H*e brings the oil lamp closer to the anatomy book that he is reading. It is Précis d'anatomie et de dissection, *by H. Beaunis. He is especially interested in the chapters dedicated to dissection. In the case of the first woman, there had been no need for deeper knowledge. The classes in fencing and dagger use that he had taken, beginning in childhood at the Baron de Francken's academy, had been sufficient. The throat of the little trollop had opened up like the necks of the black goats that he had beheaded with a single cut, using the same dagger, when still a boy, in the magic rituals in which he secretly participated, with the complicity of the Negroes on his father's coffee plantation. The slaves had called him Oluparun. But he is creative. He does not wish to repeat the stroke. Therefore, in the stifling, humid early morning in his almost monastic bedroom, he reads avidly, breathless at the excitement engendered by those pages: "Before choosing an area, total knowledge is indispensable. . . . Preferably, choose young bodies, quite young and vigorous. Make the incision in the skin and dissect the cutaneous layers in strips, detaching the tissue covering the muscle." Cut:* "couper profondément. . . . " *French is a curious language:* "profond dément." *He puts aside these discursive thoughts and continues his macabre reading. He wants to be ready.*

## EDITORIAL

IT HAS BEEN nearly 30 years since the death of Auguste Comte! How greatly humanity misses this dazzling thinker! The intellectual descendant of Hobbes, he held the goal of doctrine to be knowledge of the laws that govern phenomena! To see in order to foresee; to seek what is, to conclude what will be, this is the object of all his research. One of the incomparable geniuses of universal thought, he proved that the definitive state of the spirit is the positive state! Reason, based not on a priori principles but on experimental data. This great thinker, this modern Aristotle, the foremost exponent of positivist philosophy, despite his death will beyond any doubt be forever remembered as the greatest immortal of our century!

## COLLISION OF VEHICLES

Yesterday, on Alfândega Street, tilbury no. 104 incurred a blow from a wagon sufficient to damage it in several places. It is time for the government to put a halt to the practice of permitting the use of speedy wagons by imprudent individuals who lack the necessary experience. The danger is not only in the young age of the driver. The same deleterious effects obtain when the wagon-driver does not know how to conduct the animal through streets where there is considerable vehicular movement.

## SCIENTIFIC SECTION

The Anthropological Congress of Rome, the aim of which was to redeem man from vice and crime, has ended. The various specialists who participated in the illustrious congress reached the conclusion that the criminal is above all else a retarded person, who can be subdivided into five distinct categories: the born criminal, the alienated criminal, the criminal from opportunity, the criminal from impulse or passion, and the habitual criminal.

## CLASSIFIED

FOR SALE: Three excellent slaves, viz., a boy of 17 years of age, a fine figure, another of 35 years, quite skilled, very dexterous in his work, and a Negress of 19 years, good appearance.

CAR AND SLAVE: Am offering for sale a Victoria with harness, all in very good condition. Seeking a male slave in his middle years, healthy and free of vices, for work of all types.

IMPORTANT NOTICE: Will sell an elegant and pretty maidservant, sheltered and from a private home, who has many fine qualities. Eighteen years old, good health, excellent teeth. Can iron, sew, and cut dress patterns. The reason for selling is not such as to be of displeasure to the buyer.

THERE HAVE BEEN no further developments in the frightening crime that took place this week on Regente Street. The horrifying event has shocked the whole of Rio de Janeiro. Despite the victim being a strumpet, the violence of the murder was such that even ladies of society are consternated at the unhappy fate of the unfortunate woman. Inspector Mello Pimenta is conducting intense investigations, using every resource of modern criminology, and promises to solve the horrendous homicide soon.

## MUNDANITIES
### MÚCIO PRADO'S COLUMN

THE DAY BEFORE YESTERDAY I had the pleasure of dining with the extraordinary Sarah Bernhardt. A woman of radiant beauty and talent, Bernhardt demonstrates the intelligence and lively spirit of any man. Present, in addition to the flower of our intellectual journalism, were young men from the finest families—the sportsman Albertinho Fazelli, the elegant book dealer Miguel Solera da Lara, the studious marquis of Salles—and the renowned tailor Salomão Calif, who, despite his Oriental origins, creates with his vivacious scissors the finest Western styles. The generous host, Aurélio Vidal, owner of the Grande Hotel, where the Divine One is lodged, was surrounded by friends.

On the menu, worthy of any European nobleman's table, were *mel-ons au porto,* a *turbot Cambacérès, jambon de Prague encroûte-sauce Madère, poularde Néva,* salad, cheeses, and sorbet. A white Bordeaux '65 and a red burgundy '75 were served, both excellent years. And champagne, of course. The "pièce de résistance" came from the guest of honor, who revealed to this humble writer *entre nous* that our beloved monarch, Dom Pedro II, is still concerned about the theft of a violin belonging to Maria Luísa Catarina de Albuquerque, baroness of Avaré. Just imagine, dear reader: it is a Stradivarius!

Adopting a suggestion from Sarah Bernhardt herself, our worthy emperor will invite an English detective, Sherlock Holmès (or is it Holmes?) to solve the mystery of the disappearance of the expensive and highly coveted instrument. We knew of the famous Stradivarius belonging to the virtuoso White, but no one guessed the existence of two such rarities on Brazilian soil.

Who could have offered the beautiful baroness such a regal gift?

～

Empress Teresa Cristina Maria de Bourbon was furious. She paced back and forth in the small, intimate chamber that separated the two imperial bedrooms. She was holding the newspaper with the column by Múcio Prado folded in her hand. Her generally serene eyes flashed at the emperor.

"So, my noble husband, what is the meaning behind this lark? To make me, even more than usual, the target of ridicule at court?" She was dressed discreetly, as always in tones of gray, but at that moment the movements of her skirts gave Dom Pedro the impression of being faced with the red cape of a bullfighter. The emperor's famous beard, which made him appear older than his father, shook with uneasiness. He sought out a shopworn excuse.

"I can guarantee you that there has been some mistake. I never—"

"Mistake?" the empress interjected, furious. "What mistake? Am I not surfeited at hearing comments about your friendship with that rattlebrain?"

Dom Pedro thought of offering a gallantry, saying that at such moments of anger she was even more beautiful, but beauty was not his wife's principal endowment. Besides, anger accentuated her lameness even further. The empress's homeliness was a motif of jest among the common folk; whenever she passed by in her carriage, the rabble would say, laughing, "There goes the dragon in her wagon!" Some evil tongues affirmed that when the young sovereign saw his promised bride first arriving at the quay in Rio, he'd had to hide the tears running down his face. "Yes, he cried, and not from emotion," commented the malicious.

"So Your Majesty dared give that woman a violin coveted throughout the entire world? A jewel in the form of a fiddle!"

"Absolutely not, it's absurd! I don't know where the man dug up that piece of news."

"The same place that you launched it. From the lips of a-a-an actress!" The words came rushing out of Teresa Cristina.

"Forgive me, my dear. I see no reason for putting such a pejorative tone on the word. I went to the performance at the São Pedro Theater as a state duty. After all, Madame Sarah Bernhardt has already been received by every court in Europe. They even say she was the lover—" He cut himself off before completing the faux pas. This was not the best moment to engage in bedroom gossip.

The empress huffed in her rage.

"In addition to everything else, you have the audacity to invite an English private detective to carry out the investigations. Do you want to discredit our police once and for all?"

Aware that, in the absence of any valid argument, attack is the best defense, Dom Pedro took the role of the wounded party, lapsing into the nervous verbal tic that assailed him on such occasions.

"Quite so, quite so, quite so, quite so. . . . Well, you apparently have no desire to listen to reason. My only alternative, therefore, is to ask your indulgence and take my leave. Joaquim Nabuco is waiting for me at the Historical Geographical Institute," said His Majesty majestically and headed for the door with the dignity of an army in retreat.

⌒

The housemaid refilled the glasses with passionflower juice.

"Another piece of cornmeal cake?" asked the baroness of Avaré.

"No, thank you, baroness. Just the beverage," replied Miguel Solera de Lara, with breeding.

Thin, long-limbed, somberly but carefully dressed, Miguel had the appearance of a Spanish *hidalgo*. He exercised his profession much more for love of books than from any necessity, for he was from a well-to-do family. A dedicated son, he lived with his mother, a poor imaginary invalid who constantly bemoaned her chimerical afflictions, in a large old colonial house in the Botafogo district. Evil tongues said that the young man was the bastard seed of the marquis of Paraná; however, this insinuation was obviously nothing but an unfounded rumor. The book dealer had gone to the house on Cosme Velho Street at Maria Luísa's request to take her the order that had arrived on the latest ship. His bookstore was the largest in the city and Miguel made a point of personally attending his most important clients. The baroness was part of that select clientele. She lived in Petrópolis the greater part of the time, but she loved her house in Rio, despite the humidity and the insects. Maria Luísa Catarina de Albuquerque, the baroness of Avaré, was dazzling that afternoon. The young widow of the baron of Avaré—she was only twenty-six years of age—Maria Luísa had studied in England as soon as she had left the sisters' school, with excellent training in music and literature. She had met her husband on the ship that brought her back to Brazil.

The baron, thirty years his wife's senior, had died in a tragic hunting accident on the banks of the Piraí River. While pursing a capybara, he had bumped into the trunk of a tree and discharged his rifle into his own foot. The bullet pierced his great toe without major consequences, but his private surgeon had insisted on amputating the injured toe, and the operation provoked the gangrene that cost him his life.

After a rigorous period of mourning lasting almost eighteen months, the baroness now made a point of wearing only cheery colors. Her dress was of light-green silk, very tight, emphasizing her narrow waist and perfect body. The green accentuated her red hair and blue eyes. Miguel and the baroness were in the library, and on the table were the opened packages with the finely bound books, *doré sur tranche*, that Luísa had requested. With his long, slim fingers the book dealer leafed through the pages of *Histoire de la Révolution Française*, in four volumes, by Adolphe Thiers—the 1851 edition, from Furne at Cie, Libraires-éditeurs.

"Odd reading for a baroness," he joked.

"Listen, my dear Miguel, it's good to know what happens when the aristocracy forgets its people. Also, you know I am a noble by marriage. As many people at court are kind enough to remind me, my father was a butcher."

"I prefer to say the wealthy proprietor of stores that sold meat," Solera de Lara corrected diplomatically, displaying impeccable teeth, his smile somehow accentuating his premature baldness.

Maria Luísa picked up another book with a yellow cover.

"Ah! My Balzac has finally arrived! What a suggestive title, don't you think, Miguel?" she said with a naughty smile as she showed him *Splendeurs et misères des courtisanes*, published by Mignot in 1872. "I wonder if this should be my bedside reading."

Before the young book dealer could respond, the sound of an arriving carriage was heard outside the house. Judging by the frantic rush of the servants, it could only be the emperor. Solera fabricated a previous commitment and left by the rear door. He had no desire to embarrass the monarch.

Dom Pedro came into the library still shaken by his meeting with the empress. Maria Luísa made an exaggerated curtsy. The emperor hated those taunts.

"Quite so, quite so. . . . That's enough, Maria Luísa. This is no time for jokes. Have you seen the newspapers?"

"Of course. I found the caricature of you that Agostini published in the *Illustrated* quite amusing. The beard is perhaps a bit too long."

"That is not what I'm talking about. I refer to the note that Múcio Prado printed about the stolen violin."

"The violin? To me that's over and done with. I've already fretted enough over that theft. After all, let them take the rings, as long as they leave the fingers. . . . "

Dom Pedro was always surprised by the baroness's facility for changing moods. The Stradivarius was nothing but a toy to her—an expensive toy, nothing more. Also, it was easy to think only about fingers when the rings had been gifts.

"In any case, I think it will be diverting to receive an English detective at court," said Maria Luísa as she cut another piece of cake.

"A pity you look upon it all so lightly. The empress is like a woman possessed. Not to mention that now everyone knows the violin was a gift from me."

"How do they know?"

"Who other than I would have the courage to do something so crazy?"

"My friend, I think you are barking up the wrong tree, as they say. I could perfectly well have bought a Stradivarius. My husband left me quite a bit of money. Haven't you heard the verse they whisper at court? 'The baroness, young, talented, and pretty/ A rich widow, the most coveted in the city.'" And she added, extending the plate, "Do you want some cornmeal cake? It was just made."

For the second time that day, Dom Pedro turned on his heels and left without saying good-bye. The dignity that he summoned in that difficult moment was impressive, especially if we consider how much the emperor loved cornmeal cake.

## 5

Sarah Bernhardt had been in Brazil for almost two weeks. Today, she was acting in the *première* of Meilhac and Halévy's *Frou-Frou*, in the role of Gilberte. Dom Pedro occupied the imperial box, and the theater was in a state of celebration. Upon her arrival two hours earlier, the actress had been greeted by ardent students who threw flowers and shouted passionately, in precarious French learned from the jades in bordellos: *"Vive Madame Bernhardt!"; "Vous êtes une artiste supimpe! Vous êtes bonne à bèsse!"; "Allons enfants de la patrie! Sarah Bernhardt est arrivée!"*

At the doors of the São Pedro shortly before the performance, one could still see the Bahian women with their small trays shouting to passersby, "Sweet hominy, ma'am, good and hot! Fresh corn pudding! Coconut custard! Coconut candy!" Other vendors displayed riskier tidbits: "Shrimp patties! If you don't find any shrimp, you don't pay!" The vendors hawked popcorn, sesame sweets, coconut kisses, and other delicacies made from bananas and guava.

The house was packed. From the main floor to the uppermost balconies, Brazilians of every class had come to see the French star who had come to their shores. For many, who didn't understand a word of what was being said on stage, it was a circus spectacle, and Sarah a phenomenon every bit as mysterious as a flute-playing tiger or a tightrope-walking elephant. The play lasted over three hours, thanks to the shouted interruptions by the more excited amongst the audience; "Oh, madame!"; "Beware, Dona Sarah, he told the other woman everything!"; "It's a lie! Don't believe her, it's a lie! She read the letter when you went inside!"

At the end of the first act, many got up, thinking the play was over. When they realized their mistake, they attempted to disguise their ignorance by buying candy and a drink in the lobby, then returning to their seats.

When the curtain finally descended for the last time, over half the audience gathered at the artists' exit to see the living myth up close. In the middle of the crowd was a fragile, gentle figure of a woman, almost a girl. She was a lady-in-waiting at the imperial palace and had obtained a ticket to attend the performance. Sarah opened the door to face the multitude. Another shower of flowers, more shouts of *"Vive Sarah Bernhardt!"* Some, more audacious, approached to touch the actress's garment. Maurice Grau had to call upon all his experience to keep the crowd at a distance without appearing impolite. *En passant*, the actress was moved by the gentle appearance of the young woman. She asked her, *"Comment t'appelles-tu?"*

"Francisca," the girl said, not believing that she was actually speaking to Sarah Bernhardt. The actress took a card from her purse and, with a golden mechanical pencil that she received as a gift from the Duke of Strasbourg, wrote her name next to the inscription: *"Pour Francisca, belle et jeune brésilienne qui ma'a vue jouer* Frou-Frou *à Rio, Sarah Bernhardt."* She kissed both the young woman's cheeks, handed her the card, and swiftly got into the calash awaiting her. She was so quick that Maurice Grau had to dash to overtake her.

Francisca Meireles could not believe her luck. To her it was a miracle that Sarah Bernhardt herself, her idol since her days in the convent school, had taken the time to give her an autograph. She put the precious keepsake in her purse and walked toward Constituição Street. It would be difficult to find a cab at that hour. The coachmen, all in frock coats, were still in front of the theater hoping for larger tips. It didn't matter. For her, the night had been perfect. A girl of many abilities, her uncle, the painter Vítor Meireles, had arranged with the emperor to find a place for her as lady-in-waiting at the palace, where a generous fate had even led to her being given a ticket to the performance that evening. She opened her purse and took out the card. She was afraid it had all been only a dream. She read the inscription again; then, clutching the trophy in her left hand as if she feared it would vanish before her eyes, she continued walking, in a reverie common to young women of her age. Before she realized it, she was already at São José Street. She crossed Guarda Velha Street in the direction of the fountain, an immense construction that recalled the shape of a temple, with twenty-nine highly polished bronze spouts. It was there that the rabble from Santo Antônio Hill and from the Castelo district came to supply themselves with water. The square was deserted at that hour. The young woman, her mouth still dry from emotion, drew close to satisfy her thirst. As soon as she leaned over toward one of the spouts, she sensed the presence of another person.

The luckless girl barely has time to see the long dagger flash in the light of the street lamps. Quickly, her face is enveloped by a cape and the young woman is thrown against the parapet. The blade makes a perfect incision in the lower part of her belly and slowly rises toward the esophagus. Expertly, the man slashes the entire abdomen. The girl is not even aware of what is happening. She feels only cold, very cold, and falls into one of the two tanks, staining the fountain's waters red. He bends over the body and cuts away a flap of skin from the unfortunate lady-in-waiting. Without knowing why, he smells it before putting it away. Finally, he takes out the violin tied to his belt and covered by the cape, and carries out the same macabre ritual. This time, it is *sol,* the G string, that he rips from the instrument. He places the coiled string amongst the pubic hairs. He immediately leaves in the direction of the Santana church, executing a pathetic and melancholy czardas on the violin's two remaining strings.

~

To Inspector Mello Pimenta, it would always be Bobadela Street. He had known the narrow way since childhood and it mattered little to him that they had rechristened it. "Old Guard—is that any name for a street?" he thought. Bobadela had changed names precisely because of the Military Guard Corps, which had been installed there to maintain order among the water bearers who frequented the Carioca fountain. He crossed the street, passed by St. Anthony's convent, and continued through Carioca Square until he arrived at the fountain. He was exhausted. He had spent the night and part of the morning trying to resolve a problem of slaves who had fled to the slave district in Gávea. Secretly, Pimenta was a confirmed abolitionist, but he could not ignore the slaveowner, who came highly recommended by the chief of police. The midday sun didn't greatly bother him. What did annoy him was the fact of the girl's body not having been taken away before now. A cordon of police, the so-called dog-killers, prevented a small crowd of bystanders from gathering around the dead woman. "They look like blowflies," he snorted, more irritated still. He broke through the cordon and approached Dr. Saraiva, who was already at the scene. The coroner's eyes were puffy and bloodshot, probably from too much alcohol. Saraiva was competent, although on several occasions he had almost lost his position because of his drinking habit. Any piece of information, however secret, could be gotten out of the doctor by journalists once rum had loosened his tongue. Mello Pimenta asked, without even saying hello, "So, professor, what can you tell me?"

"Nothing good, nothing good . . ." Saraiva replied, scratching his head with a bloody hand and leaving yet another reddish streak in his white hair. "It resembles that case of the prostitute on Regente Street."

"What? Another 'windowsill woman' murdered?"

"No, no. From the papers I found, she's a respectable young woman. There's a letter of introduction saying that she was a lady-in-waiting at the palace. Her name is Francisca Meireles. She's the niece of that painter, Vítor, a friend of the emperor's, from the Imperial Academy of Fine Arts."

"That's all I needed. And what's the similarity with the other crime?"

"First, the missing flap of skin; next, the violence of the cuts. Except this time it wasn't in the neck. The murderer opened up the woman like a suckling pig." Saraiva loved culinary analogies. "Besides that, one notes the same precision in the use of the knife."

Pimenta noticed there was something in the victim's clenched left hand. The arm was hanging out of the fountain. It appeared that the girl had made a final effort to keep the object she was holding from getting wet. The policeman tried to open the small, already rigid fingers. He did not succeed.

"If I may," said Saraiva, approaching. He took the lifeless hand and hammered it against the stone fountain as if it were a walnut. The broken bones opened, bringing the wrinkled card into view. Using his thumb and forefinger, the doctor delicately withdrew the card with the actress's inscription and with a showy gesture handed it to Pimenta.

The inspector read it with interest.

"Sarah Bernhardt. Isn't she the Frenchwoman who's performing at the São Pedro?"

"Exactly. The greatest actress in the world. You haven't seen her yet?"

"Do I have the time?" He looked at the card again. "It appears this young woman was at the performance last night. I don't know if this is much help," he said, putting the card in his vest pocket.

Saraiva pulled the inspector away by his arm. "But this may help," he said, taking the violin string from his pocket. "Another musical string. Coiled, just like the other one, in the pubic hairs. Probably from the same instrument."

In the same way someone flicks a piece of lint from a jacket, the coroner removed a hair that was still wrapped around the string. He then held it out to the inspector. "A souvenir . . . "

Pimenta put it away, feeling disgust. He hadn't given much thought to the string in the first crime, but this repetition clearly indicated that he was dealing with the same madman. He must quickly find out what instrument it was and discover what kind of mental pathology could lead someone to collect flaps of skin. Perhaps these bizarre signs were clues that the unbalanced man was leaving in his path. By now the inspector no longer had any doubts that he was dealing with the same person and that he was unbalanced. Two victims in less than a month. He hoped the monster wouldn't continue at the same pace. In all his years as a policeman he had never seen anything like this. Two victims of the same murderer, with little in common. One, a prostitute; the other, a lady-in-waiting at the palace. He began imagining what similarities there could be between the two. They were young. Very young. Pretty. Both were missing a flap of skin. No, that didn't count—before their unhappy fate of chancing upon that monster, they were missing no skin. Pimenta saw that he wasn't reasoning clearly. The sun and his weariness were beginning to dull his thinking. He needed to go home, wash up, and have something to eat. He took his leave of Saraiva. "Well, there's nothing more for me to do here. Let me know if you discover anything new."

"I'm leaving shortly myself. I'm just waiting for the men to come and take away the body. I want to begin the autopsy right away, this afternoon. Even so, it won't be easy to find anything new. Unless you want to know what the girl ate before going to the theater," the doctor said, laughing, once again demonstrating his bent for that type of humor.

～

Dona Paciência was well accustomed to her husband's hours. She knew that a police inspector sometimes was away all night, and Mello Pimenta was a man dedicated to his profession. He was in the habit of joking with her about her name. "Isn't it Paciência? So be patient until I come home." She wasn't jealous, for she knew that Pimenta was out chasing criminals and not women. Paciência, at thirty-two, was an attractive woman. Not a classical beauty, she possessed what the French called *la beauté du diable*. Very pale, with large eyes and straight dark hair, in childhood her nickname had been "the little Gypsy," which she detested. While the inspector shaved with an old German razor, the sole inheritance from his father, she set the table, serving hot buttered tapioca and coffee, her husband's favorite dish.

"Be careful with the razor!" she shouted toward the bathroom.

"Why?"

"So you don't cut off a flap. . . . "

Pimenta was in the habit of discussing his police cases with his wife, and she was aware of the recent killings. He finished shaving his chin, rinsed his face in the agate basin, and came out to speak with his wife. He sat down while Paciência served the thick, steaming coffee.

"You know I don't like it when you make those jokes," said Mello Pimenta, feigning annoyance. "You sound like Saraiva."

"Drink your coffee before it gets cold." She sat down beside her husband.

"This case of the dead girls is becoming a nuisance. I don't know where to begin," the inspector complained.

"Why don't you ask for help from that English detective who's about to arrive?"

"What English detective?"

"It was in Múcio Prado's column the other day. It seems our dearly beloved sovereign invited a Mr. Sherlock something-or-other to find out who stole a very expensive violin from the baroness Maria Luísa. It's the latest *potin* in the city. Didn't you read it?" asked Paciência, who never missed the chronicler's writings in the *Journal of Commerce*. She loved gossip about the aristocracy and filled her idle afternoons with fantasies of being at court parties and *soirées*.

"A violin?" asked Pimenta, taking the catgut string from his pocket. "Could this be a violin string?"

"I don't know. It's certainly not from a guitar," answered Paciência. As a child she had learned to play a few ditties by Caldas Barbosa on that instrument. "Where did you find it?"

"At the scene of the crime," Pimenta said evasively, wishing to avoid telling his wife that scabrous part of the story. "Actually, one string near each victim." He put the string away again.

"Eat before it gets cold."

Pensive, Mello Pimenta spread more butter on his tapioca while he pondered whether it would be worthwhile to ask for the English detective's help.

# 6

The *Aquitania* was anchored at the entrance to the port of Recife, its first stop in Brazil. The city had been so named because of the *arrecifes,* or reefs, that surrounded the anchorage. The immense steamship with its four smokestacks had dropped anchor far beyond the coral, and the few passengers who were disembarking had to descend fearfully in small woven baskets. The sea was infested with sharks, which swam around the ship in pursuit of scraps of food that were always thrown to the waves by the cooks. At five in the afternoon the heat was still intense. Sherlock Holmes and Dr. Watson were leaning on the railing in search of a sea breeze.

"It seems like India," Watson grumbled. "The only time I ever felt such heat was in Bombay, when I was there in 'seventy-eight as assistant surgeon to the Fifth Northumberland Fusiliers Regiment, during the second Afghan war."

Holmes paid no attention to him. He was absorbed, concentrating on the tasks of the shark fishermen, who encircled the *Aquitania* in their small vessels. They employed an unusual system of fishing. In their boats the fishermen carried iron kettles in which they cooked enormous pumpkins, which, as soon as they were boiling hot, were tossed into the sea. The sharks, like trained seals, would catch them in their gullets, swallowing without even chewing, and dive. The intolerable heat of the pumpkins burst the insides of the animals, which then floated to the surface, already dead. The fishermen then gathered the immense sharks into their boats. To them, the entire operation was monotonous. It was a primitive but effective technique, handed down from father to son for generations. They worked in silence, perhaps from respect for the carcasses of the animals they killed.

Holmes observed, fascinated. "Look, Watson. Ingenious and primitive. The sharks are so voracious they don't even have time to notice that the prey they swallow is a fatal trap."

"I never imagined the fish was so stupid," Watson said, disdainfully, taking out his watch. "It's gone five. Tea time."

"My dear Watson, I see that you are not yet accustomed to the tropics. Instead of tea, it's better to try that coconut water that the sailors have just brought aboard. They say it's cooling and delicious."

"I'll stay with the tea. The diarrhea I had in Calcutta when I tried mango juice with milk was quite enough."

"Watson, sometimes your inability to adapt to circumstances astounds me. For my part, I already feel like a native."

"That may be. I require more time. After all, London wasn't built in a day."

"It was Rome. Rome wasn't built in a day," corrected Holmes.

"Nor was London," the doctor insisted.

The two walked down the deck toward the main dining room, Holmes, excited by the adventure of becoming acquainted with new lands, and Watson, apprehensive at his companion's excitement.

The *Aquitania*'s huge main dining room served for breakfast, lunch, and dinner as well as for dances. When the vessel crossed the equator, there had been a colossal costume ball offered by the ship's officers. Holmes, king of disguises, had won first prize, much to the despair of Watson, who hated it when his friend dressed as a Gypsy woman. The detective was unrecognizable in his long earrings and red satin skirt, offering to read fortunes. The trophy, a statuette of Neptune, was already stored in their baggage; the doctor did not want it in sight, a constant reminder of that evening. Before the party, in his cabin, Holmes had taken a large quantity of cocaine, a habit of which Watson disapproved. The detective was so affected by the drug that, following the contest, he ended the night by dancing with the captain.

In the afternoon, in the same ballroom, tea was served. The two sat at a small table near the hatchway, from which, off to the right, could be seen the outline of the city of Olinda. Sherlock marveled at the architecture of Recife. "If not for the climate, I should judge we were still in Europe," he said taking a swallow of coconut water.

"That is, if you don't look at the half-naked slaves working on the dock," answered Watson, contemplating the Negroes and sipping his tea.

As they were preparing to leave, a young steward approached, carrying a silver tray.

"Telegram for Mr. Sherlock Holmes."

The detective opened the envelope and read the message written in a beginner's English:

WELCOME MISTER SHERLOCK HOLMES PERIOD PLEASE
HELP PERIOD TWO STRANGE MURDERS OF YOUNG
WOMEN PERIOD ASSASSIN CUT OFF FLAPS OF SKIN AND
LEAVES STRINGS PERIOD MAYBE VIOLIN PERIOD
HOPE SEE YOU IN RIO DE JANEIRO PERIOD
    ATTENTIONNELLY COMMA
    INSPECTOR PIMENTA

"Curious, very curious," murmured Holmes, putting the telegram in his pocket.

"What is it? News from England?"

"No, from Rio de Janeiro. A policeman asking for my assistance. It seems that fate is once again leading me to an encounter with a most horrible crime," replied Holmes, taking out his pipe and beginning to fill it. "I believe that the case of the stolen Stradivarius is going to be overshadowed by these recent events."

Watson was irritated at his friend's interest in the telegram. "I thought you were going to take advantage of this trip to clear your head of the complex police problems of London. You need to rest, Holmes. After all, even Christ rested on the sixth day."

"It was God who rested, Watson. And on the seventh. . . . " Holmes informed him, leaving for the main deck.

~

Eight A.M. Júlio Augusto Pereira, marquis of Salles, had already changed clothes at the Boqueirão Bath House, on Luiz de Vasconcellos Street, and was stretched out on the sands of Saudade Beach. He was only thirty-eight, but he nevertheless suffered from attacks of gout. Dr. Ribamar, his physician, had recommended sea baths as an infallible prescription for the malady that now and again afflicted him. As he led an intemperate life and it was not easy for him to rise at that hour, the marquis, on his days for therapeutic immersions, merely extended even further the late hours of the previous night and headed straight for the beach. The physician would have done better to prescribe an abstemious diet, cutting out the wines and brandies that so delighted the noble bohemian, but as he was a companion in the marquis's revelries, it was difficult to suggest a more rigorous regimen. "Sea baths, my friend. For gout, there's nothing better than long sea baths. The curative powers of iodine are beyond dispute," said Dr. Ribamar, at a table in Paschoal's sweet shop, drinking Armagnac at the nobleman's side.

Already half intoxicated, the marquis replied, "That's why I like you, doctor. Imagine, a physician at court—Vilella, who takes care of Dom Pedro's erysipelas—said that, in my case, alcohol was harmful."

"Nonsense. Vilella is of the French school. My treatment is much more modern," asserted Ribamar, much to the marquis's relief.

"Excellent! So let's have a few more drinks, then off to the whores!" And their carousing would continue until the early hours of morning. The marquis of Salles loved to frequent the "upstairs women," and despite being quite rich, as a lark was in the habit of running off without paying, once his desires were satisfied. He was already well known in certain locations. When he would arrive at Sabão Street, the young girls would call out through the *persiennes* to their unsuspecting peers, "Watch out, that man's a welsher!"

Júlio Augusto had been lying on the beach for more than an hour. He was beginning to feel drowsy and was wondering whether he should go home to cure his queasiness or have another plunge in the waves. In the distance, ploughing through the waters of Guanabara Bay, a pair of rowers from the Cajuense Regatta Club passed by, heading in the direction of Cavalos Beach. While he was thinking, De Salles heard, far off, the voices of people conversing in French. He turned and, to his surprise, made out Sarah Bernhardt, in a long bathing costume. She was walking, conversing animatedly with Maurice Grau. Surely the Frenchwoman was unfamiliar with the local customs. It was not usual for ladies of quality to bathe at that hour. By seven in the morning, families were rarely to be seen on the sands. Despite his surprise, he beckoned for them to approach. Grau was wearing a daring bathing costume, with a shirt with very short sleeves and black breeches that ended at the knee. Sarah was wearing ample breeches made of baize and a loose-fitting blue blouse with a mariner-style collar. She also had on rope shoes, tied at the ankle, like Roman sandals. On her head she wore a large hat tied to her chin with a silk ribbon. The couple went on talking without paying any heed to the marquis.

"*Non, c'est ridicule!*" shouted Sarah, irritated.

"*Écoutez, le mal est déjà fait. Maintenant il faut y aller,*" her secretary tried to convince her.

"*Bonjour, Madame Bernhardt. Monsieur Grau, comment ça va?*" the marquis said, rising. "I don't know if you remember me, Júlio Augusto Pereira, marquis of Salles. We were together at the dinner in the Grande Hotel, just after *Camille.*"

"*Ah, oui, le marquis de Salles, bonjour, monsieur,*" said the Divine One, visibly annoyed.

"May I ask, madame, to what our beaches owe the privilege and honor of your morning visit?"

"To my ill humor, monsieur, to my ill humor. My private doctor is in the habit of saying that there is nothing better for overcoming neurasthenia than the sea air."

"Well, I thank your irritation for this unexpected pleasure. It's unbelievable, the Divine Sarah Bernhardt on the beaches of Rio! Were I to gather into bottles these sands trodden by such a magnificent presence, I would find greater success with them in Paris than a pilgrim with flasks of water from Lourdes!" fawned the marquis.

Sarah and Grau exchanged glances and, after an instant, burst into guffaws.

"Ah, monsieur, only a Brazilian could make me laugh at this hour of the morning, after what I have gone through the last two days," complained Sarah Bernhardt.

"May I inquire what has happened?" asked the marquis, who had spent the last forty-eight hours in one of Senhora Barbada's brothels in the Jardim Botânico district.

"Imagine, *monsieur le marquis,* that in yesterday's performance when we came to the fourth act of *Adrienne Lecouvreur,* Martha Noirmont, a second-class actress to whom I gave employment as an act of charity, had the audacity to insult the audience by reciting her role mechanically, almost asleep. The last straw was when she made certain responses to me at the wrong time. Inexcusable."

"I can imagine how upset madame must have been."

"No, no, you cannot, monsieur; not even Eugène would be more enraged," said Grau, referring to Eugène Scribe, author of the play. "Sarah was vexed to the point of slapping her a few times, and breaking a parasol over her head."

"I'm sorry about the parasol," remarked la Bernhardt.

"The problem," the secretary went on, "is that Martha took the incident seriously. Yesterday she lodged a complaint at the police station, and Madame Bernhardt has been summoned to make a statement this afternoon. Can you conceive of a more disagreeable situation?"

"Except that I'm not going. That's final, I won't go."

"Sarah, be reasonable. I'm sure it's only a formality. They've even assured me that our lawyer is of the highest quality," argued Maurice Grau.

"May I ask who he is?" intervened De Salles.

"A certain Monsieur Nabuco. Sizenando Nabuco," replied Grau, his tongue twisting around the name. "He was in attendance at the play and was recommended by our impresario. Do you know him?"

"Of course. Madame could not be in better hands. Sizenando is the brother of the deputy Joaquim Nabuco. An abolitionist, but very competent."

Sarah diverted her gaze to the ocean. "Well, if it is absolutely necessary, we shall see. After lunch. For now, since we are at the beach, let's go into the water. I've never seen such a lovely landscape. It reminds me of the poet: *luxe, calme—*"

"*—et volupté . . .*" concluded the marquis, sensually kissing the Divine One's fingertips.

Surprised, Sarah Bernhardt withdrew her hand. "I see that the marquis is quite familiar with Baudelaire."

"Whenever I read '*L'invitation au voyage,*' I think that he was speaking of Brazil."

"Let's go in, Maurice," said Sarah, pulling her secretary toward the waves. The couple ran along the sand, which now was beginning to heat up.

"I hope you enjoy your swim. Take care with the sun, and with the sea, which is treacherous at times. And don't go beyond the protected area," concluded the marquis, pointing to the yellow rope attached to a buoy some thirty or forty meters beyond the breaking waves. The rope served as support for bathers.

"*Au revoir, monsieur le marquis!*"

"*Au revoir, madame,*" waved the dissolute nobleman, thinking that the Frenchwoman, despite her age, was still a corker.

⁓

Never had such an uproar been seen in the station house of the third police district of Rio de Janeiro, at the corner of Lavradio Street. It was already past four, and at any moment Sarah Bernhardt, the greatest actress in the world, would enter to answer a summons.

To Inspector Mello Pimenta, the highest official at the station, it was all merely a nuisance. The contretemps he faced investigating the crimes of Regente Street and the fountain were enough to deal with. Vítor Meireles had used his influence at court to speed the proceedings, placing every possible resource at his disposition, but Pimenta knew that this would be of scant help. He had not yet been able to connect the clues that linked the two murders. An infernal hubbub coming from outside caught the policeman's attention:

"It's her! It's her!"

"Good lord! She's beautiful!"

Suddenly, as if she were a ray of light coming in through the door, Sarah Bernhardt, dressed entirely in pink, her cheeks reddened from the morning sun, approached the desk. Pimenta rose to receive her.

"*Mello Pimenta, à vos ordres. Asseyez-vous, madame, s'il vous plaît.*"

"*Ah, quelle surprise! Vous parlez français?*"

"No, madame. Just that sentence, which I rehearsed all morning."

Pimenta stepped around the table and pulled up a chair for the actress.

As soon as Sarah was seated, the chair, a precarious piece of furniture with crooked legs, took on the stature of a throne. Beside her, standing, were Maurice Grau and the lawyer Sizenando Nabuco.

"It doesn't matter, inspector. I'll serve as interpreter. I'm the attorney Sizenando Nabuco. I represent madame in this lamentable episode. Surely you know with whom you're speaking."

"Of course, Dr. Nabuco, of course I do. Unfortunately, I was obliged to register the incident, because Mademoiselle Martha Noirmont insisted on lodging a complaint. Here is a copy of the statement dictated yesterday to the scribe Lousada," said Pimenta, indicating a functionary in a threadbare brown suit, seated at the end of the room, as he handed a sheet of paper to the lawyer. Lousada, a pale, weak-looking figure, almost hairless, had been police scribe for more than twenty-eight years and feared anything that might stand in the way of his pension. He rose and left quickly for the jail, grumbling that he had to take food to the prisoners.

"*Salope,*" hissed Sarah between her teeth, referring to her fellow thespian.

Sizenando pretended to be reading the document with great attention.

"It's deplorable . . . deplorable . . . the inspector must understand that this is nothing but a fantasy on the girl's part. She is very new in the profession. She didn't understand that Madame Sarah Bernhardt was merely carrying out her role."

"Her role?" Pimenta asked, startled.

"Yes. The slap and breaking the umbrella were part of the text. With the enthusiasm that she brings to all her creations, perhaps madame exaggerated a bit. Do you know *Adrienne Lecouvreur?*"

"I've never met the lady," said the inspector, who was not a theater lover.

"It's the name of the play, inspector. It deals with a great

French actress of the last century who had a torrid romance with the Count Maurice de Saxe, marshal of France. It is natural that another great French actress, while embodying the character, may have allowed her emotions to burst forth in a gesture of passion! Who are we to judge her enraptured interpretation? Would our nation's Justice have us succumb to this farandole and transform us into judges and executioners of the muse Melpomene?" roared the defender of the arts melodramatically, brandishing the paper.

The complainants and petitioners for certificates of poverty who were amassed in the station applauded frenetically. They hadn't understood a word, but the eloquence of the jurist was proof enough of the actress's innocence. Pimenta imposed order on the scene. "Silence! Do you think the precinct house is a nosocome for dunderpates?" he shouted, to show that he too had a good vocabulary. "If you go on with this bedlam, I'll put you all in the hoosegow!" He sat down again. "I'm sure the incident can be surmounted, Dr. Nabuco. After all, we don't want Madame Sarah Bernhardt to take away a bad impression of our country. I was obliged to issue the summons to comply with the law. Now that I have heard your explanation, I consider the matter closed."

"Thank you, inspector," the lawyer said magnanimously, storing the copy of the complaint in his pocket.

Mello Pimenta knew perfectly well that there was nothing to be gained from attacking a stone wall headfirst. The Nabuco family's influential friendships and the importance of the actress would merely lead to the complaint being filed away in one of the dusty drawers of the Court of Justice of Rio de Janeiro.

"*C'est tout?*" asked Sarah, rising.

"*Oui, madame,*" ventured Pimenta, in French. He stood up to accompany them. "If it's not a nuisance, I'd like to ask if Dona Sarah by any chance remembers this card," said Pimenta, taking from his vest pocket the crumpled paper with the actress's inscription.

"But of course," replied Sarah. "I gave this autograph to a pretty *jeune fille* who was at the theater exit. The sweetness of her appearance caught my attention. Your daughter?"

"No, madame. Unfortunately she is one of the victims in a tortuous case of murder on which I am working."

"How horrible!"

"Did you notice whether anyone was with her?"

"Ah, no! When I leave the theater, I see nothing. I get directly into the waiting car. I stopped only because that girl was truly different. I'm very sorry, inspector. I hope you catch the savage who did it. Good luck with your investigations, or, as we theater folk say in France, *merde!*"

"*Merde* to you, too," replied Pimenta, shaking the actress's hand vigorously.

Sarah Bernhardt left the station, accompanied by her entourage, as if exiting from the stage in the second act of *Ruy Blas.*

# 7

*The kerosene lamp casts shadows on the walls of the room. He looks at his doleful contour, made gigantic, and smiles. With his hands, he creates childish images of rabbits and foxes, which the flickering flame projects in silhouette. He again fixes his specter on the wall. This is the image they bear on their retinas before dying. He does not comprehend what drives him to do it but he knows he must continue. If they do not stop him, he will go on killing. Each time, the messages he leaves become more obvious, but no one seems to understand. From his frequent reading, he knows by heart the passage from the anatomy manual by Le Pileur,* Le corps humain, *that deals with the lungs. He declaims aloud, as if it were poetry: "An essential organ for respiration. There are two, although they receive oxygen through the same channel and blood from a single vessel. They should be considered the terminal expansion of the branching of the tracheal artery. Or, if we prefer, as two crowns of the same tree. They occupy the greater part of the pectoral cavity, which can be considered their housing or mold. . . ." He remains silent for a time, listening to his own breathing. He must have spent almost an hour hearing the air entering and departing from his body. Later, he raises one of the hardwood boards from the floor and verifies that the bottle with the flaps of skin is still in its improvised cache. He returns the board to its place. From the cupboard, he takes out the whetstone and the long knife. Sitting on the edge of the bed, which is as hard as a cot, he begins sharpening the knife with long strokes, in a slow cadence.*

*Whetstone, tombstone. Nameless gravestone. Whetstone, founda-*
*tion stone, philosopher's stone. Precious stone, pristine, precise.*
*Cornerstone, whetstone, stone. He increases the rhythm, coming*
*and going, sharpening faster and faster. He is panting, excited, his*
*brow is exuding sweat. He grasps the hilt of the dagger more*
*tightly in his hand, and, visualizing his next encounter, plunges*
*into the stertor of orgasm. His exhausted body falls back on the*
*narrow bed. Stone. One stone fewer on the playing board.*

~

The bookstore Aphrodite's Retreat, owned by Miguel Solera
de Lara, on Ouvidor Street, as much as or more than the Garnier, was the principal meeting place for the city's intellectuals,
almost all of them contributors to the newspapers. The sui
generis name was owed to the fact of the store's having once
belonged to a retired professor of Greek who was fascinated
by mythology. Above the door, bedecked with Hellenic
motifs, could be seen a classical painting of the goddess
emerging from a shell. The painter had placed an open book in
Venus's hand, as if she were reading one of the precious volumes in the collection. Miguel had found the idea picturesque
and, upon buying the shop, had kept the drawing and the
name.

Through there passed daily such figures as Olavo Bilac,
Guimarães Passos, José do Patrocínio, who edited the *After-*
*noon Gazette*, Aluísio Azevedo, the marquis of Salles, Angelo
Agostini, and the greatest bohemian of them all, Paula Nei.
Nei was an unusual case, for he had never published a line. His
fame had been born and had grown exclusively on Ouvidor
Street. He was known for the poems and epigrams he recited
for his friends in the cafés, and he also distinguished himself

by his appearance: small, thin, ugly, very myopic, he always wore the same bowler hat, tilted back on his head.

As evening fell, they began arriving at the Retreat. They were going to read, to their friends, new poems or old ones as yet unpublished. From time to time even Machado de Assis graced them with his presence. In the days when he contributed to the *Marmota*, he had appeared more often. After the success of his novel *Epitaph of a Small Winner*, he was wont to come by less frequently. He would say, in jest, that the quality of his work was incompatible with the persiflage of that band of bohemians. Actual books they purchased sparingly, preferring to read the latest publications right there, standing beside the bookshelves. Paula Nei had even gone so far as to use a bookmark to know at what point to continue his reading the following day. When Miguel Solera de Lara complained, he had replied in high dudgeon, "Oh, so? Would you prefer me to dog-ear the page, spoiling the volume? What the devil kind of bookseller are you?"

For this and other reasons, Miguel dreamed of going to live in London. Perhaps to open a small bookshop in the East End. Mad about England and an incurable romantic, Solera de Lara had the eccentric notion that it was his duty to bring a touch of culture to the less-favored English classes. He was not wanting for money. Only his pseudo-infirm mother tied him to Brazilian soil. His friends, all with one foot in France, mocked the bookseller.

"I don't know how you come by that Anglophilia of yours," sneered the marquis of Salles. "Don't you know that everything you're thinking of is in Paris?"

Miguel did not argue. It was pointless to speak of Shakespeare to the ears of Molière.

∼

At two in the afternoon, there were few people in the bookstore. Anonymous customers leafed silently through the latest new publications. A few decorators came to choose books by the meter for their nouveau-riche clients. Of the group, only Guimarães Passos was present and was reading aloud to the bookseller his latest satiric poem about an extremely rich businessman who had not been able to fulfill his marital duties on his wedding night. The pair's guffaws drew reproving looks from those customers present. Guimarães said good-bye to the bookseller, promising to return at dusk.

Outside, the usual tumult caused by street peddlers could be heard:

"Live turkeys with b-i-i-i-i-g fans!"

"Old bottles bought!"

"Onion man! Onions!"

"Sweet buns. Sweet buns hot from the oven!"

"Sherbet, sherbet for a penny,

If you haven't got the coin, you don't get any."

Suddenly, Sarah Bernhardt came into the bookstore, accompanied by her American impresario, Edward Jarrett; by her friend and confidante, the actress Marie Jullien; and by the actors Berthier and Philippe Garnier. Sarah, after almost a month in Brazil, had exhausted the reading matter she had brought with her, and Aphrodite's Retreat had been recommended to her as the best place in Rio to restock her supply of books in French. They were returning to the hotel after lunch at La Renaissance, owned by the French chef Pierre Labarth. Jarrett did not want to stop at the bookstore as he wasn't feeling well.

"Just for an instant, *mon chéri*. I want to see if a book by my friend Émile has arrived," said Sarah, referring to Émile Zola.

Solera de Lara came to attend her, delighted to see the actress in his shop.

"Madame, I cannot express the pleasure it gives me to receive you in my humble bookstore."

"I have heard it's not all that humble. They told me you always have the newest French editions."

"I do what I can, but sometimes the ships are delayed," the book dealer replied modestly. "Which book in particular are you looking for?"

"*L'oeuvre* by Émile Zola. It seems to be causing the greatest uproar in Paris, because Cézanne, a friend of Émile's for years, thinks he himself was portrayed in the character of the painter in the work. They say the two are no longer speaking," whispered the actress in a gossipy tone.

"Unfortunately, madame, the book has just been published. I have ordered it, but it hasn't arrived yet. I have *Germinal*, from last year. Actually, quite interesting. It's about a miners' rebellion. I don't know if you're familiar with it."

"Yes, I've read it. And it's not a rebellion, it's a strike," Sarah corrected.

"Aren't they the same thing?" the bookseller asked, put out.

"For some, yes," replied Sarah, mildly irritated. "I don't want to take any more of your time. If you don't mind, I should get back to the hotel: my impresario, Mr. Jarrett, is feeling somewhat ill." And she added, as if talking to herself, "I fear he is suffering from yellow fever." Then to Miguel: "Good-bye, monsieur."

As she turned to leave, she bumped into a short, plump lady, attired, however, in the latest style, in a dress embellished with seven rows of ruffles. Sarah dislodged a package that the woman was carrying. The contents of the package scattered on the floor, exposing a book and several wide playing cards.

"Oh, *pardon*! How clumsy I am!" said Bernhardt in apology.

"*Ce n'est pas grave, madame,*" said the lady, stooping to pick up the book and cards.

Sarah bent down to help her and exclaimed in delight as she saw the deck of cards: "*Mon Dieu!* It's the Marseilles tarot! Don't tell me you read cards!"

"Just as a hobby. Allow me to introduce myself. Mercedes Leal. You, of course, need no introduction. I came here to fetch the order that arrived on the latest steamer. Miguel told me it has been in for days. Well, with your permission, madame," the lady said, heading toward the door.

Sarah took her by the arm. "Ah, no! Don't you believe in fate? Neither of us is leaving until you read the cards for me."

Her companions protested.

"Sarah, I really must get back to the hotel. The doctor is waiting for me," said Jarrett.

"It's true, Sarah. We still have to rehearse before the show," added Berthier, who had secretly made an appointment in his room with a young admirer.

"Then the two of you go ahead. I'll follow later with Philippe and Marie," decreed the Divine One with finality. She said good-bye to the two men and turned to Miguel: "Do you perhaps have a more private place where we can read the cards?"

"Certainly, madame. My study, in the rear."

Saying this, he drew aside a curtain and went inside with the small retinue.

～

Mercedes Leal sat at a small table across from Sarah Bernhardt and began to shuffle the cards with the dexterity of a professional.

"A new deck. It must be thoroughly shuffled."

Around the table, Miguel, Garnier, and Marie Jullien observed in silence. Mercedes asked Sarah to cut the deck and began laying out the cards on the table. As soon as the great arcana were in place, Mercedes turned over the first card and hesitated: "Madame must understand that this is just a hobby. Nothing that one can really believe in."

"Why do you say that? Did you see something terrible in my future?"

"Well, these are new cards. I haven't read the book yet. I place more trust in my old Grimaud by Madame Normande. Perhaps we should shuffle again."

Sarah stayed her hand before she could pick up the cards.

"No, Mercedes. Read what you see. My future can't be all that horrible."

"Of course not, but nevertheless, if I were you I would take some precautions." She began to read the colored figures in front of her: "The Jongleur, or Magician, appears upside down, just above the Archpriestess. Strength, beside the Emperor and the Empress, above the Star, shows what we all know: you are a woman of great power, talent, and seduction. Immediately after, the Crazy Man and the Devil."

"I see that I'm in good company," joked Sarah, and everyone around the table laughed nervously.

Unperturbed, Mercedes Leal continued, "What worries me is the Final Judgment, followed by Death, the Hanged Man, and the Tower. As you know, these interpretations depend heavily on the intuition of the person reading the cards."

"Mercedes, what are you trying to tell me?"

"Nothing, madame, nothing, but I have a strange premonition that you should not return to Brazil. I see an accident, on a later voyage, a fall with grave consequences. The Tower indicates this." Saying this, Mercedes Leal gathered up the cards and stored them with the book. In the small room, one could have heard the buzzing of a fly.

La Bernhardt broke the spell by getting up.

"Well, at least I have nothing to fear for this season. Just as well, as the house is already sold out for every performance. *Merci,* Mercedes. Forgive me for taking up your time."

"I hope madame does not take these things too seriously. It's as I said, if it were with my old deck, Madame Normande's, but this one—"

"I know, a new deck," Sarah Bernhardt interrupted. "Unlike the casinos, to read the future we should not put our faith in a new deck. Don't miss me tonight in *Le passant.* I promise not to slip." She showed her lovely teeth in exaggerated laughter, said good-bye to Miguel, and left, still laughing, for Ouvidor Street.

# 8

Next to the Repository for Cadavers of the Third Order of Penitents, on Carioca Square, at the beginning of Assembléia Street, stood the appropriately named Morgue Bar. Despite the name, it was one of the liveliest places in the city. With its wrought-iron tables and marble tops, its loud conversations, a piano forever occupied by some night owl, the occasional late-night guitar, and air beclouded by the finest cigars from Havana and Bahia, the truth is that the place had atmosphere. Known also as the "Beer Hall of the Dead," the Morgue Bar was one of the preferred spots for the city's bohemians. They went there for the German proprietor's sausages and especially for the beers—particularly Dois Machados, Porter, Carlsberg, and Guinness, all imported from Europe.

One of the most assiduous denizens of the Morgue Bar was Olavo Bilac. That night, the house was filled. At their usual table in the rear, along with the poet, were his friends Guimarães Passos, Coelho Neto, Paula Nei, Agostini, Aluísio Azevedo, Salomão Calif, the marquis of Salles, José do Patrocínio, and Albertinho Fazelli, who was paying the bill. This was an indispensable detail, for the German, tired of putting things on the cuff, had posted a clearly visible sign beside the cash register saying: VIADO SÓ AMANHÃ (credit only tomorrow). What he didn't know was that in Portuguese "credit" was *fiado,* while *viado* was a slang term for a homosexual. The spelling error was due to the proprietor's Germanic origin: he invariably confused *v* with *f*. No one had taken it upon himself to correct the picturesque mistake.

Another constant figure in the circle was Chiquinha Gonzaga, a talented composer who had enjoyed great success the year before with her operetta *The Country Court*. An exquisite pianist, Chiquinha from time to time would adorn the end of the night with her popular songs and *chorinhos*. Everyone adored the composer, whom Paula Nei considered "our George Sand." This was because, in defiance of convention, she only traveled in masculine circles and had had the courage to leave both her husbands. The scandal had shocked both nobles and the bourgeois, one more reason for the band to take Chiquinha Gonzaga to its bosom. In self-mockery, the group had dubbed itself "the gang."

Paula Nei, in his inimitable style, was reading aloud the new code of conduct that had been published in the newspaper *The Country*.

"It is prohibited to place pots with flowers in the window, as they may, if knocked over, cause serious injury to passersby. Masquerades will only be permitted during carnival. Horses shall not gallop through the streets, save the cavalry in cases of urgency. Public urinals shall be constructed to prevent citizens' carrying out their necessary functions on the sidewalk. And, finally, all cuspidors shall be removed from the streets," he concluded, miming the act of spitting in Calif's hat and evoking laughter from his friends.

They went on to discuss the arrival of Sherlock Holmes, who was due in Rio the following day. The marquis of Salles had been designated by the emperor to meet him at the quay. Albertinho, who was a shameless liar, almost said that he had met the detective on one of his trips to London, but he restrained himself, remembering that he might find himself face to face with the Englishman.

"It appears he's coming in the company of a doctor, one Doctor Watson," informed José do Patrocínio, who had heard the news in the offices of the *Afternoon Gazette*.

"How so? Is the man sick or a hypochondriac?" asked Bilac.

"Neither one nor the other. The doctor is merely an inseparable friend who lives with him," replied Patrocínio.

"Curious. Could he be a poof?" ventured the marquis of Salles, who thought about nothing but such things.

"That's all we need, an English bugger," grumbled Salomão Calif, the tailor. "The shit-stirrers we already have are more than enough. Would you believe that the other day one of them wanted me to make him pants with the fly at the rear to facilitate his vice? 'I'll pay whatever it costs . . . there's money, Mr. Calif, there's money. . . . '"

"Knowing your appreciation of coin, I don't need to ask if you satisfied his wish," shouted Guimarães Passos from the other end of the table.

Everyone laughed at the quip. If there was anyone with no reason to doubt the tailor's generosity, it was Guimarães Passos. Salomão had made several suits and frock coats for the poet, without yet seeing the color of his money. One day, put out with his friend, who owed him for almost an entire wardrobe, he told Passos he would make him no more clothes until the poet paid what he owed. Despite their long friendship, Salomão gravely stated that Guimarães's credit was suspended but magnanimously pledged to go on making any changes or small alterations that the poet might need. A week later, Guimarães entered his friend's shop.

"Is your promise still good to do small alterations?"

"Of course," said the tailor.

Passos immediately took a small sack of buttons from his pocket and placed it in Salomão's hands.

"Well, then, I'd like you to sew an English cashmere suit onto these buttons."

The story was told by Calif himself, who had burst into laughter and had ended up making another suit for the poet.

Olavo Bilac returned to the subject of Sherlock Holmes.

"Seriously, I've heard that the man's deductive abilities are extraordinary. I've learned that Inspector Mello Pimenta is also going to seek him out to ask his help in the case of the murdered women."

"Good thing, too. I wasn't happy about such a brilliant mind wasting his noodle looking for a fiddle," said Paula Nei.

"Not a fiddle—a Stradivarius. It's worth a fortune," corrected De Salles.

"Not as much as the lives of those young women," retorted Bilac.

At that moment, Inspector Pimenta came into the bar. He knew them all well, for he always came to have a beer after duty. Bilac, remembering that the inspector was looking for him, got up and tried to conceal himself among his friends.

"Relax, Mr. Bilac. There's nothing outstanding against you. It's all newspaper exaggeration. After all, if our young men could no longer write manifestos, what would become of Brazil? I just came in to have a beer," stated Pimenta.

"And it's on us, inspector," said Albertinho Fazelli, gesturing at the waiter.

Bilac, now at ease, sat down again, saying, "A curious coincidence, your coming here at this very moment. Do you know we were just now speaking of the murdered girls? Quite a worriment, isn't it, inspector? There's even talk that you plan to ask the help of Sherlock Holmes, who is here at the invitation of the emperor."

"I'm not saying yes and I'm not saying no," answered Mello Pimenta, irritated that the news was already being bandied about.

"Look, Pimenta, everybody already knows the story," said the always irreverent Chiquinha Gonzaga. "Paiva, the fellow at the post office, took it on himself to spread it around that you sent a telegram."

Mello Pimenta was so indignant that he choked on his beer.

"Betraying confidentiality! How could that scoundrel have the audacity to reveal the contents of my correspondence? That's a crime!"

"We know, but Paiva, in addition to being a public servant, is the brother of the Count D'Eu's governess. No one can lay a finger on him," explained Coelho Neto.

"Not even a zealous police inspector and pursuer of poets," said Bilac with a knavish expression.

They all burst into guffaws, including Pimenta. He finished his first glass of beer and immediately Albertinho Fazelli asked Laurindo, the waiter who always served the group, to bring them another mug.

"Young Bilac is right. As my telegram to the Englishman seems to be in the public domain, there's no reason to deny it. I actually did ask the English detective for help. Only I don't know if he's going to be able to give me any of his time. After all, he's come to Brazil at the behest of Dom Pedro."

"No self-respecting detective could fail to be interested in two such odd crimes," said Aluísio Azevedo, lighting a cigar. "I would just like to know what the fellow's specialty is."

"I can be of some help there," answered Pimenta, his tongue loosened by the second large mug of beer, "as I also asked Scotland Yard for information. . . . "

Thanks to the beer, the pronunciation of the English police agency's name came out almost perfect. The group, interested, drew even closer. Fazelli ordered another round. The marquis of Salles ventured, "I'll bet it's deduction. A good detective has to have the ability to arrive at conclusions, based on clues, using only logic and reason. Am I right, inspector?"

Mello Pimenta agreed. He was enjoying being the center of attention.

"I might add, marquis, that it's not as easy as it appears. I would even like to take advantage of this highly intelligent group to offer a demonstration. I'm going to speak about a very famous case and see who can discover the solution, having the same clues."

"An excellent idea!" said Aluísio Azevedo enthusiastically. "It's like a guessing game."

"Not guessing, Mr. Aluísio, deduction!" pontificated Mello Pimenta, installing himself at the table.

He was master of the situation. The bohemians, even those at nearby tables, came closer to drink in his words and a few more liters of beer. Pimenta took another swallow, wiped the white foam from his mustache, paused, and began, "As I said before, it's very difficult. Something for professionals. Don't be upset if you fail to come to any conclusion. Needless to say, I'm going to omit names and places." Then, in a more somber tone, he began reciting an old police-procedure conundrum, making himself the protagonist: "A woman was found dead in her home, in the bathtub, with a bullet in her heart."

"She must have done something to deserve it," groused Alberto Fazelli, who did not hold the weaker sex in high regard. Coelho Neto told him to be quiet, and Mello Pimenta continued: "The bathroom floor was wet, indicating that some kind of struggle had taken place before the shot. When I got there, her poor husband told me he was the first to find her. He had heard the shot, gone in her direction, seen she was bleeding profusely, and had run to find some bandages. When he returned, his wife was already dead. He then went to the living room and had me summoned."

"Poor man. . . ." commented Salomão Calif, who worshipped his family.

"Carefully examining the scene, I saw there were traces of three sets of footsteps made by the husband's wet shoes."

"And how did you discover your murderer?" asked José do Patrocínio impatiently.

"Well, inside the house, I noticed on the table in the dining room an uncorked bottle of port wine, with a dark stain on the label. The entrance mirror was broken. Immediately I turned to the husband and arrested him. Why?"

"Because the wine was poisoned!" said Albertinho Fazelli hastily; he often spoke before he thought.

"Albertinho, the woman died from a gunshot," Bilac reminded him.

"Because the bullet was poisoned!" insisted Fazelli, who was obsessed.

"If this were a contest in nonsense, not deduction, you'd easily take first prize," said Paula Nei.

"Had the husband drunk any of the wine?" Bilac wanted to know.

Mello Pimenta shook his head solemnly.

"He broke the mirror when he saw his reflected image. He

must have been very badly dressed," offered Salomão Calif. Even Albertinho Fazelli found the tailor's professional distortion absurd.

No one had any further suggestions for a solution to the puzzle. Pimenta lit a cigar offered by Guimarães Passos and smugly took a long puff, savoring both the Havana and his success.

"The footprints. The solution is in the footprints," said Chiquinha Gonzaga.

"Don't be asinine, Chiquinha. What do footprints have to do with it?" jeered Aluísio Azevedo.

"Dona Chiquinha is right," agreed Pimenta, mildly irritated.

Chiquinha Gonzaga continued: "All of you are muddleheaded. The inspector said that he found only three sets of footprints. Now, if the husband came from elsewhere in the house as he claimed, there would be four sets of tracks on the wet floor. The first when the husband entered the bathroom and went up to his dead wife. Another to fetch the bandages, another to return to the bathroom to try to help the woman, and finally the fourth set when he went back to the living room to summon the police. Since the inspector found only three sets of footprints, it's a sign the husband was already in the bathroom when he discharged his weapon after a brief struggle with his wife, who tried to defend her life."

Everyone in the Morgue Bar was amazed at the composer's powers of deduction. Paula Nei shouted, "*Viva* Chiquinha Gonzaga, our detective in skirts!"

"*Viva!*" shouted customers and waiters, in unison.

"More beer for the living in the Beer Hall of the Dead!" requested Alberto Fazelli.

Amidst the excitement, only Pimenta seemed less than pleased at seeing his mystery case unraveled by a woman. Interrupting the festivities, the marquis of Salles asked, "Inspector, what do the open bottle of port, the stain on the label, and the broken mirror have to do with the story?"

"Nothing. That was just to give the case more atmosphere," said Mello Pimenta, embarrassed, looking sideways at Chiquinha and evoking laughter from his listeners.

Even the German, the bar's owner, applauded the composer:

"The next *rround* is on the *Haus*," he bellowed in his thick accent. "This *girrl* is *very besser* than Beethoven."

It was never ascertained if the German was comparing the intelligence or the musical gifts of the two composers.

It was clear to Pimenta that Chiquinha Gonzaga was stealing the evening. To transform the situation and avenge himself on the pianist, he began diverting the course of the conversation.

"The crimes I am investigating now are much more complex. Two pretty young women, almost girls, brutally killed, without anything, apparently, that ties one to the other. The first was a prostitute, the second a lady-in-waiting at the palace. Both of them victims of the same barbarous murderer."

"How do you know that it's the same person?" asked Guimarães Passos.

Immediately, Pimenta was sorry he had brought up the matter. The clues left by the monster were not yet public knowledge. If not for the beers, he would certainly have kept his counsel. Now it was too late to turn back, and the policeman forged ahead.

"Because of the flaps of skin. . . ."

"What flaps of skin?" asked Olavo Bilac, curious.

"The murderer cut off a flap of skin from each victim and took it with him."

A frisson of revulsion ran through the bar. Pimenta was pleased with the reaction he had caused.

"Perhaps Dona Chiquinha would care to examine the cadavers. She may be able to help me with her brilliant powers of deduction," he added perversely.

"An excellent idea," said the marquis of Salles, excited at the prospect of becoming acquainted with the charnel house.

"As for me, I don't see why not," answered Chiquinha Gonzaga.

"Nor I," said Paula Nei, emboldened.

"I'd very much like to, but I can't. I forgot the keys to my house and I don't want to wake up the domestics," said Alberto Fazelli, excusing himself.

"I have to go home to sleep, too. I have a fitting early tomorrow," stated Salomão Calif, avoiding the funereal experience.

"If we're going, let's be on our way," said Olavo Bilac, rising.

"Calm down. There's no hurry. Where they are, no one will take them away. First, I'm going to finish my cigar. It's disrespectful to smoke up the dead," affirmed Mello Pimenta, taking a long puff.

～

Of the group, only Guimarães Passos, Paula Nei, Coelho Neto, the marquis of Salles, and, of course, Chiquinha Gonzaga went to the Third Order of Penitents morgue, making

their way through the short stretch of Assembléia Street to
Carioca Square. Presenting his credentials, the inspector had
the night watchman open the heavy iron door that lent the
place an even more sinister appearance. Hearing the creaking
of the gates, Coelho Neto considered making up some excuse
and beating a hasty retreat; nevertheless, he stood his ground,
fearful of the mockery of his friends. The six of them proceeded in silence through the twisting corridor that led to the
repository. A strong smell of formaldehyde reinforced the
odor of death. They came to the entrance to the mortuary
room and Pimenta called out to the individual charged with
the night watch.

"Gervásio! Gervásio, wake up!"

Gervásio appeared, groggy from sleep, his hair tousled.
Everyone was surprised at the sight that stood before them.
Gervásio was a dwarf. He was thirty years old and was at most
a meter and a half tall. He belonged to a traditional circus family and was once billed as the smallest dwarf in the world, but
he had been forced to give up his artistic career as the result of
the calamity that is the nightmare of all professional dwarfs:
Gervásio had started growing. At first, when he noticed that
he had risen from ninety-eight centimeters to a meter and two
centimeters, he had attempted to hide it, shrinking into himself
whenever he entered the circus ring, but his father and his
brothers, all dwarfs, quickly spotted Gervásio's deceptions.
Endowed with the integrity characteristic of the circus world,
the family had refused to participate in the fraud. Amid tears
and sobs, the ill-fated dwarf had said good-bye to his friends,
broken off with the bearded lady, with whom he had been involved for years, and departed to face the hostile and gigantic
world. After much searching, the only employment he had

found was this, mortuary attendant at the Third Order of Penitents morgue, and even so it had been through the influence of a charitable priest who was moved by the tiny artist's plight. At first, Gervásio found it strange living with the dead, all of them taller than he. But now, after five years, he moved nimbly among the cadavers.

"Hello, inspector, isn't it kind of late? Aren't you afraid of waking up my customers?" joked the Lilliputian attendant in a falsetto voice.

"Forgive me, Gervásio. You know very well that Justice never watches the clock. I need to show my friends here, great investigators all, the bodies of those two young women."

"Of course, inspector. I'm always very happy to be of service to you," the dwarf said sincerely, for Pimenta was the only one who didn't make the obvious jests about his stature. "The girls are in very good condition. I just hope the shipment of ice isn't delayed."

Gervásio was referring to the blocks of natural ice that came from the United States. They arrived in large chunks, in the hold of ships, carefully swathed in thick layers of sawdust. The ice was stored in special depositories in the Santa Luzia district, where, with the necessary precautions, it was immediately placed in deep pits. Incredibly, loss was minimal, no more than 30 or 40 percent at the end of five months. The problem was that sometimes the steamers were delayed, which occasioned great inconvenience for morgues and ice-cream factories. The dwarf agilely pulled open two large drawers, exposing the bodies of the girls, and removed a small bundle wrapped in brown paper from one of the drawers.

"So that's where I left my sandwich," the attendant commented to himself.

The group was aghast at the scene. With the exception of Bilac and the marquis, who possessed a morbid curiosity, all repented of having accepted the inspector's invitation and wanted to leave as quickly as possible. They pretended to be unruffled, but Pimenta knew perfectly well the sensation of uneasiness and dread that the place evoked in his guests. He had felt it himself, many years before, at the start of his career, the first time he had visited the morgue. Yet despite their violent deaths, the two girls, enfolded in long white sheets, appeared as if in a deep slumber. Those present almost felt they were in a boarding school rather than a morgue, and were secretly spying on a girls' dormitory.

"How lovely they are," murmured Bilac.

"What monster could have visited such savagery upon them?" Guimarães Passos asked himself.

"That's what I would like to know," said Mello Pimenta. He turned to Chiquinha Gonzaga, savoring the vengeance of having brought the composer there, and asked, "Well, 'colleague'? Would you care to examine the bodies?"

"The inspector knows very well that I'm not a specialist. Furthermore, the only curious fact has already been pointed out. The missing flaps of skin," replied Chiquinha, unable to take her eyes off the dead girls.

"And the strings," said the inspector.

"What strings?" asked the marquis of Salles.

"Didn't I mention that? Coiled in . . . on the body of each of them was found a string from a musical instrument," said Pimenta, taking the strings from his pocket. "I just don't know what instrument."

Chiquinha Gonzaga yanked them from Mello Pimenta's hands.

"Listen, inspector. For this there was no need to bring us to this place filled with shadows and sadness. They're two violin strings. I can tell you more than that: they're the first and the last ones, *sol* and *mi*." She handed the strings back to the inspector and turned toward the exit: "Can we leave now, or do we have to stay in this macabre version of Madame Tussaud's?" she said, harshly, referring to the famous wax museum in London.

"Let's go, all of us. Enough horrors for one night," added Coelho Neto, grabbing the arm of Olavo Bilac, who went on staring at the bodies of the two young women. "Come along, Olavo."

"They're so beautiful. . . . " murmured the poet.

Gervásio closed the drawers and accompanied them to the door.

"Stop by any time, inspector. You know how much I like a good chat, and my guests aren't very talkative."

He asked the watchman to help him close the heavy gates and stood observing the departing group from behind the bars. As soon as they had disappeared down Assembléia Street, the dwarf took the brown package from his pocket and calmly finished eating his sandwich.

## 9

For the traveler arriving by sea, the city of Saint Sebastian of Rio de Janeiro was a dazzling sight. The whole of the shoreline, adorned with luxuriant vegetation, was covered with palm trees, ferns, *muricis,* and trees undreamt of by European minds. As soon as the ship crossed the bar and entered the Bay of Guanabara, between Governor's Isle and Sugar Loaf Mountain, the wayfarer would begin to see the districts of Botafogo, Catete, and Glória, which already displayed some large-scale constructions. The waters were dotted with small boats that came out to meet the steamers, their sailors yelling a welcome. Between the hills of Castelo and São Bento could be seen, in the distance, the rooftops of the city; what most attracted the attention of those arriving, however, was the whiteness of the sandy beaches.

Leaning on the railing of the main deck of the *Aquitania,* the detective Sherlock Holmes and Dr. John Hamish Watson took all this in. The doctor was wearing a suit of brown wool with a vest and felt hat made of the same color. The detective sported dark clothing, over which was a checkered cape lighter in tone, and a cap of the same weave, which constituted an unvarying part of his wardrobe. It was only seven A.M., and at this time in winter the temperature was quite pleasant, around seventy-three degrees. As the ship had not yet docked, the passengers waited in the small boats that would ferry them to the quay. Distracted by the scenery, imagining what life must be like in that city, Sherlock did not notice that, from one of the boats, someone was shouting his name. Watson was obliged to break into his thoughts.

"Holmes, I think they're calling you."

"Who?"

"I don't know. Someone."

"Where?"

"It appears to be from over there, from that boat," said Watson, pointing.

Below, in the small boat, Júlio Augusto Pereira, the marquis of Salles, waved to the detective. He had barely slept and his features betrayed the fatigue of the lugubrious previous night. In addition, he hated boats and only a request from the emperor could have gotten him out of his bed and into so nautical an enterprise. He balanced himself in the boat as it rocked to the rhythm of the waves and, cupping his hands around his mouth, yelled again, in English, "Mr. Sherlock Holmes! I am looking for Mr. Sherlock Holmes!"

"Here I am!" replied the detective, waving his arms.

The marquis ordered the boatman to draw closer to the *Aquitania*.

"I've come to meet you by order of the emperor. I hope you had a pleasant journey."

"Excellent, thank you."

"Speak for yourself," grumbled Watson, who had hated every moment on board. Besides that, as he was wont to say archly, his stomach didn't have its sea legs. Not even the home remedy of drinking an egg yolk with a glass of sherry in the morning had stopped the doctor from expelling all the Pantagruelian meals served on the ship.

"Watson, see that our baggage gets ashore. Meanwhile, I'll

say good-bye to the captain." Before Watson could object, for he detested it when Holmes treated him like a servant, Holmes had disappeared through a door on the deck.

~

The progress of the *Aquitania* to the Pharoux quay took place without incident. The baggage was placed on a cart, while De Salles and the two visitors climbed into the marquis's landau. As the carriage made its way through the center of the city, Watson said in surprise, "Curious. I don't see any Indians in the streets."

The marquis of Salles was amused at the doctor's wonderment.

"Nor will you, Dr. Watson. We are almost civilized by now," he said ironically. "Furthermore, the Indians are as free as nature; they're of little use for domestic labors. We rely on the slaves. For the most part the blacks do well enough, even if some are quite ... quite—" He could not find the word in English. He murmured to himself: *"Preguiçosos ... preguiçosos ... how could I say preguiçosos in English ... ?"*

"Lazy," offered Holmes, with perfect aplomb.

Watson's astonishment was surpassed only by that of the marquis of Salles.

"What? So Mr. Sherlock speaks Portuguese?!"

"I suppose so," replied Holmes, speaking now in the language of Camões.

An intrigued Watson, who despite living with the detective for seven years had yet to accustom himself to such revelations, asked, "Where the devil did you learn to speak this language?"

"In Macao, in China, a year before meeting you. I spent almost six months there, studying mysterious Oriental poisons, and the greatest specialist in the subject was a Portuguese scientist, Nicolau Travessa."

"I've never heard of him," said Watson, not without a certain disdain.

"Of course not, Watson. How would a surgeon in Her Britannic Majesty's army know about exotic poisons?"

"This Nicolau Travessa truly understood the subject?" asked De Salles, with his fascination for indecorous matters.

"Travessa was a misunderstood genius. He was born in Lisbon, to a wealthy family, but his spirit of adventure soon took him to Goa, in India, from which he was expelled."

"Why?" inquired the marquis.

"For having used his own body in experiments with the venom of the *naja* snake, which cost him one eye and paralysis in his left leg," related Holmes respectfully.

"He tried the poisons on himself?" Watson asked, horrified.

"Like all great scientists, Travessa made his own system into an experimental laboratory. From Goa he left for China. Over the years he tried arsenic, cyanide, lead carbonate, strychnine, curare, and even *conum maculatum*, which is a rare poison extracted from a Japanese fish. During my long stay in Macao, I learned a great deal from this simple and dedicated man. A pity that science does not do justice to him."

"And just where is this exemplar of toxic substances now?" asked the marquis of Salles.

"He died, unfortunately, while testing on himself a concentration of venom from African scorpions," answered Holmes, with emotion. Despite being a dispassionate man, he was always moved at the memory of the sage from Lisbon.

During the remainder of the trip, Holmes was able to

demonstrate his command of the language to the charmed marquis. Because he had learned it in a Portuguese colony, he spoke with a thick Lusitanian accent. The landau stopped in front of the Hotel Albion and the coachman, a young man of barely twenty, stepped down to help the passengers. Holmes was the last to descend from the carriage, supporting himself on the youth's arms.

"Thank you, young man. I see that your brother had tuberculosis and died of the disease a short time ago. I'm sorry," concluded Holmes. Observing the shock on the part of the coachman and the other occupants of the landau, the detective continued: "I sense that you are perplexed at my deduction, but it is elementary. I note a red stain on your frock coat, definitely the result of hemoptysis. It can also be observed that the clothing in question is quite loose on you, which shows that it belonged to another person. As is the habit among less privileged families, the younger brothers inherit the garments of the older. Therefore, it is obvious that this jacket, stained by the effusion of blood, belonged to your unfortunate brother, cut down by that terrible disease."

Absolutely speechless, the marquis of Salles turned to the coachman. "Are Mr. Holmes's observations correct?"

"No, sir. I'm an only child. The jacket belonged to my uncle, who's an apothecary. That's why it has this here stain, from mercurochrome."

Holmes, who was already entering the lobby of the hotel, ignored the young coachman's stammered explanations.

～

The Hotel Albion ceded nothing to its old-world counterparts. It was located on Fresca Street—the word means cool—which owed its name to the fact that it was the constant beneficiary of ocean breezes coming from the sandbar, and the rear of the hotel looked out to sea, which meant the rooms were always quite airy. The floor at the entrance was covered with travertine marble and the main foyer, where the concierge's desk was located, was decorated with stylish furniture imported from France, all of it upholstered in tapestry or silk. Florentine mirrors ringed the area, increasing even further the room's dimensions. On the tables, which were set with white lace cloths, enormous porcelain vases laden with tropical flowers gave the arriving guest the impression of having passed through the gates of paradise. To the left of the entrance was an immense billiards room, frequented by gentlemen of society, who would meet there after their workday. To the right, a tearoom that served, in addition to the most refined English selections, the best French patisserie, all on silver trays and in delicate porcelain dishes. Everything at the hotel was imported, from bedclothes to toothpicks.

The marquis of Salles approached the guest counter with Holmes, while Watson kept a watchful eye on the baggage being carried in by three uniformed Negro boys.

"The Crown has reserved rooms for Mr. Sherlock Holmes and Dr. John Watson," advised the marquis.

Inojozas, the efficient concierge and an indispensable figure at the Hotel Albion, presented the room keys. Thin, very elegant, with waxed mustaches and black hair plastered to his head with brilliantine from Argentina, this astute employee could solve any problem. The gratuities he received from grateful lodgers far exceeded his salary. It was said that, if the recompense was commensurate, Inojozas could even place five virgin cocottes in the bed of any traveler, despite the strict vigilance of the proprietor and the unlikeliness of finding so many maidens engaged in the oldest profession.

"These are the best rooms in the hotel," he said, bowing and scraping, and he gestured for another employee to accompany Holmes and Watson.

"I doubt that," retorted Holmes. "The best ones must be occupied by some millionaire plantation owner. The doctor and I well settle for, how do you say in Portuguese, 'second best'?"

"I believe it is untranslatable. If you need anything, just let me know. My name is Inojozas, at your service," added the concierge, changing the subject in impeccable English.

"Well," said the marquis of Salles, "I'll let you rest a bit. We have a luncheon at the palace at one-thirty, with Madame Sarah Bernhardt. Generally, His Majesty lunches at eleven o' clock, but as the steamer was late, Dom Pedro will defer to you. I know that the emperor is eager to tell you about the case involving the violin belonging to the baroness of Avaré. I'll come by at noon to fetch you, as the Boa Vista palace is rather far from here. Mr. Holmes, Dr. Watson, it's been a pleasure," concluded the marquis of Salles, departing. He took a flower from one of the vases, placed it in his lapel, and walked briskly toward his landau.

~

The table for the luncheon was placed in the solarium, in one of the wings of the palace. For obvious reasons, the participants were few: Sarah Bernhardt, her son, Maurice, Sherlock Holmes, Watson, the emperor, the viscount of Ibituaçu, and the marquis of Salles. Edward Jarrett, the actress's American impresario, also invited, was unable to attend, as Sarah's fears had been confirmed: Jarrett was suffering from yellow fever.

The viscount of Ibituaçu was a friend of long standing of the emperor's. A wealthy plantation owner from the Paraíba Valley, he was owner of a large and magnificent Roman-style house on Laranjeiras Street, at the center of a splendorous park, where he spent several months each year. A confirmed bachelor, the eccentric nobleman loved to give parties in his mansion for the city's bohemians and literati, from which stemmed his acquaintance with De Salles. Dom Pedro valued his friendship because, thanks to him, the emperor was kept well informed of what was going on in the bars and cafés. As soon as they arrived, Holmes and Sarah Bernhardt recalled to mind previous meetings.

"I have never forgotten your Lady Macbeth two years ago, at the Gaiety in London. The sleepwalking scene, besides leaving the audience delirious, had the English actresses dying of envy."

"*Mon cher* Holmes, charming as ever." She turned and addressed herself in English to Dr. Watson: "And how is my dear doctor? I hope you have taken seriously my suggestion to describe in book form the fantastic adventures of your friend."

"I have thought about it, madame. For now, there is no time."

Dom Pedro II, displaying his habitual restraint in dress, was wearing a black frock coat and white gloves. He began by apologizing.

"I beg your indulgence at the empress's absence, but Teresa Cristina isn't feeling very well. If not for her migraine, I would have offered my illustrious guests a large banquet."

Everyone at the table knew this was a lame excuse, as the matter to be discussed would surely not have been pleasing to the empress.

The ensuing conversation could have taken place in the

Tower of Babel, as Watson spoke in English; Sarah Bernhardt and Maurice in French; the marquis, the viscount, and the emperor, in all three languages. Holmes, expressing himself correctly in the Portuguese of Portugal, seemed more a Lusitanian businessman than an English detective.

"I am delighted to be in your country," he told the monarch.

"A pity the reason for your visit is professional," replied Dom Pedro, wishing to broach the subject of the violin. He courteously translated the phrase for the others.

Sarah Bernhardt took advantage of the opportunity to praise the Brazilian sovereign.

"I love Your Majesty's genteel manners. Very different from those of another ruler I know, Franz Josef of Austria. He's a detestable man. I had a chance to see how harsh and unkind he is with his wife, Empress Elizabeth, who happens to be his cousin. She married while still a girl, when she was barely fifteen. An affectionate young woman who never had anything but disdain for the ridiculous court etiquette of Vienna. After I saw the coarse manner in which he treated his wife, I refused to go on stage at any theater where Franz Josef was present."

There was an uncomfortable hush among the Brazilians in the solarium. Unwittingly, Sarah Bernhardt had committed a monumental faux pas. Dom Pedro, son of the Austrian princess Leopoldina, was Franz Josef's cousin. The emperor himself assumed the task of breaking the chill by changing the subject.

"I read in your memoirs that madame performed in North America six years ago and met President Lincoln's widow."

"Yes, Your Majesty. In unpleasant circumstances." She turned to the guests, who were immediately transformed into her audience. "Imagine, I was aboard the *L'Amérique*, when I decided to take a breath of air on the main deck. It was very cold that morning. As I was walking, my path crossed that of an older lady, dressed in black, whose expression was one of resignation. Suddenly, an unexpected wave dashed itself against the ship with such force that we were thrown to the floor. I managed to clutch onto the leg of a bench, but the unfortunate lady was swept forward. I got up and was in time to grab her by the skirt. If not for that, the poor woman would have gone headlong down the stairs. I said, 'You could have been killed!' She answered, 'Yes, but unfortunately, God was not willing.' And she added, 'I am Lincoln's widow.' Think of the irony of fate: her husband, the President, had been assassinated by Booth, an actor, and Bernhardt, an actress, had just prevented her from going to meet her beloved husband. For the rest of the crossing I didn't have the courage to say a single word to her."

Sarah narrated the incident with such drama that, at the end, her listeners almost applauded. It fell to their host, once again, to dispel the tension. In a jovial tone, Dom Pedro announced, "I hope Madame Bernhardt and Mr. Holmes like the food. I ordered a meal with some of our typical dishes. There will be *feijoada* and *vatapá*. Our guests can choose from among one and the other."

"*Merveilleux!* What are they?"

At a signal, several liveried valets approached with trays. The emperor did the honors. Pointing first to the *feijoada,* he explained and translated, "These are *feijões pretos,* black beans, *haricots noirs,* cooked with several kinds of meat: pigs' feet and ears, dried meat, pork loin, ribs, pork sausage, and other varieties. The meat and beans are served with kale, slices of orange, manioc flour, and white rice. Quite good."

"And the other dish?" asked Maurice Bernhardt with the natural curiosity of the French for the exotic.

"*Vatapá*. A Bahian speciality. A delicious delicacy for those who prefer seafood. *Vatapá* is made from slices of fish, shrimp, cornmeal mush, peanuts, and coconut milk, and seasoned with coriander, parsley, bay leaf, nutmeg, ginger, scallions, garlic, onions, tomato, and lots of red pepper. It's cooked in *dendê* oil."

"*Dendê?*" asked Holmes.

"Palm oil. *Dendê* is a small native coconut that yields a highly extravagant oil," the emperor explained euphemistically. "The *vatapá* is served accompanied by a type of dressing called *acaçá* or white cream, made from rice flour and thick coconut milk. A veritable dish fit for the gods. *Madame et messieurs,* the choice is yours."

Sarah Bernhardt, an experienced traveler, avoided the highly spiced *vatapá* and chose merely a small portion of bean broth and rice. Maurice imitated his mother. The Brazilians divided themselves between the two dishes, except for the emperor: claiming doctor's orders, he requested a green salad. Sherlock, who though thin was a hearty eater, mixed the *vatapá* with the *feijoada* and sprinkled on several spoonfuls of red pepper and a liberal amount of palm oil. The aged viscount of Ibituaçu had contracted a certain indisposition in Germany, most likely venereal in nature, as he was constantly in doctors' offices, invariably hurling imprecations against women. For that reason he was obliged to follow a strict died based on chicken soup. As he was an inveterate jokester, he decided to amuse himself with the detective's voracity and began to direct Holmes's appetite.

"My dear Sherlock, try another rib with red pepper. It's sublime."

"Thank you," said Holmes, chewing.

"A slice of fish. This one here, with the most *dendê*. *Dendê* is very good for the heart."

"Thank you," said Holmes again.

"Don't overlook the peanuts with the *vatapá*. Excellent for the circulation."

"Thank you," said Holmes, devouring it.

"Don't spare the sausage and the cornmeal. An infallible recipe for easy digestion."

"Thank you," said Holmes yet again.

"I'd like to offer you, at my house, a *sarapatel*. It's a regional dish from Pernambuco and I have a cook from the northeast who's a specialist."

"Thank you," said Holmes, burping discreetly. He went on eating, following the viscount's counsel to the letter. Only Dr. Watson, pensive, was not yet eating. He continued to stare at the delights of the imperial table.

"So, Watson, you're not eating? It's delicious," affirmed Holmes between two huge forkfuls.

Watson stared dubiously at the enormous platters. His culinary experiences, from the time of his service in India, made him wary. Ever since, he had avoided bizarre spices and meats of any kind. He responded by looking fixedly at the dishes.

"I haven't decided yet whether I'll eat the yellow stuff or the black stuff."

"If I may offer some advice, doctor, I suggest the beans, the rice, and the kale, without the meat," said the marquis of Salles, with the experience of a survivor of more than a thousand banquets. Later, taking advantage of a moment in which everyone was distracted by the food, he asked the detective about the case of the murdered girls.

"I have heard that our police inspector has asked for your help in a gruesome case that he's investigating."

"Correct," admitted Holmes, engulfing a shrimp. "I found his telegram curious and, as a detective, was intrigued by what I have been able to learn of the case. I eagerly anticipate meeting him. Without, of course, neglecting the principal reason that brought me to Brazil," he added, smiling at the emperor.

Dom Pedro replied, "Quite so, quite so. . . . Naturally, if Mr. Holmes could help our police in this case, we would also be very grateful. After all, one of the victims is the niece of a friend of mine, Vítor Meireles, one of our most talented painters."

The luncheon proceeded without further comments worthy of note. For dessert, fruit was brought, and Holmes accomplished the phenomenon of eating an entire pineapple and two mangoes. After coffee, brandy, and cigars, the emperor accompanied his guests to the door.

"If I may, I'd like to ask Mr. Holmes and Dr. Watson to remain a little longer. I'd like to discuss this matter in greater detail. Afterward I'll have you taken back to the hotel."

Sarah turned to the detective.

"Good-bye, Mr. Holmes. Don't fail to see me at the theater. I'm almost regretting the day I must leave for Argentina. I know I shall miss enormously this warm Brazilian public."

"There can be no doubt, madame. If I have time. I am certain that, as always, it will be an unforgettable experience," said Holmes, enchanted.

Dom Pedro took his leave of everyone, gracefully kissed Sarah Bernhardt's hand, and withdrew with the two Englishmen.

~

The three installed themselves in a small reading room, one of the emperor's favorite hideaways in the immense palace. It was a discreetly furnished room, where Dom Pedro kept cherished objects and family remembrances. Delicate antique statuettes decorated the setting and the walls were covered with paintings by Vítor Meireles, Almeida Júnior, and Araújo Porto Alegre. On one of the tables were tin soldiers, in a formation that re-created the famous battle of Tuiuti, in the Paraguayan War, where the famous general Sampaio had died heroically. Holmes lit his pipe, while Watson, intrigued, looked at a yellowed photograph of Dom Pedro surrounded by Indians. The aborigines were naked and over his dress uniform His Majesty wore an embroidered mantle, with the pallium made of toucan crops.

"Fantastic!" exclaimed the doctor.

"Do you like it? A shame the daguerreotype is already somewhat faded."

Holmes came over and examined the framed portrait.

"Fortunately, the daguerreotype is a thing of the past. With the advent of the new colloidal process, using a solution of nitrocellulose, invented by my countryman Frederick Scott, photography has begun to keep pace with the modern times in which we live," said the detective, spouting erudition. "Photos have been of great help to us in the identification of criminals."

"May I ask Your Majesty the story behind this daguerreotype?" asked Watson, still intrigued.

"It's very old. I took it, as a relic, to the Centennial Exposition in Philadelphia, in 1876, to add to the brilliance of Brazil's pavilion. It appears we cut a fine figure," the emperor boasted. "In fact, it was on that occasion that I met—"

"Alexander Graham Bell, inventor of the telephone," interrupted Sherlock Holmes.

"You know of that meeting?" asked Dom Pedro, surprised at the detective's knowledge.

"Of course. Bell himself told me of the episode with the telephone: 'To be or not to be. . . .' "

Dom Pedro explained, upset.

"This is an injustice that history will surely visit on me. It was not I but Bell who spoke Shakespeare's phrase into the telephone. I was so nonplussed at hearing Bell's voice coming clearly through the apparatus that I idiotically started repeating, 'That is the question. To be or not to be, that is the question,' when I saw that the gadget actually talked."

"Your Majesty must forgive it if the anecdote is recounted incorrectly," said Holmes, relighting his pipe. "As my father used to say, 'If the myth is more picturesque than the fact, tell the myth.' "

The emperor sat down in his favorite armchair and gestured for his guests to install themselves on a small sofa.

"I know you must be fatigued from your journey and I don't want to take up any more of your time than is necessary. I would like to quickly relate the facts about the stolen violin. I don't even know where to begin."

"Try to begin at the beginning, Your Majesty," urged Holmes, nonchalantly crossing his long legs and with his movement knocking over a small table holding a collection of Sèvres porcelain.

"It was nothing," Dom Pedro said, ashen, not even blinking despite the pieces having been a gift from Bonaparte to Marie Louise of Hapsburg, in the royal family for years. The emperor turned his eyes from the broken shards, which seemed to have no effect on the Englishman, and began his narrative: "Since the 1870s a marvelous Cuban violinist named José

White has frequented our court. White studied in Paris with masters such as Alard, Reber, and Taite. He even won first prize in violin at the conservatoire. I became enchanted with his talent and took him under my protection. Together with the pianist Artur Napoleão, White created the Brazilian Society of Classical Concerts, which has given us some unforgettable moments."

"I hope to be able to share some of them," interjected Holmes.

Ignoring the Englishman's unseemly interruption, Dom Pedro continued.

"Well then, the last violin made by Antonio Stradivari, at ninety-three years of age, shortly before his death, was an instrument called, with good reason, 'the Swan Song.'"

"Interesting, I always thought it was the Muntz, which he made at ninety-two," said Holmes, who though an amateur was well versed in the subject.

"That's what was thought for many years, but in 1822, the Swan Song was discovered, having been manufactured in 1737. It's marvelous that at that age Stradivari achieved in his final work the perfect formal equilibrium of each part. The instrument's broad and powerful sonority is almost unbelievable. The sole detail, incidentally, and it is a poignant one, that betrays the tremor of his aged hands is the slightly unsure intaglio of the two *f*-shaped openings that form the acoustical system of the top. This last work of the great master ended up in the hands of a Professor Bertuzzi, in Milan. In 1840, the Swan Song was taken to Paris and acquired by the businessman Jean-Baptiste Vuillaume. Forty years later, the famous violin was once again in the hands of a violinist, the Frenchman Claude Miremont. Finally, after passing through some other owners, the Swan Song went on auction at the Hotel Drouot, in Paris, and the Maison Gand et Bernardel acquired it." Dom Pedro paused and poured himself a chalice of wine from the island of Madeira. "I hope I'm not being tiresome," he concluded, noting the detective's stifled yawn.

"Much the opposite; as a musician I am fascinated by this information," said Holmes, cautiously uncrossing his legs.

The emperor continued.

"For some time my friend Maria Luísa Catarina de Albuquerque, the baroness of Avaré, had expressed the desire to have a Stradivarius. You know how a woman's whims are. When they get an idea in their heads, nothing will dislodge it."

"I know very well. That's why I'm still a bachelor," agreed Holmes.

Dom Pedro took another sip of wine and resumed the narrative:

"Well then, I spun a plan with my protégé, José White. I advanced him twenty thousand francs, the price of the violin, and White went to Paris to buy it as if it were for himself. When he arrived back here, without anyone's knowledge, my dear violinist handed me the Stradivarius and kept a perfect imitation secretly manufactured in Santa Catarina, one of our southern states, by a family of luthiers, descendants of Germans, who make extraordinary instruments. Thus I was able, discreetly, to make the gift to the baroness. That's all. Maria Luísa's wish was satisfied. *Tout est bien qui finit bien.*"

"Except for the fact of the famous Swan Song having been stolen."

"Exactly," concluded Dom Pedro, his brow dotted with sweat.

Sherlock Holmes rose and began walking around the room

with long strides, under the apprehensive gaze of the emperor, fearful for the rest of his porcelain.

"Before anything else," declared the detective, "I want to say how much I admire Your Majesty for his role as patron of the arts. I was already familiar with the musical talent of Brazilians, for I had occasion to attend the première of *Il Guarani*, at La Scala in Milan. I was only seventeen, but I recall it as if it were yesterday. It was a Saturday and a fine rain was falling."

The emperor almost spilled the bottle of Madeira.

"You don't say, Mr. Holmes! What an extraordinary coincidence. Then you met Carlos Gomes?"

"From a distance, in the aisle. I was there with my parents, who were great friends of Maestro Terziani. At the end of the performance we went behind the scenery to greet the maestro. I was absolutely electrified. It was my first trip to Italy and my first opera. I will confide a secret, emperor. *Il Guarani* awoke in me a passion for music."

"Fantastic!" Dom Pedro exclaimed.

Holmes walked back and forth in the small chamber, brushing against precious objects.

"Getting back to the violin, it seems to me that it's time we had a talk with the baroness, Maria Luísa. I want to know exactly how the instrument disappeared."

"Nothing simpler. I shall tell my personal coachman to take you to her residence. Actually, she's already waiting for you," said the emperor. "However, don't count on much help from the baroness. Between us, Maria Luísa is an *enfant gâtée*. Her husband, the old baron of Avaré, acceded to her every wish. To her, the violin was just another plaything. She lamented the loss, but her pretty little head is already busy with other diversions. Now, if you will excuse me, I have certain commitments that cannot be postponed," concluded the emperor, rising and accompanying Holmes to the door.

"Let's go, Watson," cried the detective.

The doctor, who had been dozing peacefully, awoke with a start.

"Of course! Of course. Hmm. . . . Quite interesting, the story of the daguerreotype," stammered the doctor, unwittingly revealing at what point in the meeting he had fallen asleep.

Holmes said good-bye to the monarch.

"I hope my investigations prove successful. For now, all that remains is for me to thank Your Majesty for the magnificent luncheon. The delicacies conferred upon us are magic. I feel as light as a feather."

He made an elegant bow with his cap, saluting the emperor, and when he turned, his cape knocked from its pedestal a precious vase from the West Indies Company which graced the room. With a quickness unsuspected in a gentleman of seventy-one, Dom Pedro II executed a catlike leap and grabbed the relic in midair before it could shatter on the marble floor.

Holmes, passing through the gates on the way to the carriage, did not even notice the emperor of Brazil prostrate on the floor of the entrance hall.

~

The liveried slave came into the music room where Maria Luísa Catarina de Albuquerque, baroness of Avaré, was fingering the harpsichord that had belonged to the family of her deceased husband.

"There're two men outside wanting to speak to ma'am."

"What do they want?"

"I don't know, ma'am. I only know one of them speaks some funny language and the other is a Portuguese. The Portuguese keeps telling me, 'I'm home, I'm home.' Does he think he lives here?"

Immediately, the baroness understood that "home" was "Holmes," and gestured for the servant to show the two men in.

Despite the impressiveness of the large house in the Cosme Velho district, with its gardens and its waterfalls, what most caught the attention of the detective and the doctor was the beauty of Maria Luísa. They were not expecting to find, in Brazil, eyes so blue and hair so red. Besides this, the baroness was wearing a *décolleté* beige dress that accentuated the generous curve of her bosom. Holmes approached, kissed her fingertips, and introduced Dr. Watson. While the doctor enjoyed the view that revealed itself from the small verandah, Holmes and the baroness seated themselves on a settee.

"Would you care for coffee? It's freshly ground. These sweet-potato candies are from Castellões, one of our best confectioners," informed the baroness, pointing to a table covered with these delicacies. Watson declined from his place at the verandah, and Sherlock, who never refused food, helped himself to the sweets and coffee.

"Assuredly, the baroness is already aware of the purpose of our visit," said Holmes, sipping his coffee.

"The emperor informed me of your arrival. But I don't know what I can say to facilitate the investigation."

"A great deal. The baroness would be astonished how small details that escape the layman's eyes can be significant to one who has developed the exercise of deduction. For example, I can state that the baroness is a widow, that your husband was the owner of an appreciable fortune, that he died as a result of a hunting accident, that he was hunting beside a river, that he was quite a bit older than you, and that when he died he left you all his goods."

Maria Luísa, speechless, almost spilled her cup of coffee.

"That's amazing! How did you deduce all that?!"

"I read it in the *Complete Brazilian Peerage* that I found in the hotel."

Recovering from her surprise, the baroness took a glazed walnut from the serving tray and asked, "How can I be of use to your investigation, Mr. Holmes?"

"I'd like to know from where exactly the violin disappeared," answered Holmes, eating more sweet-potato candy.

"It wasn't here at the house. I noticed that one of the instrument's tuning pegs was loose, making its tuning more difficult, and I asked one of my servants to take it to the Viola d'Ouro shop, belonging to an Italian master who has lived in Rio de Janeiro for years."

"What is the gentleman's name?"

"Giacomo Peruggio. He's an absolutely trustworthy person. He knows everything about violins. Besides being a wizard of a craftsman, Peruggio is an excellent violinist. He sometimes performs at the Mozart Club, which is often visited by our emperor."

"May I speak with the servant who took the instrument to the shop?"

The baroness rang a small bell and asked that the domestic be summoned. Minutes later, a Negro wearing high boots and a scarlet redingote came into the room. He was holding a top hat and spoke with the voice of a basso-profundo.

"You called, *sinhá*?"

Holmes and Watson were startled by the huge figure standing in the threshold. The Negro, forty years of age, must have measured almost two meters tall, and the padded redingote could not hide the man's powerful muscles. His shaved head and a scar that ran from his left eye to the corner of his mouth gave him an even more frightening appearance. The baroness introduced him.

"This is Mukumbe. He's my guardian angel. He was my father's slave but today is a free man, manumitted by me as soon as my father died. Mukumbe is my factotum: coachman, butler, messenger, and bodyguard. I don't know why, but I feel safe in his company," said the baroness, laughing.

The Negro opened his mouth in a wide grin full of white teeth, and his face became as sweet as a child's.

"Mukumbe, this is Mr. Holmes and over there is his friend Dr. Watson. They want to ask you some questions about the violin."

"Of course, *sinhá*."

Holmes approached the giant.

"I only want to know if by any chance you noticed someone following you, when you went to the repair shop."

"No, sir. There's not a man living or a ghost who comes after me when I walk through the streets."

"I can understand why," murmured Holmes. "Are you sure the violin was in the case?"

"Yes, sir. I saw it when *sinhá* stored it before giving it to me. It was right after we played a waltz here in the parlor."

"I forgot to say, Mukumbe is also an exquisite pianist. He plays the harpsichord and the organ, when there's a Mass here in the chapel."

Sherlock almost chocked on his fifth piece of sweet-potato candy. Watson, observing from the terrace, not understanding the conversation, inquired, "What is it, Holmes?"

"The Nubian plays the piano," said the stupefied Holmes, in English.

"And I also speak English," added Mukumbe, in an unmistakable London accent.

"It's true," said the baroness. "When my late father sent me to study in England, he insisted that Mukumbe accompany me as chaperon."

"And I'm not a Nubian. My family comes from the Congo. My father was king of the Yoruban nation, imprisoned by the Zingala and sold to the Portuguese."

"And what type of music do you play?" asked Holmes, returning to the earlier topic.

"It depends. In the chapel, of course, sacred music. When I play with *sinhá*, waltzes and polkas, but what I like most are the maxixe and the samba."

"Maxixe? Samba?"

"They're round dances brought from Angola. If *sinhá* will permit, I can give a short demonstration." Mukumbe looked at the baroness as if asking her approval.

"Of course, Mukumbe. Even though the harpsichord isn't very adequate for the purpose. Don't take too much of Mr. Holmes's time."

Even before Maria Luísa could finish speaking, the giant sat down at the instrument and began to improvise. The rhythm was gripping. His enormous hands ran over the keyboard like spiders. Without realizing it, Holmes began keeping time by tapping his pipe on a Louis XV console beside the harpsichord. Mukumbe ended by performing a *chorinho* by Ernesto Nazareth.

"A pity I left my violin at the hotel. I would love to learn those new rhythms," explained the detective, continuing his drumming, which had already left an indelible mark on the console.

"I am sure there will be no lack of opportunities," promised the baroness, rising. "If you have no more questions, I ask your permission to retire. I have a riding lesson shortly. Mukumbe will see you to the door and, as soon as you wish, can take you to the Viola d'Ouro in one of my carriages."

"I am beholden to you, baroness. Tomorrow, without fail, I shall seek out the Italian. Good-bye."

"*Obrigado,*" said Dr. Watson, pronouncing in a heavy accent the only word he knew in Portuguese.

# IO

*H*e execrates kiosks. Those crude wooden stalls had proliferated throughout the entire city, monuments to filth and sin. Fetid little towers befouling the streets. He hates with even greater intensity the kiosk he sees from the window of his room. Often, when night falls, as now, he spends hours on end, the lights turned out, watching the movement of the passersby who, like thirsty animals, come to wallow around that shrine of vice. He abominates the ground around the kiosk. He is disgusted by the sludge formed by the thick spittle of the rabble that gathers at that putrid pavilion, hawking and drinking cheap rum. Drinking and *spitting, forming a viscous carpet around the cloaca. He hates the decadent drunkards for whom the kiosk is an oasis amidst an alcoholic mirage. He detests the mediocre shop assistants who come there to buy tickets for the Grand Drawing, as if the kiss of money could transform them from toads to princes. The greatest repugnance, however, he reserves for those who come to buy pornographic postcards. There are obscenities of every sort. Naked women, their sex on display, with an idiotic smile on their lips, women lying supine, the heads of immense dogs stuck between their thighs. Women rubbing themselves against enormous wooden phalli, and even women with women. And always laughing. The same perverse idiot's laugh. Whores. They're all whores. He thinks again about the young woman at the fountain. So she was a lady-in-waiting at the palace? A pity, but she was in the street at that hour. If she was in the street, she was a whore. Whore, whore. Aren't they all whores in their souls? He looks at the kiosk again. As if to challenge her limits, a woman comes and leans against the counter. She is a very light mulatto, almost white. He glimpses the delicate features of her face, delineated by the streetlights, and is startled by the girl's beauty. The young woman laughs at something the kiosk owner says. Surely an infamous proposal. The laughter slices into his ears like a blade. One more whore. She walks away, carrying a bottle of milk. He quickly leaves for the street in search of his prey.*

～

Holmes awoke to the sound of grenades exploding. He imagined it must be a group of rebels trying to overthrow the regime. He leapt from the bed and, crossing the bedroom, unsteady from sleep, half-opened the door leading to Dr. Watson's room. He saw his friend, a light sleeper like all doctors, in a deep slumber. Nonetheless, the shots and explosions continued, growing louder and louder. He went to the window. The street was calm and deserted at that hour. It was only then that he realized it was not grenades. The explosions he heard were coming directly from his abdomen. It was the palm oil finally taking effect. The detective began to experience the devastating result of the shrimp, sausage, peppers, peanuts, and sweets. Suddenly, he could feel a sharp, delicate pain coming to life in his entrails. By now he was perspiring heavily. He opened the bedroom door and walked at a quick pace toward the toilet.

Minutes later, partially recovered, he returned to the room. He was weakened, but he didn't want to wake Dr. Watson because of a mild digestive indisposition. He drank a glass of water and felt a little better. Sleep had fled. He decided to go for a walk and avail himself of the evening cool. He pulled his trousers over his nightshirt, put on his deerstalker, threw his cape over his shoulders, and left the room on tiptoe so as not to wake the doctor. At the hotel door, he took a deep breath and, still debilitated, went down Fresca Street toward Santa Luzia. The sea air helped him recover little by little. The long stroll was doing him good. Accustomed to walking in London for hours on end, he didn't realize that he had come some distance from the hotel. After a time, he arrived at the Campo dos Frades passageway, at the corner of the promenade. There he stopped under a gas streetlamp, feeling a sense of relief, and lit his pipe. He leaned against the lamppost and took a long puff.

⌒

The girl was exhausted. She had done two performances of the revue *The Woman-Man*. Her role was small, almost that of a chorus lady, but Oscar Pederneiras, who had seen her on-stage, had been enchanted with her vitality and had promised her a good role in *Zé Caipora,* with the actor Machado, next season at the Príncipe Imperial Theater. She was still quite young and could wait for principal roles. After the theater, she had stopped at Isidoro's kiosk, on Lavradio Street, near Bernardo de Vasconcelos, to buy the bottle of milk that she would drink warm, alone at home, before going to sleep. As always, the Portuguese had directed a few off-color witticisms at her. The young mulatto woman found amusement in those harmless bits of foolishness that he repeated every time in an end-of-night ritual. Now she was carelessly walking along Nova dos Arcos Street, taking no notice of the figure, so pale as to be almost transparent, who stealthily followed her. As soon as she turned at Visconde de Maranguape Street and came to the promenade, he attacked. Covered by his immense black cape, he looked like a gigantic bat swooping down upon the girl.

This time, however, chance favored the hunted rather than the hunter. When the executioner in black alighted next to his victim, his foot slipped on one of the loose paving stones and he lost his balance. The young woman turned quickly, with the agility learned on the stage, and threw the bottle of milk in his face. Then she took flight in a headlong dash, screaming for help.

Holmes, at the next corner, advanced rapidly in her direction. He grabbed the hysterical girl and clutched her to his chest. She went on screaming, pointing at the dark form.

"There! A man! He tried to kill me! Help! Help!" screamed the terrified girl.

The detective saw that the attacker was holding a long dagger. At that distance he was unable to make out his features. He told the girl, "Stay here!"

The man had turned and was running down the street. Holmes set off after him like a shot. A few curious souls began to turn lights on and come out of the houses across the way. The assassin stopped. He looked at Sherlock, who was coming nearer. He found himself trapped between the detective and the men coming toward him. He turned to the first building before him, and, using the point of the dagger, prised open the lock on the heavy gate, disappearing into the structure. It was the National Library.

With more than one hundred thousand volumes, dispersed among forty-two rooms, the National Library was the emperor's pride. Holmes stopped at the entrance to the building. There was a musty smell in the air. He could hear the monster's footsteps echoing on the marble floor. He shouted, "This is Sherlock Holmes! Halt or I'll fire!" It was a bluff, for the detective had left his revolver at the hotel. The killer paid him no heed.

Without hesitating, Holmes went in pursuit. He passed the niche housing the marble bust of Dom João VI and saw, in the distance, the black form slinking away among the third-story corridors that housed the forty-five thousand books of the theology section. The detective ran, taking no precautions, and this haste nearly cost him his life. When he passed under the arch that divided that area, he was almost buried under an immense bookcase that his quarry had attempted to topple onto his head. He escaped by pure reflex, and the floor was strewn with precious works, such as the polyglot Bibles of Ximenes and Arias Montanus. He saw the madman run past Greek and Latin Classics, pass through Moral Sciences, and climb a small spiral staircase. In a flash, Sherlock covered the space separating him from the stairs. He took the steps three at a time. On the floor above, the beast, at bay, opened a door leading to the bathrooms. Without hesitating, the man hurled himself through the window overlooking the grounds behind the building, leaving a trail of shattered stained glass. Holmes, who had almost overtaken him, prepared to leap through the broken glass, following the same path. It was then that he saw the sanitary vessel of French porcelain decorated with interlaced red roses. The sight immediately awoke in him a violent colic, but he still hesitated between launching himself through the window and sitting down on the receptacle. The hesitation lasted only a few seconds. Unbuttoning his trousers, he yielded to the imperious call of nature, remaining there, humiliated, long into the night. The palm oil had accomplished a feat that not even his archenemy, Professor Moriarty, had achieved: stopping Sherlock Holmes.

~

The name of the young mulatto woman was Anna Candelária. The love child of a mixed-breed washerwoman, she had been reared by a priest, Marcial Fiúza, in Itaguaí, near Rio, and the gossiping women of the town, ever ready to speak ill, said that the priest was the girl's father. All because Father Marcial, of Dutch forebears from the state of Pernambuco, had very red hair and green eyes. By one of those ironies of fate, Anna Candelária had the same emerald green eyes as the priest. Pure coincidence, doubtless, but to the self-righteous church ladies it was conclusive proof.

Father Marcial had a habit little appreciated by the residents of Itaguaí. On Sundays, after Mass, he would stroll around the church square and, thrusting his hands through the opening in the pockets of his cassock, scratch his groin. Then he would dissemblingly lift his fingers to his nose, sniffing and babbling in ecstasy, "Better than ever! What pleasures! Today it's better than ever!" These were the same hands that he held out for passersby to kiss who came to ask his blessing: "God bless you, my son . . . oh, it's better than ever . . . today it's better than ever . . . God bless you, my daughter . . . oh, what pleasure . . ." And he would go on sniffing and blessing all day long.

As soon as she was fifteen, Anna Candelária ran away to Rio de Janeiro with a street peddler who was passing through the town. Now, at twenty-two, living alone in a small rented room on Marrecas Street, she for the first time missed Itaguaí. There, her life had never been threatened. If not for the tall man with the Portuguese accent, she would be dead. She had not stayed behind for her rescuer, of course. As the profession of theater actress was confused with that of prostitute, she wanted no trouble with the police. She sat on the bed, her heart still racing, and thought again about the tall man in the peculiar checkered hat. Perhaps she should have waited. He was attractive, the tall man, with his angular features that seemed carved with a knife. Though not handsome as such, he was very attractive. And, after all, he had saved her life. Anna Candelária sighed, lay down, and pulled the bed cover over her. "No sense crying over spilt milk," she thought, and quickly remembered the bottle of milk she had thrown in the assassin's face. She blew out the light of the lamp and, minutes later, was sleeping the peaceful sleep of angels and the daughters of priests.

⁓

The Viola d'Ouro was located on Ourives Street. Although the site was traditionally occupied by jewelers, Giacomo Peruggio, the proprietor, had chosen the street because he believed that his own activity was also one of jewelry making. A native of Cremona, cradle of the Amati, where the most famous violins in the world were born, he had come to Brazil in 1866, the day he turned thirty. He was planning to go to North America, but when he got to the port, the ship that was about to set sail was heading for South America, and he did not hesitate; he embarked with his wife and their few pieces of luggage. In his life, Giacomo solved everything in this same fashion. When he decided to marry, he courted a girl from his land for five years. He determined to ask for the young woman's hand in marriage. Her father, a small farmer, was succinct.

"In my family, marriage goes by age. First the eldest, then the younger ones."

"So be it. I'll take the eldest." And he married the young woman he met that day.

The Viola d'Ouro sold and repaired every type of stringed instrument, but Peruggio's true passion was violins. Besides having learned his trade in the land of Stradivari, in a small shop near the house where the great master was born, Giacomo was also a reasonably adept instrumentalist, and whenever the occasion presented itself he played in the various musical societies that existed in the city. In fact, being thin, very blond, and with long, unruly hair, he resembled a maestro more than an artisan.

That afternoon, leaning on the rear counter, he examined the strings that Inspector Mello Pimenta had given him.

"There's not the slightest doubt," he said in his Italian accent. "They are violin strings. *Sol* and *mi,* the first string and the last."

"Are you sure?" asked Pimenta, still annoyed at Chiquinha Gonzaga's having been correct in her assessment.

"Absolutely, inspector. I know this better than the back of my hand. Look, these strings are very fine, made of gut, very different in texture and size from viola, mandolin, or guitar strings. They are also of excellent origin. Can I ask where you found them?"

"Yes, you can. But I can't answer. They're part of a confidential investigation."

"Ah, then they must be connected with the dead girls," said the luthier, demonstrating that in Rio de Janeiro nothing was very confidential.

"Has anyone been here of late to buy strings to replace them?"

"No, inspector. If anyone had come, I would certainly remember. For one thing, I know every violinist in the city."

"Please, if someone does come looking, don't fail to let me know."

The inspector asked Peruggio to return the two strings and was preparing to leave when a weary Sherlock Holmes entered the shop, accompanied by Dr. Watson. Instead of a pipe, he carried in his hand a green coconut from which he took long draughts. The coconut water had been the suggestion of Inojozas, concierge at the hotel, as the best curative to free him of the gastric indisposition of the evening before. Watson had urged Holmes to try tincture of camphorated opium, but the detective preferred the more exotic treatment.

"Inspector Pimenta, I presume," stated Holmes.

Pimenta was startled.

"That's right. How do you know who I am?"

"I was at the station house looking for you and they told me I would find you here. I'm Sherlock Holmes and this is my friend Dr. Watson."

"So you're the famous English detective? I was going to look for you at your hotel this very day. I hope you received my telegram," said Pimenta, surprised by the fact that Holmes was expressing himself in Portuguese. He turned to Dr. Watson: "I didn't know that you two spoke our language."

Watson, who didn't speak it, remained silent.

"Only I," replied the detective. "Dr. Watson doesn't understand anything you're saying."

"It was good to find you. I greatly need your help. Just imagine—"

Holmes interrupted the inspector.

"One moment, please. First I should have a small chat with Mr. Giacomo," he said, turning to the Italian.

Peruggio was beside himself with joy. It was not every day that he took part in such exciting affairs. Murders, a stolen Stradivarius, mysterious violin strings—all of it being discussed in his shop. He blessed the day he had changed ships.

"Of course, Mr. Holmes. I'm at your disposal."

"I should like you to explain to me how they stole the baroness's violin from here," said the Englishman.

"My own carelessness, Mr. Holmes. My own carelessness. . . ." lamented Giacomo. "I put the instrument on my workbench, at the back of the store, and when I went to fetch it the next morning it had disappeared. The rear window had been smashed."

"If I may ask, I don't fathom why you left such a precious violin within the reach of the malefactor," said the detective, expressing himself like a perfect native of Lisbon.

"Mr. Holmes, I know they steal everything here: food, boots, clothing, even bandores, but I never imagined that those illiterates would steal a violin," stated the Italian. Neither Holmes nor Pimenta was convinced by the explanation.

"Frankly I feel that your negligence has caused great displeasure to the baroness, and of course to the emperor," replied Holmes, coldly.

Giacomo was beginning to perceive just how much his error could harm him. He loved showing off for Dom Pedro, playing his violin at the musical clubs and the concerts on Glória Street. He began to weep and to tremble in an exaggerated manner.

"Oh, Dio, Dio, Dio. . . . The baroness will never forgive me! What will become of my life?!" And, like a good Italian, he started banging his head against the wall.

Watson, who understood nothing of what had been said thus far, opened his bag, took out a small vial, and threw himself upon Peruggio, shouting, "Good heavens! It's malaria. Quick, Holmes, help me with this quinine!" And before anyone could stop him, he poured the entire contents of the medicine container down the poor wretch's throat. "That's why in the tropics I'm never without my bag," concluded the doctor, proudly.

"Watson, I regret to inform you that this poor Italian was merely having an attack of nerves, quite common among people of Latin origin," explained Holmes.

"Well, no one told me he was Italian," grumbled Watson sullenly, closing his bag. "Do you expect me to understand this pagan language?"

Sherlock resumed the interrogation.

"Have you any idea of who might have stolen the violin?"

"None," replied Giacomo, spitting out the bitter taste of quinine.

"At what time was the violin stolen?"

"I don't know for certain, between eight P.M. and eight A.M."

"I should like to examine the place from which the instrument was purloined," requested the detective.

Peruggio accompanied them to the small workshop in the rear. Holmes took a magnifying glass from the pocket of his coat and began to minutely study the workbench. Watson, who was familiar with his friend's methods, was phlegmatic, but Pimenta followed the detective's every movement, mesmerized. After the bench, Holmes began to study the window. Caught on a nail sticking out of the windowsill was a slender thread of black cloth. Sherlock carefully removed the cloth from the nail, holding it between his thumb and forefinger.

"Curious, quite curious. . . ." said Holmes, bringing the lens closer to his fingers.

"What is it? Did you find something suspicious in that piece of cloth?" asked Pimenta, electrified.

"No. In my fingernail. It must be a splinter from the coconut," replied the detective, discarding the torn piece of cloth and sucking his fingertip.

Sherlock carefully searched the rest of the room without finding anything of relevance. Returning to the front of the shop, he and Pimenta said good-bye to Peruggio. Watson, still disgruntled, also shook the Italian's hand, shouting, "I'm very happy it's not malaria! For these attacks of nerves, I recommend herb balm!" he said with the British certitude that, by speaking loud enough, every human being on the planet can be made to understand English.

Pimenta was about to say something, but he was interrupted by the sound of a gigantic Negro entering the shop, almost tearing the door from its jamb. He was ready to pull his revolver from his pocket when Holmes reassured him.

"Be calm, inspector. This is Mukumbe, who works for the baroness and is at my disposal."

"An errand boy came to tell me that the marquis of Salles is at Amorim's Café and invites the gentlemen to have a drink," Mukumbe informed them, unperturbed.

"If it's not inconvenient, I would like to discuss with Mr. Holmes the case I'm handling now," said Mello Pimenta, putting away his weapon.

"Then come with us to the café," invited Holmes. "If the customs here are like those of London, the tables of public houses are always a fount of information."

Pimenta was not very taken with the idea, for he would have preferred to conduct the investigations on confidential terms, but given the detective's enthusiasm there was no way to refuse. Giacomo Peruggio accompanied them to the exit.

"Mr. Holmes, tell the baroness Maria Luísa not to think ill of me."

"You may rest assured of that, Mr. Peruggio. I had no intention of frightening you. The baroness knows it was not your fault."

Peruggio, grateful, dramatically extended his arms. Holmes availed himself of the gesture to leave the empty coconut in the hands of the Viola d'Ouro's owner.

~

Amorim's Café was located in the Canecas passageway, at the corner of Rosário Street. It was famous for its cool beverages and cold foods, in addition, of course, to its coffee. It also served the best wines and liqueurs. Amorim, the owner, was an enormously fat man, in his forties, with a mustache whose points curled upward. He was dressed in white trousers, a shirt, waistcoat, and an apron about his waist, like the French garçons he saw in photogravures. The apron was so large that Paula Nei was wont to joke, "Amorim, it looks like a shroud covering the vast meals that lie in your belly."

Amorim would laugh and go on squeezing between the tables to personally serve his preferred customers.

He would sometimes ask awkward questions, as now, with a group of plantation owners who were sipping genipap liqueur and discussing prices of their latest harvest. One of them, "Colonel" Mendes Freire, was the youngest in a family of seven children. Curiously, despite the fact that his parents were white and all his brothers and sisters quite blond, Mendes Freire was very dark, almost black, with kinky hair. Amorim could not resist.

"Colonel, there's something I've been wanting to ask you for a long time. How is it possible that your parents and your brothers and sisters are so white and blond and you came out like that, so dark?"

Mendes Freire drank his liqueur and explained, speaking to Amorim and his friends.

"It's an almost supernatural story. My mother was two months pregnant and went to spend a few days at my grandfather's plantation. One day, when she was walking in the environs, a delirious Negro slave came from the fields and tried to overtake her. My mother dashed for the plantation with the slave running behind her. She was able, thank God, to make it to the house and my grandfather's men seized the poor crazy

Negro. I was born with this color and this hair because of the scare my mother had."

Mendes Freire's friends shook their heads, touched. Amorim respectfully opined, "The colonel will pardon my saying so, but I have the impression that the Negro caught the good lady."

The plantation owners dissembled, holding back a fit of laughter, and before Mendes Freire could protest, Amorim moved away to get Holmes, Watson, and Pimenta and to lead the group to the marquis of Salles's table.

As soon as he saw the newspaper that Júlio Augusto Pereira, the marquis of Salles, was reading, Pimenta quickly perceived that there was no longer any reason for being secretive about the case of the dead girls. Everything was on the front page of the *Afternoon Gazette,* under the title "Collector of Skin." The marquis greeted the three men and handed the newspaper to Sherlock Holmes while he complained to the inspector.

"I see that you withheld some rather picturesque facts when we went to the morgue. What trust, inspector," he said, ironically.

"I see nothing picturesque in this repulsive story," replied Mello Pimenta.

Júlio Augusto was referring to the more scandalous side of the news item, for the newspaper had told all, including the morbid detail of the musical strings that the monster left coiled in the poor girls' pubic hairs. The inspector silently cursed Professor Saraiva. Only Pimenta himself and the doctor knew the exact location where the killer had placed the strings. He had not even told his wife. The inspector wondered how many bottles of rum it had taken to loosen the coroner's blasted tongue. There was also, on the second page of the *Gazette*, a caricature of Sherlock holding an enormous pipe. Below the drawing, the story related the English detective's arrival. Holmes took the newspaper and read avidly, translating for Dr. Watson.

"So you can see, I have nothing new to tell you," said Pimenta, unhappily.

"But I have," informed Sherlock, when he finished reading.

"What do you mean?"

"Yesterday, I had an encounter with the murderer."

The inspector was astounded.

"Where? How?"

"At the National Library. Unfortunately, I only managed to see him from a distance."

"Please, tell us everything, Mr. Holmes," asked Júlio Augusto.

Sherlock Holmes related in minute detail the previous night's episode, only omitting the reason he had been prevented from continuing the case. He claimed that when he got to the window the monster had already disappeared in the city streets.

"I only regret that the mysterious girl did not wait for me. She was quite lovely, a very light-skinned mulatto with large green eyes, wide hips, and generous breasts," sighed the detective, rapt.

The marquis found the Englishman's ecstasy amusing.

"You are not the first, and certainly will not be the last, foreigner to become enchanted with our mulatto women. In fact, many of your countrymen have given up everything for a dark-skinned girl of mixed race." And he recited, "Dark women with the delicate lineaments of a Hindoo, with large scintillating eyes veiled by a bewitching expression of melancholy, their hair as black as a raven's wing, possess the captivating grace of the sylph and the sensual gaze of the doe. . . ."

Pimenta saw that the conversation was getting out of hand and returned to the main theme.

"There is only one thing the newspaper did not mention. Several people who live near the places where the girls died told the police that they heard the sound of someone playing a violin in the streets."

"If he goes on tearing out the strings, the problem will very quickly solve itself," said Júlio Augusto.

"That's it!" exclaimed Holmes, striking the table and waking up Watson, who was dozing.

The inspector appeared not to understand.

"How so?"

"Don't you see it, my good man? The violin has four strings: G, D, A, E," he explained, designating the notes by letter, English-style. "If he's already used two strings, there are still two left."

"You're trying to tell me that the murderer plans, for no reason at all, to kill two more girls?"

"You put it very well, inspector, 'for no reason at all,' because this man has lost his reason. Only in some sick recess of his mind does he find the pretexts for this bloody outrage. I hope the two of us, working together, can stop him," said Holmes.

"We all hope so," added the marquis of Salles.

Sherlock turned to Watson and translated the entire conversation. The doctor was deeply affected.

"What a horrible thing. The man kills these women like that, with no motive?"

"Yes, Watson. In all my career I have never seen anything similar. To brutally take the life of these young women, always in the same manner and without the slightest purpose. This is a deranged man who enjoys killing in series—what I would call a 'serial killer.' Just so: serial killer," decreed Sherlock Holmes, coining the expression.

After repeating the recently created neologism several times, he turned to Júlio Augusto and asked, "How would you say 'serial killer' in Portuguese?"

"*Assassino serial?*" ventured the marquis in a terrible translation.

"Whatever it is, it's necessary to stop him," stated Mello Pimenta.

Holmes lit his pipe. An idea was beginning to germinate in his head.

"Have you by chance given any thought to the possibility that our killer must be the same man who stole the baroness's violin?"

Pimenta cursed himself for not having imagined as much. It made sense. Actually, it was the only thing in this entire mad business that made sense. The demented man who was killing the girls was the same one who had stolen the violin. He did not know just how this revelation would help, but it was obvious that the Englishman was right. Both things had begun at precisely the same time. What he couldn't understand was why the madman left the strings in the pubic hairs of his victims. "Why? Precisely because he's crazy, that's why!" he thought to himself. A thousand ideas went through his head. Could the assassin be a professional musician? There were so many musical societies in the city! Where to begin? First, he would see if there was some violinist with a file on record with the police. Sherlock Holmes interrupted his thoughts.

"Inspector, one thing above all continues to intrigue me profoundly."

"What is it, Mr. Holmes?"

"Where do you think I could find that mulatto woman again?" replied Holmes, with the melancholy look of a man in love.

## I I

*H*is Siamese cat, which usually wanders among the rooftops, is sleeping peacefully today in the wicker basket beside the door. He pays no attention to the cat. Lying in his narrow bed, he loses all notion of time. He has lain there supine for over two hours, staring fixedly at the ceiling. It is a spiritual exercise he performs whenever the hatred in his soul begins to wane. He lies down, entirely naked, and, eyes closed, imagines the hatred once again taking hold of his being. Little by little, the sensation invades his body. It begins in his toes and creeps up his legs. Along with the thought, he fixes the hatred in each fold, in each curve, in every pore of his body. The hatred penetrates his muscular thighs and continues to rise. Now it envelops his sex. He never understands why hatred hardens his genitalia. With the hatred comes the heat. The hatred and the heat grow in equal measure. He perceives the *division that manifests itself during the exercise. When the hatred reaches the solar plexus, he feels his body on fire, while the upper part remains cold, like dead flesh. Two distinct hemispheres of a single cocoon. At that moment, he knows he must concentrate even harder, silently repeating like a sacred mantra: hate, hate, hate. Little by little, the hatred proceeds, pursues its path, its destiny, envelops his head until it reaches the tips of his hair. Every hair bristles. The sheets on the bed are drenched in sweat. The process ends. The essence of being, replenished by purest hatred. Rarely does he need to resort to this exercise. One thing alone saps his hatred: fear. He had felt fear last night. Fear that the English-man would overtake him, discover him. In the distance he saw the ridiculous cap, the checkered cape, and he was afraid. Afraid of dying, afraid of living. He doesn't want to be caught, he knows he doesn't want to be caught. Even so, there is something that drives him to leave the clues that will surely lead to disaster. They are too obvious. That fat, obtuse policeman sees nothing, but the English-man will read the messages easily. Sherlock Holmes will not fail to see the screaming spoor that he leaves in his path. He rises and be-gins drying himself on a linen towel. He is sweating so much that he soon needs another towel. He takes the ancient dagger from the box hidden in the armoire and runs its cold blade along his fore-head, relieving the feverish sensation he still feels. The woman and the detective couldn't have recognized him; there was the cape and the darkness to cover him. Nevertheless, he is frustrated. She was lucky. Very lucky. That was the only reason he was not able to pierce her soft breasts with the sharp blade of the dagger and pull out her lungs. The half-breed woman had seven lives, like cats. Or was it nine? Do cats have seven lives or nine? He doesn't recall. He goes over to his Siamese, asleep in the wicker basket. In one hand he holds the animal by the head and with the other opens its belly with a single blow of the dagger. It is so fast that the cat dies without even opening its eyes. One life. So cats, like whores, have only one life after all.*

⌒

As she had already been honored by various Brazilian thespians, Sarah Bernhardt decided to pay a surprise visit, accompanied by her troupe, to a theatrical presentation in Rio de Janeiro.

The play chosen was the revue of the year, *The Woman-Man*, precisely the one in which, in the role of a soubrette, was the mulatto girl Anna Candelária, who had so charmed Sherlock Holmes. It was being staged at the Santana Theater, on Constituiçâo Square in the Rossio district, where Sarah Bernhardt was performing at the São Pedro de Alcântara. The high point of the revue was based on a case that had occurred in the city a year earlier: a man had appeared at respectable homes, dressed as a woman, to work as a servant. When the disguise was uncovered, a scandal had erupted that gripped all of Rio. The episode was being portrayed in the show that paraded the year in revue. The principal music was by Chiquinha Gonzaga and the book was by Valentim Magalhães and Felinto de Almeida. The audience burst into guffaws when the excellent comic actor Vasques, swaying wantonly in women's clothes, interpreted a sung monologue and ended by saying:

> I'll explain things, as I ought,
> In terms that are contextual:
> In my form and in my thought
> I'm really quite unsexual

After her own play, without even changing clothes, Sarah left the São Pedro and entered the Santana Theater almost at the end of the show, when the entire company was participating in the tableau "Maxixe in the New City." It was a triumphant entrance worthy of the Divine One. As soon as the illustrious visitor's unexpected presence was noted onstage, Heller, the impresario of *The Woman-Man*, stepped to the proscenium, interrupted his actors, and ordered the maestro to attack the *Marseillaise*. There was veritable delirium. Sarah climbed to the stage and presented Cinira Polônio, one of the principal actresses in the cast, with a bouquet of flowers secured by green and yellow ribbons, the Brazilian colors. The audience, enraptured, rose to its feet to applaud Sarah's gesture. Vasques could not resist: he approached, embraced, and kissed the Frenchwoman. Then he ran around the stage screaming, "I kissed Sarah Bernhardt! I kissed Sarah Bernhardt!"

The party ended with French and Brazilians fraternizing at a dinner overflowing with wine and guitar, offered by Heller at the Restaurant de la Terrasse. The sophisticated Heller ordered Roederer Cristal, a *cuvée de prestige* and the only champagne in a transparent vessel, an invention of Czar Alexander II so that his guests could appreciate the liquid in its bottle.

The following afternoon, Sarah arrived at the theater still feeling the effects of the previous night's revel. How impetuous these Brazilians were! All of them madly in love with her. They told her that, the week before, a plantation owner had ridden three days and nights to attend her play. When he got to the ticket office, the house was sold out, as always. The plantation owner made a scene, insisting that he was not leaving without seeing "the famous artist who came from France." To placate his wrath, the manager offered him a place where he could stand, at the rear of the theater. Calmer, the planter took his ticket and headed for the entrance. Before he disappeared through the door, he turned to the manager and asked, "By the way, what does the woman do? Does she sing or does she dance?" The actress had laughed heartily at the incident.

Sarah Bernhardt communicated with her team of technicians through the intermediary of the interpreter Sarmento, a functionary contracted by the theater, who had lived in Paris for two years. Sarmento, thickset and with no neck, was a native of the interior of the state of Ceará. While still very young, moved by a spirit of adventure, he had signed on as a mariner with the New Zealand Shipping Company and had set out to see the world. For fifteen years, in divers countries, he had exercised the most varied professions. He had pulled a rickshaw in Hong Kong, been a *banderillero* in Barcelona, a water carrier in Bombay, a stagecoach driver for Wells Fargo in Missouri, a shaman in Peru, a croupier in London, a gondolier in Venice, a distiller in Glasgow, a singer in the Tyrol, a grave digger in Istanbul, a miller in Coimbra, and, finally, a kept man in Paris. During this time he learned to speak Mandarin, Spanish, Hindustani, English, Italian, German, Turkish, and French, languages that Sarmento commanded with a perfect Ceará accent.

Sarah called everyone to the stage to polish the final details of *Le maître de forges* by Georges Ohnet, in which she played the role of Claire de Beaulieu. It was one of her greatest successes, and, as the consummate professional that she was, she wanted everything to be just right. She noticed that a chair was missing onstage, and, through Sarmento, asked Pipoca, the prompter, where the missing piece of furniture was.

"It'll be here tonight," was the man's laconic reply.

"And the proscenium rug?"

"It'll be here tonight."

"Where is the table lamp?"

"It'll be here tonight."

"And the cushions are missing, too."

"They'll be here tonight."

Without losing her aplomb, Sarah turned to Sarmento.

"Tell Monsieur Pipoca to immediately put all the missing objects onstage, now. If not, tonight it is I who won't be here."

She turned and began to discuss the text with the cast. Before she could start the rehearsal, she was interrupted by Pimenta, who was arriving at the theater.

"To what do we owe the honor of this visit, some other complaint against me?" asked Sarah, from the stage, always through Sarmento's mediation.

"Naturally not, madame. I came to find a gentleman who works here. I ask your forgiveness for the interruption," said Pimenta, touching his hat and taking the hallway leading to the musical rehearsal room.

He was looking for a violinist named Haroldo Borges. Borges had been arrested four times for violently beating his wife. The complaints were lodged by a neighbor, a military man, who on several occasions had come to the rescue of the musician's wife, and the beatings had earned Borges two months in jail. The inspector went to the room that the orchestra used for rehearsals. Several musicians were conversing, while others were tuning their instruments. The discussion, as always, centered on the low salaries they were paid. All fell silent at Pimenta's entrance.

"I'm looking for a violinist named Haroldo Borges," said the inspector.

A thin figure with a sunken face answered from the rear.

"Yes?"

"I'm Inspector Mello Pimenta. I'd like to have a private talk with you."

Without saying a word, Borges stored his violin in its case and went slowly to where the policeman stood. The pair went toward the artists' entrance. When they arrived at the small door, Borges threw the case with the instrument at Pimenta and attempted to dash into the street. The fat policeman pinned him against the doorjamb.

"Where do you think you're going in such a hurry?" inquired Mello Pimenta, grasping him by the arm.

"Anywhere that there's no police injustice."

"Injustice?"

"It was Gouveia again, wasn't it?"

Mello Pimenta didn't understand. He didn't know any Gouveia, nor was he an admirer of injustice.

"I don't have the slightest idea what you're talking about. Who is this Gouveia?"

"The sergeant in the Court Police who lives on my street. It's always him."

Mello Pimenta was beginning to grasp the situation. Gouveia was the military man who lodged the complaints whenever Borges beat his wife.

"My concern has nothing to do with your domestic squabbles. I'm investigating two crimes and I want to know about your movements on the days of the crimes."

Pimenta took out his notebook. Unfortunately for him and fortunately for the violinist, on the days of the killings Borges had been in Juiz de Fora, considerably distant from Rio de Janeiro, doing a short season with the string quartet that he had organized to augment his meager monthly income in his free time. In his stead had been Lima, a master of seven instruments who normally replaced his colleagues whenever they went off to earn a little extra money. Mello Pimenta put his notebook away in his pocket, saying dryly, "You may go. And, before I forget, don't ever again have the effrontery to beat a defenseless woman and accuse the police of injustice."

Haroldo Borges directed a doleful look at Pimenta.

"Inspector, do you know my wife, Marieta?"

"Of course not."

"She weighs more than two hundred and twenty pounds and measures close to six feet tall. Do you think that with this puny body I would be able to beat her?"

"Then what's this story of beatings?"

"Well, inspector, she betrays me with that sergeant Gouveia, who lives on my street. Every time I complain, Marieta gives me a drubbing. Then the sergeant goes to the station house and lodges a complaint to the contrary. Just yesterday I took a beating," related the violinist, opening his shirt to reveal his body covered with bruises. "When I saw you, I panicked. I thought Gouveia had already gone to the police and that you had come to arrest me. I can't bear to go to jail unjustly again."

"And why do they believe that man's story at the station house?" the inspector asked incredulously.

"You know: Gouveia is a sergeant, a soldier of the Court Police. He has lots of friends there, and I'm merely a violinist."

"You can rest assured that I'm going to take steps to see that you're not persecuted any longer," promised Pimenta, moved by the musician's story. "But I'm going to give you some advice, my friend. Leave the woman, find another companion."

"I can't, inspector. I'd like to well enough, but I can't. Marieta is very jealous. She's said that if I leave her she'll kill me," explained Borges in a low voice, as he buttoned his shirt.

Mello Pimenta said good-bye, thinking about taking some toffee with peanuts to his Paciência, an extremely loving wife. He walked away feeling pity for the cuckolded violinist.

## 12

Rodrigo Modesto Tavares had gained the title of viscount of Ibituaçu in an unconventional manner. A very rich man, already of a certain age, he was an habitual figure at the palace, forever flattering the sovereign. One beautiful April morning some five years earlier, Dom Pedro had just inaugurated one more branch of his beloved railway. With him were various dignitaries, ministers, senators, counselors, marshals, and, obviously, Rodrigo Modesto Tavares, who made it an iron rule to appear at all such ceremonies at the emperor's side. His Imperial Majesty was radiant in his dress uniform. The band, with great pomp, interpreted a few military marches. A multitude had gathered to see Dom Pedro II. The resplendent sun and the limpid azure of a cloudless sky added further solemnity to the moment. On the crowded reviewing stand, the monarch was preparing to begin the inauguration ceremony when something unexpected happened. Just after the applause that succeeded the national anthem, in the instant of silence that followed, Dom Pedro inadvertently loosed a noisy flatus. General embarrassment on the stand. The authorities didn't know what to do faced with that inopportune accident. It was then that Rodrigo, with the flatterer's quick wits, said in a loud voice, "A thousand pardons, Majesty. It was I. It happens to me now and then. I suffer from meteorism." And he assumed, with dignity, the thunderous imperial flatus.

Ministers, senators, and marshals envied Rodrigo Modesto's presence of mind. Deep inside, they moaned, "Damn! Why didn't I think of that?!" The grateful monarch granted to the friend who had saved him from humiliation the title of Viscount with Grandeur. So that the denomination of the new noble would reflect the event, Rodrigo was named viscount of Ibituaçu, which in Tupi-Guarani means "big wind."

The viscount's mansion, in the Laranjeiras district, was one of the city's most sumptuous residences. Constructed in the middle of a forest, surrounded by coconut palms and floss-silk trees, it was situated on the highest point of land, standing out amidst the luxuriant vegetation. Invitations to the parties that Rodrigo Modesto Tavares, viscount of Ibituaçu, offered at his residence were greatly sought after by all of society, but Rodrigo preferred to surround himself with artists, bohemians, and intellectuals. And so it was tonight, at the dinner honoring Sherlock Holmes and Sarah Bernhardt. The gang had come, from Bilac to Paula Nei, the most amusing of the group. The viscount had also invited the baroness of Avaré and some pretty and elegant young ladies, to offset the decidedly masculine majority at the reception. Sarah Bernhardt was accompanied by her son, Maurice, but Sherlock Holmes had come alone. Dr. Watson had stayed at the hotel, with the excuse that he needed to bring his correspondence up to date. In reality, he hated these soirées that went on into the late hours of the night. The always irreverent Paula Nei, upon seeing the detective without his habitual companion, said, "Look at this, Pythias came without Damon. I thought that wherever the teakettle went, the cup went with it."

After the dinner, they went into a large hall that the viscount mockingly called the crystal room because of the immense Viennese chandelier that illuminated the space. They spoke in French, a language commanded by all, including Sherlock Holmes. A pleasant surprise awaited them: seated at the piano, providing musical background for the evening, was Ernesto Nazareth.

Nazareth, a young pianist and composer of twenty-three, made his living giving private lessons and performing at parties. He had already published several songs, and polkas like "Fountain of Sighs," "People! Did the Tax Catch On?" and "Your Enchanting Eyes" had found great popular acceptance. At the moment he was interpreting his most recent creation, the waltz "Dora," which he had composed for Teodora Amália de Meireles, whom he was to marry in a few days. With a lock of hair falling onto his forehead, Ernesto recalled Chopin, of whom he was in fact a profound admirer. As soon as he finished, Rodrigo Modesto asked him to play another very successful polka, "The Hummingbird." Impressive in the young pianist's compositions was the note of melancholy that permeated even the gayest maxixes.

The viscount of Ibituaçu was happy. The night was a *réus-*

*site* without precedent, even at his house. In homage to Sherlock Holmes, Miguel Solera de Lara had vanquished his customary shyness and had recited in a masterful fashion passages from "The Triumph of Life," by Shelley, his favorite poet. All were enjoying themselves immensely. Bilac approached Sarah Bernhardt, accompanied by Guimarães Passos.

"Madame, if you will permit me, I would like to present the young poet of whom I spoke to you at the dinner at the Grande Hotel. Olavo Bilac."

"Enchanted, madame," said the poet.

"Your friend has praised you most highly. Who knows if one day I may serve as your inspirational muse?"

"The suggestion comes too late, madame. I have already committed the audacious deed in the form of a sonnet. It is called 'Fedora,' and I plan to publish it in the magazine *The Week*," replied Bilac.

Enchanted, the actress asked Bilac to recite it for her. The poet didn't have to be begged, and in a polished French recited the verses that ended:

> *Tu sais tous les secrets des abîmes du coeur,*
> *O toi, qui sais mêler, pour monter ta douleur,*
> *Le cri d'une lionne aux sanglots d'une femme!*

Enthusiastic applause from all the guests, and Sarah, touched, kissed the young bard's brow. Bilac was beside himself with happiness. The marquis of Salles, who always had a surprise for these occasions, offered to declaim something.

"By whom?" asked Artur Azevedo, who never left the side of his "Divine One."

"You don't know him. It's an author still unknown, born in Uruguay but a countryman of madame because he was the son of a French consul. His name is Isidore Ducasse. We studied together at the École Polytechnique in Paris, at the end of the sixties. He wrote a long poem under the pseudonym of the count of Lautréamont. The work was published, but unfortunately his editor never had the courage to distribute it to the bookshops for fear of being sued," said the marquis, who loved to create unusual atmospheres.

By now the curiosity of those present was palpable. Everyone wanted to know more details about that enigmatic writer. Solera de Lara, as a bookseller, was more interested still.

"What is the book called?"

"*The Songs of Maldoror.* Luckily, I have an autographed volume that was given me by Ducasse himself. A rare thing, Mr. Miguel, very rare. . . ." goaded the marquis.

"I can't stand so much mystery. Read us a passage from this damned poet immediately," requested Sarah Bernhardt.

"On second thought, madame, I don't know if I should. My friend's verses may shock the sensitive ears of the ladies."

The women in the room protested vehemently. Chiquinha Gonzaga made herself their spokeswoman.

"Marquis, we're in the nineteenth century. There is nothing left to be revealed by your scribbler," she said disdainfully.

"Very well, since you insist, here is a fragment of what Maldoror counsels in the first canto. . . ." said the marquis of Salles, coming to the center of the room and beginning to recite in his velvety baritone voice:

One must let
his fingernails
grow
for two weeks.
Oh, how sweet to brutally yank from its bed a child

still without a shadow of down above its lip
and, with eyes wide open,
pretend to run a hand smoothly over its cheek,
brushing back its long hair!
Then, suddenly, at the moment it least expects,
to sink one's long nails into its soft breast.
Without it dying, however,
for if it died,
we would not later see the marks of its suffering.
Next, it is necessary to drink its blood, licking its wounds
and, all this time, which should last an eternity,
the child cries.
Nothing is as good as its blood, extracted thus, still hot,
except its tears bitter as salt—

"I think we've heard enough," interrupted Miguel Solera de Lara.

A sensation of unease swept through the room. The young women invited by the viscount fanned themselves with their painted *éventails*.

"Now I understand the editor's reluctance to distribute such wretchedness," said the viscount of Ibituaçu.

"Well, I did warn you," said the marquis of Salles, not succeeding in hiding his smile of contentment at the awkward situation he had created.

Sarah Bernhardt, serving herself another glass of champagne, came to the author's defense.

"Well, I thought it was excellent. I'd like the marquis to lend me the book."

"With pleasure, madame. I am delighted that my friend Isidore has found a champion of such importance."

Sherlock Holmes broke the spell by asking innocently, "Does anyone mind if I smoke my pipe?"

"My dear Mr. Holmes, after the marquis's presentation, you can even smoke opium without shocking anyone," concluded Paula Nei. The tension in the room dissipated as everyone laughed at the bohemian's observation, much to the viscount's relief.

⌒

As always happened at such gatherings, at a given moment the party divided into two groups: men to one side and women to the other. Except for Chiquinha Gonzaga, the baroness of Avaré, and Sarah Bernhardt, who preferred to join the men, and Maurice Bernhardt and the marquis of Salles, who obviously chose the company of the ladies. Maurice, like the marquis, was an incorrigible womanizer and had already been involved in complications owing to his temperament. He had been standing in the hotel lobby offering gallantries to the young women passing by, when a young man accompanying one of the ladies took umbrage and gave him a couple of violent shoves. The intervention of the manager was necessary to prevent the incident from having more serious consequences. Now, along with the marquis, the contretemps already forgotten, he chatted with the young women, who asked a thousand questions about Paris and about his mother: "Is it true she keeps a lion in her house?" "Is Pigalle really as they say it is?" Maurice answered, sometimes lying, sometimes telling the truth, but always with the marquis's complicity.

In the vast library, amidst Havana cigars and French brandy, Sherlock Holmes, after narrating his near-encounter with the "*assassino serial*," as the marquis had translated it, was also satisfying his listener's questions. Aluísio Azevedo wanted to confirm the rumor that had spread throughout the city.

"Is it true, then, that the violin thief and the mad killer are the same person?"

"I presume so. Taking into account the strings that were found, it would be a great coincidence if both things happened at the same time, and I don't believe in coincidences," stated the detective, taking a puff from his pipe.

"And why does he leave the strings next to the victim and cut a flap of skin from her side?" asked Olavo Bilac, intrigued.

Chiquinha Gonzaga, lighting a discreet cigarette, offered, "But it's elementary, my dear Olavo. The man has left clues deliberately, as a challenge. He probably has an unconscious urge to be caught."

Holmes was startled by the composer's shrewd reasoning. He had some time ago come to the same conclusion.

"Congratulations, Miss Gonzaga. I think exactly the same thing."

"But why would he steal precisely my violin?" asked the baroness Maria Luísa, who was following the conversation with keen interest.

"I don't know yet. There could be several motives. First, because it's a Stradivarius. It's obvious that our criminal wants to call attention to himself. It also may have been the first instrument that he came across."

"And the flaps of skin? Why does he insist on this sinister collection?" asked Aluísio Azevedo, standing beside his brother.

"It can't be because he's an art collector. Neither of the victims was tattooed," joked Alberto Fazelli, ever inopportune.

"The flaps of skin are also a message. A cruel message from the 'serial killer,'" affirmed Holmes solemnly.

As the neologism had never been heard by any of those present, Aluísio Azevedo asked, "'Serial killer'? What does that mean?"

"I've never known of a similar case; that's why I created the term to designate someone who kills several people sequentially, always in the same manner and without the slightest apparent motive. That's why it's so difficult to apprehend him."

"Serial killer, '*sirialquíler*,'" murmured Paula Nei, Brazilianizing the accent.

Coelho Neto, who had little interest in sensational stories but loved to observe people in order to transform them into characters in some future novel, changed the subject to a more everyday topic.

"So, Mr. Holmes, what do you think of our Brazil?"

"A fascinating place, truly fascinating. I'm charmed by the national customs. The people are extremely cordial. I feel quite at home. There is something, however, that I don't understand," added Holmes.

"Tell us, Mr. Holmes," requested Coelho Neto.

"The dress. I can't understand why all the men wear black, European style, in a tropical country."

The detective had touched upon a sensitive point. The custom of imitating the waistcoats and heavy frock coats of colder climates was cause for amazement and joking among visitors, and even the satirical magazine *The Meddler* had published cartoons criticizing the practice.

"Mr. Holmes will forgive us, but civilization has its costs. *Il faut souffrir pour être beau. . . .*" answered the baroness of Avaré.

"Well, for my part, I regret not having brought less heavy clothing. I should like to find a tailor who could make me some light-colored suits."

"Salomão Calif!" shouted the men in the room in a single voice.

Guimarães Passos explained.

"He's the best tailor in the city and a very good friend of ours. When you like, I can take you to him," volunteered Guimarães Passos.

"I should be very grateful," said Holmes. "Another thing that is quite impressive is the beauty of the women. The girl whose life I saved was a stunner. I just saw her briefly, but my trained eyesight could see that she was a mulatto with very light skin, slightly wavy black hair, tall and slender, with a firm body and large green eyes."

Sarah Bernhardt interjected.

"How odd, Mr. Holmes. The other night I went to a revue and in the cast was a young mulatto woman who looked just like that. It had been a long time since I'd seen such a beautiful woman."

"There is no shortage of pretty mulatto women in the city," stated Paula Nei.

Holmes, nonetheless, was hooked.

"At what theater?" he asked.

"I don't recall the name. It's very near mine."

As there were several theaters in the Rossio area, no one knew for certain to which one Sarah Bernhardt was referring.

"It must be the Santana, where they're doing *The Woman-Man*. The music is by our own Chiquinha," ventured Aluísio Azevedo, a specialist in the genre.

"Exactly," said Sarah, remembering. "I just saw her in passing, on the stage, but afterward we all went to dinner. As I understand it, her role is small, but they assured me she's a girl with talent."

"The only mulatto in the cast is Anna Candelária, a very pretty girl who's just starting out," informed Chiquinha Gonzaga, lighting another cigarette.

Holmes took out his notebook and wrote down the name of the young woman and the theater.

While Albertinho Fazelli was trying to convince Holmes not to be overly optimistic, for in his experience various mulatto women could answer to that brief description, Maurice Bernhardt came into the library. He was accompanied by the marquis and several young ladies who were laughing excitedly.

"*Maman,* I had a marvelous idea. Why don't we have a séance?"

"At this hour, son?"

"It's the best hour. The hour of the spirits. I've already told the girls: when I'm present, the glass always moves."

Except for Sherlock Holmes, who didn't believe in the supernatural and at the moment could think of nothing but the mulatto girl, everyone liked the idea. Immediately, the viscount of Ibituaçu removed everything from a round table and pulled it into the center of the room. The others brought chairs while the baroness of Avaré, having gone to the secretaire, wrote and cut out pieces of paper with the letters of the alphabet.

"Could a spirit perhaps appear who could tell us where my violin is?" she joked.

Paula Nei drained his champagne glass and turned it upside down in the center of the table, surrounded by the small pieces of paper bearing the letters. The viscount ordered the servants to put out the lights, save for a single candle holder burning near the bookcases. Bilac, the marquis, Paula Nei, Guimarães Passos, Maurice, and some of the young ladies took their places at the table. The others remained standing, forming a circle around the small group. Those seated placed a finger on the upturned wineglass. They remained in that position, thinking about souls and ghosts, for several minutes without anything unusual happening.

"The spirits are taking a day off," suggested Paula Nei.

"They're probably miffed at not having received a formal invitation from the viscount," added Guimarães Passos.

"Concentrate. It's necessary to concentrate," said Maurice Bernhardt, covering up the muffled laughter of the girls.

"There's still a lot of light. Mr. Holmes, would you be so kind as to put out the candles, over there?" requested Maurice.

Holmes, absorbed in his thoughts, did not hear the young man's request. It was Sarah who took upon herself the task of blowing out the candles. Only a beam of light illuminated the room, casting shadows on the group.

The ensuing silence, amidst the darkness, was broken by a scream of terror coming from one of the women. Before anyone could light the candles, a resounding slap was heard.

"You low good-for-nothing. Go put your hand on your mother's leg!" exclaimed the girl sitting next to Maurice, as she got up.

When the lights returned, Maurice Bernhardt, embarrassed, was still rubbing his face. The young Frenchman was up to his old tricks.

~

Inspector Mello Pimenta took out his cambric handkerchief and wiped his brow once again. He never sweated from the heat; the perspiration was due to the reprimand that he was receiving, at that moment, from his chief. He was in the office of the Central Bureau, at 36 Lavradio Street, where his station was also located. A fly was circulating annoyingly overhead. The chief of police, Judge Coelho Bastos, seated at an enormous mahogany desk, smoothed his mustache while he spoke coolly, without looking Pimenta in the eye.

"You understand that my situation is rather delicate. Even today, the newspapers haven't forgotten the case of the stolen crown jewels."

Coelho Bastos was referring to the disappearance of jewels belonging to Empress Leopoldina, Baroness Fonesca da Costa, and Princess Isabel, which had disappeared from the palace some years before, when Trigo de Loureiro was chief of police. Later, it became known at court that the pilferer was Manuel de Paiva, the brother of Pedro de Paiva, chamberlain to the emperor, and the case had been hushed up, but Bastos still remembered the ridiculous caricatures of the police which *The Meddler* had published.

"As if it weren't enough that I learned about the stolen Stradivarius through the newspapers. It seems Dom Pedro no longer has confidence in his chief of police even to solve the robbery of a stolen fiddle," said Coelho Bastos, disparaging the instrument. "And then a murderer comes along to complicate things."

"A *sirialquíler*," corrected Mello Pimenta, using the catchphrase that Paula Nei had spread the length and breadth of Ouvidor Street.

"A what?" asked the chief of police.

"'*Sirialquíler*.' It was the name Sherlock Holmes gave to this criminal who kills in series," answered Pimenta, shooing away the fly that had just landed on his nose.

"Sherlock Holmes. One more proof of His Majesty's lack of confidence. I don't know why we need an English detective in these parts," complained Coelho Bastos, trying to crush the same fly on his desk, using his blotting pad.

"The judge will forgive me, but I think that, in this specific case, we're going to have to call on all possible help. Thanks to him, we now know that the violin thief and the murderer are the same person."

"What else do we know?"

"Very little. I was at the palace investigating the poor girl who died at the fountain. She was an orphan, aided by her uncle, and, from what they tell me, led a quiet life. She had no female friends or suitors. She kept to herself, off in the corners reading saccharine French novels. A nice, proper type of girl."

"And the other one, the woman on Regente Street?" asked Coelho Bastos.

"The opposite. I went to the brothel where she worked. I spoke with a ne'er-do-well known as Ladies' Backside who takes care of the house, from whom the girls have no secrets. He told me that the girl, despite not even being eighteen, drank a lot and gave herself to anyone. She didn't have regular customers."

"And our usual informants?"

"We shouldn't expect anything from that side. I tell you, Mr. Bastos, it's not going to be easy to discover the man because he kills without motive," concluded Mello Pimenta, frightening off the fly that, at that instant, was attempting to enter his ear.

"How so?"

"It's the first thing we learn in the police, Mr. Bastos—to discover the motive of the crime."

"Motive. You say motive? The motive is that the guy is off his nut, that's all!" Coelho Bastos simplified.

"It's not that simple, judge, to discover the motive of a deranged person," explained Mello Pimenta, again drying his forehead with the handkerchief.

The chief of police stood up, irritated.

"Then go to the asylum, talk with the doctors, talk with crazy people, take the Englishman with you if you think it's necessary, but catch this maniac before I too lose my mind!"

In his irritation, Coelho Bastos had given Mello Pimenta a good suggestion—it wasn't a bad idea to speak with an alienist at the Dom Pedro II Asylum, in the Praia Vermelha district. To see firsthand how those afflicted in their mental faculties acted, perhaps even talk with one of them, find out what they thought and how they conducted themselves. He must attend to that posthaste, for it was no longer possible to allow the monster to continue acting freely. Two women had died and everything indicated that the murderer was far from completing his bloody task.

"Anything else?" asked Judge Coelho Bastos, interrupting the inspector's thoughts.

Mello Pimenta, familiar with the chief's explosions, knew when it was time to withdraw.

"No, Your Honor," he replied ceremoniously.

"Then a good afternoon to you."

The inspector bent forward in a small salute and left, slamming the door and inadvertently crushing the fly that tried to follow him.

～

There could be no doubt: Salamão Calif had the best clientele in the city. There were more famous tailors, like Luiz Maria de Mattos, on Ouvidor Street, who performed miracles with the emperor's embroidered uniforms; Adolpho Ornellas, on Ourives; Teixeira, at the Swan of Gold; and even Braga, a tailor on Hospício Street who created the cassocks for His Eminence Dom Pedro de Lacerda, bishop of Rio de Janeiro. But the city's dandies placed their trust only in the scissors of Calif. His tailor shop was located on Uruguaiana Street, next to Hippolyte Effantin's barbershop.

It was there that Holmes, Watson, and Guimarães Passos headed after lunch. As they passed Hippolyte's door, Watson stopped.

"Holmes, while you order your clothes, I could take the opportunity to get a shave and haircut," he said, observing the large mirrors and *pompier* chairs that were the barber's pride.

"A fine idea, Watson. As for me, I'm going to let my hair grow, but I don't think this more romantic style would look very good on you," said the detective.

He was about to follow Guimarães Passos, when Watson called to him.

"Just a minute. You know I don't speak a word of this language. Explain to the man how I want my hair cut."

"Watson, it's time you learned something. All you have to do is go in and tell the barber: '*Barba e cabelo,*' which means 'shave and haircut,'" said Sherlock, walking away before the doctor could protest.

In the center of the tailor shop, where dozens of bolts of English cloth were piled on the counters, Salomão Calif was waiting for them, with outstretched arms.

"Mr. Holmes, Guimarães, welcome," greeted the Arab.

"I told Mr. Holmes that you were the best tailor in the city. Don't disappoint me," warned Guimarães Passos.

"Don't believe him, Mr. Holmes, a friend's exaggeration. What type of clothes would you like? I have here the most lovely flannels and cashmeres from your country. What do you prefer?"

Holmes replied as he ran his hand over the proffered fabrics.

"Neither one. I'd like you to make me four suits of white linen."

"Linen?" Guimarães and the tailor were startled.

"But here no one of quality wears that," argued Calif.

"It's something for hoi polloi," added Guimarães Passos.

"Then I shall set the fashion," stated the Englishman stubbornly.

"So linen it shall be," said Salomão, fetching the measuring tape and coming up to Holmes in front of the mirror.

"And white, don't forget. I can't understand why you don't wear lighter clothes, appropriate for the heat of the tropics."

"What style, Mr. Holmes? Have you something in mind?"

"Nothing very special. Make the frock coats loose, with space for the revolver I use when I travel beyond Aldgate," requested the Englishman, referring without explanation to the outskirts of London. "I want the pockets deep, as I always carry my pipe and magnifying glass with me."

Salomão Calif began to take Sherlock's measurements. When he kneeled to measure their inner seam, he was impressed by the volume that filled one of the trouser legs.

"I see that Mr. Holmes is extremely fortunate," he commented, with the traditional adulation of tailors.

"Don't talk rubbish, Mr. Salomão. That's my pipe," explained Sherlock Holmes.

Calif became flustered at Guimarães Passos's guffaws; he knew that the story would be recounted later at the Globo Café. As he went on efficiently measuring the Englishman from head to foot, he said, "I know that Mr. Sherlock must be tired of speaking about the subject, but I can't help asking: How are the investigations going? Is there anything new about that 'sirialquíler'?"

"For the time being, everything is the same, but patience is a virtue," said Holmes, proud that his expression was already being used everywhere.

"Do they at least know the type of weapon the killer uses?" the tailor asked eagerly.

Sherlock Holmes answered, subtly, "It is known for certain that it is a cutting instrument. It may be a razor, a bayonet, a dagger, a knife—or scissors," he concluded, picking up the enormous crossed blades that Salomão carried attached to his belt. "Yes, it could very well be a pair of scissors like these," he added.

"Come now, Mr. Holmes, the Turk here even suffers when he cuts his cloth," jested Guimarães Passos.

Holmes smiled.

"I am only making merry with your friend. I know very well he is not the assassin, for the fellow is much taller than he. Don't forget that I saw him from a distance in the National Library."

After a cup of coffee, Guimarães Passos and Sherlock Holmes said good-bye to Salomão Calif, who was still trembling at the detective's jape.

"Good-bye, Mr. Holmes. I will advise you as soon as the suits are ready to try on."

"Before I forget, I should also like a cap like mine, made of the same material. Is that possible?"

"Of course! I'll order it myself at the Ao Chapéu Monstro, on São José Street. It's the best hat shop in the city."

The pair left the tailor's shop and headed for Hippolyte Effantin's establishment, where Watson, seated in the barber's chair, a towel around his neck, was saying for the hundredth time.

"*Barba e cabelo.*"

The exhausted barber was asking, "Do you want me to trim your hair or a complete cut?"

"*Barba e cabelo.*"

"But it is just to trim?" asked Hippolyte once again.

"*Barba e cabelo,*" shouted the exasperated Watson, louder each time.

This would not be the occasion when the good doctor would go back to his good and venerable Prince Danilo cut.

# 13

*H*e had amused himself, silently, at people's indignant reaction to a few lines of a poem. How small the human soul is. Didn't they understand that Maldoror, like him, had been born perverse? They are shocked by the circumscribed iniquity of an obscure poet but are unmoved by the cruelty they see manifest in the city as they pass happily through its filthy streets. What would they *say if they knew they were in the same room as a being much more cruel than any creation in books? They would probably refuse to believe it, averting their eyes as they do when they trip over the Negroes and dirty beggars they encounter in their path. If the landscape is terrible, close the window. For him, it is different. He feeds on that quotidian misery. The misfortune of others is always a heavy balm for his solitude. The hell of others is his paradise. He finds amusement in the priests' sermons that always place Good above Evil, as if they were not two sides of the same coin. For him, Good is Evil. Cruelty, after all, is only a point of view. They call what he does to whores cruelty. Why? It's no different from what he has just read, searching for inspiration, in a manual on carving meat. Again, he picks up the small book lying beside the bed and reads the marked passages, droning as if in prayer:*

*"First the skin is removed. The breast, after removing the cartilage, is cut along the ribs, following the areas that offer no resistance to the knife. The shoulder is cut into slices above and underneath. . . . The leg is cut on a diagonal until arriving at the bone, and, grasping the handle thus formed, one continues removing the flesh until only the bare bone remains. . . . The head is then cut off, which is served whole. . . . The ribs and neck are delicate portions. . . . The backbone is cut into two halves and the ribs are separated, remaining attached to it. . . . Locating the joints, the rest is cut into slices, leaving the haunches for last. . . . A heavy blow with the knife through the scapula easily separates it from the framework of bones. . . . If further cutting is necessary, the smaller parts can be separated and the ribs or skeleton disjointed and divided into pieces. . . . The split is made beginning at the neck, running along the backbone, and then the slices are made transversely. The liver and kidneys are also divided into small pieces and offered to those who like them. . . . Always be sure the carving knife is well honed. . . ."*

*He closes the booklet and places it carefully on the table. At no time is this ritual called cruelty. It is not cruel simply because the sacrificed animals are used for food. That, therefore, is the differ-ence. Eating. Perhaps he should also eat. Finally taste flesh. The idea fills his mouth with saliva.*

*He picks up the blade and plunges into the night to sate his new-found appetite.*

∼

At that hour Constituiçâo Square was beginning to empty. People leaving the various theaters quickly summoned their coaches and returned home, some still laughing, others seri-ous, depending on the show they had attended.

At the door of the Santana, wearing his new white suit for the first time, stood an impatient Sherlock Holmes. He was alone. He had got rid of Watson by making up a story that he had been invited to a secret meeting with Mello Pimenta. The photos on the posters at the entrance confirmed Sarah Bern-hardt's information: the young woman was the one Sherlock was looking for. He had already attempted to meet with Anna Candelária for several nights, but fate had dictated that each time the detective should arrive late at the theater. This time, to avoid further disappointment, he had arrived half an hour before the end of the performance. Leaning against the wall next to the artists' exit, Holmes awaited the woman whom he could not get out of his head. He was beginning to worry. Sev-eral players had already left and, thus far, no sign of Anna Candelária. He had confirmed the name with the doormen the other times he had come seeking her. Now, two of them were talking as they closed the foyer grille.

"Did you see who's there again?"

"Who?"

"The Portuguese . . . waiting for the mulatto girl."

"You think I don't know? He's already asked me at least ten times when the show was supposed to end."

"Why do you suppose he's dressed all in white at this hour?"

"I don't know, something the Portuguese do."

Holmes was preparing to refill his pipe when Anna Candelária appeared. She immediately recognized her benefactor.

"Hello! How good to see you again. I feel I owe you an apology."

"Apology? And why should the young lady apologize?"

"For the other night. After all, you saved my life and I didn't even wait to thank you," she said, with a dazzling smile that completed the definitive conquest of Holmes's heart.

"Under the circumstances, it's perfectly understandable. I imagine the young lady must have been shaken by the occurrence."

Ever since Anna had read in the newspapers that her savior was the famous Englishman, she had been seeking a way of meeting him. She had almost gone to the police station to learn of his whereabouts.

"How did you discover that I work here?"

"Do you forget I'm a detective?" asked Sherlock, also smiling in a captivating manner. "Sherlock Holmes, at your service."

"Anna Candelária," she said, extending her hand.

Holmes kissed her fingertips without taking his blue eyes from the green eyes of the beautiful mulatto girl.

"The young lady would afford me immense pleasure if she were to accept an invitation to dine with me and some acquaintances. Inspector Mello Pimenta will be there, and since we have begun investigating jointly those horrible crimes, the presence of Miss Anna, as the sole victim who escaped the assassin's fury, is indispensable," argued Holmes, using the episode as a pretext.

"Please, call me Anna."

"Of course, provided that to you I am simply Sherlock," ventured the Englishman, surprising himself with the intimacy proffered to the girl, as generally the maximum that he permitted, even with Watson, was to be called by his surname. Leading Anna Candelária by her arm, Holmes beckoned to a cab.

~

The Botanical Gardens on Rodrigo de Freitas lake was one of the most beautiful spots in Rio de Janeiro. It had begun as a small garden created by the marquis of Sabará next to the lakeside gunpowder factory that he ran. When a visitor would express the desire to see it, a soldier from the factory would accompany him, walking around the flowery retreat and describing the various flowerbeds that gave such pleasure to the marquis. There were tea plants, spices, and seeds, brought from the Île de France in 1809. Later, the gunpowder factory was transferred to the Estrela foothills, where conditions allowed production of some 165 tons a year. The garden of exotic plants had been enlarged to a league in length and was now annexed to the Royal Museum. The serene beauty of the lake lent it an incomparable appearance. Rodrigo de Freitas lake only became uncomfortable with the sudden perishing of massive numbers of fishes, a phenomenon that occurred whenever the supply of oxygen dropped, contaminating the area with an unbearable odor. There was a project, forgotten in the bowels of some government bureau, for enlargement of the canal that connected the lake to the sea. A palm-lined street led to the entrance, and next to the iron gates, between pillars decorated with marble vases, was an ancient wild pear tree.

Almost directly across from the gate, on Jardim Botânico Street, stood the Chalet Campestre restaurant. Nestled in groves of leafy trees, the Campestre served meals at any hour of the day or night, and, as it remained open until the early morning hours, was a favorite spot for night owls. Outside, the tables were situated beneath the trees, which boasted swings greatly appreciated by the ladies. Inside was a semicircular English-style bar with a mahogany countertop, a mirrored wall behind it, a machine with two spigots for beer on tap, where one could savor the cold beverage, and, off to the side, an immense billiards room. The owner, J. R. Macedo, a former seminarian, had infinite patience with the bohemians' slowness in settling their accounts. He had only cut off the credit of Fernando Limeira, known as Sorrel, a young man from an excellent Minas Gerais family, who had spent a few years studying in Europe at his father's expense. He had a long, red face, whence his nickname. Fernando absolutely refused to work and lived by his wits while he sought to obtain public employment as an amanuensis. His stratagems to find money were not always of the most conventional kind. Once, when a new streetcar line was about to be inaugurated in Laranjeiras, Sorrel went into a bar and asked to speak to the owner, a corpulent Portuguese with few friends. He introduced himself solemnly.

"Pleased to meet you. Fernando Limeira, of the Botanical Garden Railroad Company, assistant to Marshal Carnaúba."

"I don't know you," said the Portuguese brusquely.

"I'll explain the reason for my visit. You must have noticed that our company has opened a new streetcar line running through your street here."

"I don't care."

"I know, but imagine how much your business would increase if one of the stops for our vehicles were exactly at the door of your bar. You would also come to have a floating clientele, because of the passengers descending at your door," Limeira explained to the Portuguese, who was already mentally calculating the extraordinary profit he would make.

"And how much is this story going to cost me?" asked the Iberian, who knew very well that nothing came free.

"It's very cheap, only four hundred *mil-réis*."

"That's a lot."

"True. Because of your great amiability, I'll let you have it for one hundred and fifty. But I'm an honest man who keeps his word. You can pay me only after the streetcars begin stopping at your door."

The agreement made, he withdrew, carrying his case filled with old newspapers, which he used only to lend dignity to the role he was playing. Late that night, when the street was empty, he returned and painted the lamppost in front of the bar white. This was the sign used by the railroad company to indicate obligatory stops to the drivers.

The following day, Fernando Limeira was received in the packed bar by the euphoric Portuguese.

"This is wonderful! The streetcar stops and the people swarm in here like flies! Like flies! You're a man of your word, a rare thing these days. Here's what we agreed on," he said, happily handing over the haggled-down sum in coins and wrinkled bills.

"I don't do this for the money but to support Marshal Carnaúba's policy, who bends every effort to broaden evermore the ties that link our two peoples," declared Sorrel magnanimously, as he pocketed the hundred and fifty *mil-réis*. He left quickly, for he knew that the Portuguese's joy would be short-lived.

As soon as the streetcars arrived at the station and mentioned that there was a new stop on their route, the supervisors saw at once that it was a swindle. By the end of the afternoon, employees of the company had painted the post black again and the streetcars returned to their original stops, to the despair of the Portuguese.

At the Campestre, Fernando Limeira also did a little mooching, in addition to his not having paid his bills for over a year, which had led J. R. to put an end to the abuse. Indignant, Sorrel spread a different story: he said he no longer went to the Campestre because the prices were excessive.

It was precisely for the Chalet Campestre restaurant, in the Botanical Gardens district, that Sherlock Holmes and Anna Candelária headed. A happy circle, laughing and talking loudly, was waiting for them. Seated at one of the outdoor tables were Inspector Mello Pimenta and a large number of the gang. The marquis of Salles was the first to greet the couple.

"Mr. Holmes, I see you finally found the one you were looking for. You were right, the girl is truly a unique beauty," he conceded, inspecting the woman from top to bottom with his expert eye.

Anna Candelária, an actress and a woman of liberal habits, was very much at ease. Holmes, however, seemed exceedingly discomfited by the situation. He was not accustomed to female company and blushed to the roots of his hair when he felt the girl take his hand. Bringing chairs from a neighboring table, they joined the group. Amused at the Englishman's uneasiness, Chiquinha Gonzaga said to Anna, "So, girl? It seems that you've made our detective's head spin."

"Who am I, Dona Chiquinha, to do such a thing? But I'm immensely grateful. If I'm alive today, it's thanks to him." She added, turning to Holmes, "Isn't that so, Sherlock?"

Sherlock Holmes felt a shiver run from head to foot upon being addressed in that manner. He still didn't know how to deal with such intimacies. Macedo himself came to take their order and, in the Englishman's honor, insisted on offering the wine with his compliments. Mello Pimenta didn't even wait for dessert. After all, the dinner was being held to discuss the case of the murdered women. As soon as the main dish was served, he interrupted the amenities and pleasantries to ask Anna Candelária, "I don't understand why you didn't go to the station house to relate your encounter with the killer."

"I was afraid, inspector. As you very well know, in Brazil our profession is still confused with that of prostitutes. I didn't know how I would be received."

"I can assure you that the police treat everyone with respect and courtesy. Even prostitutes," declared Mello Pimenta hypocritically.

Chiquinha Gonzaga almost choked on the chicken she was eating.

"Pimenta, if you plan to stay here with the gang, you'll have to cut out the bunkum."

Paying no attention to the group's laughter, Mello Pimenta continued.

"Could you give me a description of the assailant?"

"Impossible, inspector. It was night and he was covered by

a cape, with a hat pulled down over his head. All I remember are his eyes, which seemed to flash in the darkness."

"You didn't see what type of knife he was carrying?"

"No, I only know it had a long blade."

"Did he say anything when he approached?"

"Not a single word."

"It looks as if it's going to be difficult to discover this killer. From what we've seen, it could be anyone," said Olavo Bilac.

Sherlock Holmes agreed with the poet and decided to show off a bit for Anna Candelária.

"It's true, Mr. Bilac. Anyone. Even someone who at this very moment is calmly eating right here in this restaurant, observing us from a distance."

In silence, everyone looked around, examining the other customers. Sherlock continued.

"He might even be sitting at our table," he declared mysteriously.

"What? Do you think he's one of the gang?" said Albertinho Fazelli, startled.

"I don't think anything. I'm merely saying that, for all we know, it could even be you," concluded the detective.

The marquis of Salles intervened before Fazelli fainted.

"Come now, let's not exaggerate, Mr. Holmes. I've been with Alberto on several nights' revels, and I've never known his eyes to flash in the dark."

Holmes pretended not to understand.

"Don't forget, marquis, our man is crazy. He may have a double personality. By chance, before traveling I read a book called *The Strange Case of Dr. Jekyll and Mr. Hyde,* which deals with precisely that."

"Then, am I also a suspect?" joked Guimarães Passos.

"Why not? I know only that the murderer cannot be either

me or Dr. Watson, as we weren't here when the crimes began, nor, of course, Anna Candelária," said Holmes, looking tenderly at the girl.

"Because she's a woman?" asked Alberto Fazelli, for whom reasoning was always a challenge.

"No, because she was nearly one of his victims."

On the other side of the table, Chiquinha Gonzaga showed interest.

"So you don't exclude women? Finally we're equal to men at something!"

"Why not? The 'serial killer' could perfectly well be disguised. We know of the uncommon strength characteristic of the insane at moments of crisis," said Sherlock Holmes, trying to light his pipe and burning his fingertips, as he couldn't take his eyes off Anna.

Mello Pimenta thought it was time to get the conversation back on track.

"Speaking of the insane, Mr. Holmes, my chief, Judge Coelho Bastos, without intending to do so, made a suggestion that could bear fruit. He advised us to visit the asylum. Perhaps by speaking with an alienist or even with one of the patients we may find an inspiration."

"An excellent idea, inspector. I had already thought of that myself," lied Sherlock Holmes.

"Then I'll make an appointment with the director of the asylum. As soon as I'm informed of the day of the interview, I'll send word to you."

After coffee, they discussed the lack of security in Rio de Janeiro.

"This year alone, counting the two young women, there have already been fifteen homicides," said Mello Pimenta.

"It's part of living in a large city," said Guimarães Passos.

As always, Alberto Fazelli paid the bill. As they were preparing to leave, they heard a disturbance at the restaurant door. It was Fernando Limeira, Sorrel, who had arrived totally intoxicated and was arguing with Macedo. The owner of the Chalet Campestre kept repeating, "I've told you, Fernando, I think a lot of you, but if you want to eat you have to pay cash."

"With these absurd prices you charge?" shouted Limeira, pushing aside the waiters who were trying to lead him out.

"I don't charge anything absurd. You're the one who's always ordering the most expensive thing on the menu. It's food that's expensive, not the service."

Fernando Limeira straightened his crooked tie and rose to the occasion.

"You're right. Let's come to an agreement." He put his hand into the inside pocket of his frock coat and, pulling out a piece of raw meat, bellowed: "How much does the 'service' on this steak cost?"

The entire restaurant broke into raucous laughter, along with Macedo. It was impossible to quarrel with Sorrel for very long.

～

Sherlock Holmes and Anna Candelária left the Chalet Campestre in a rented victoria. The Englishman offered to drop Anna at her house, but, after giving her address, the girl stated with the directness of artists, "It's still early. Before going, I'd like to see your hotel. They've told me the apartments at the Albion are stunning."

Holmes found himself with divided emotions. He was overjoyed that Anna wanted to accompany him, but he felt shocked at the idea. He would never dare make such a suggestion to the young woman, yet it was exactly what he desired. The two continued in silence to Fresca Street.

While Holmes distracted the night doorman by asking for totally useless information, Anna Candelária slipped past to the stairs. As soon as they got to the room, she sat down on the bed.

"Good heavens, how soft it is! And the room is much prettier than I thought." She patted the pillows. "Come here close to me."

Awkwardly, Holmes placed himself at her side. On impulse, Anna took Sherlock's face in her hands and kissed his lips at length. The detective's heart raced. Not even in the pursuit of the most terrible criminals had he felt such emotion. He was unaccustomed to the situation. He stood up, stored in the dresser drawer the Beaumont-Adams revolver that was his constant companion on dangerous missions, and, feigning unconcern, asked as he opened his coat, "May I offer you something? Tea, sherry, cocaine?"

"Cocaine?"

"Yes, an excellent stimulant. I learnt its use with Sigmund Freud, a doctor in Vienna. We studied the technique of hypnosis together at Dr. Charcot's clinic in Paris. My friend Sigmund is an unshakable defender of the miraculous properties of coca," said Sherlock Holmes in self-justification, taking from his pocket a small box and a silver straw, preparing for a *prise*.

"I'd have thought I was stimulant enough," said Anna Candelária suggestively, taking the objects from the detective's hands and putting them on the small table by the bed.

She again pulled Holmes toward the bed. She kissed him a

second time, with still more intensity, opening his shirt. Sherlock affectionately pushed her away.

"Anna, there's something terrible that I must confess."

"What is it, my love?"

"I'm a virgin."

Anna Candelária couldn't believe what she had just heard. Holmes appeared to be over forty, and in the tropics boys of eleven were already rubbing up against the family's young women slaves. On the plantations they lost their virginity with the young slave girls even before they had hair on their faces.

"Sherlock, how old are you?"

"I was thirty-two in January," replied the detective, who looked older than his years.

"I don't understand. Did you take some vow of chastity?"

"By no means. It's just that, until I met you, I never had any interest in sex. My mind was always focused on criminology."

Anna was both moved and flattered.

"You mean I'm the first woman in your life?"

"Yes, except for Violet," said Holmes.

"Who is Violet?"

"My mother."

The beautiful mulatto had tears in her eyes. Tenderly, she touched his thick brown hair.

"Do you understand now why I was going to resort to cocaine?"

Anna smiled, touched by his childlikeness.

"My love, those drugs just dispel desire. What you need is something to make you relax."

So saying, she took from her purse a small blue packet with yellow trim and showed it to the Englishman.

"What's that?" asked Sherlock Holmes.

"You're not familiar with it? They're Indian cigarettes, made from *cannabis*, an Asiatic plant. It also grows very well in our climate. You can buy it at any apothecary," explained Anna Candelária, opening the roll of waxed paper and preparing a cigarette.

"And what are they good for?"

"For almost everything. The instruction paper says they're excellent for snoring, sleeplessness, lack of appetite, asthma; it's a miraculous medicine. Besides that, it's wonderfully soothing on the nerves," said Anna, extending the cigarette to Holmes.

"Thank you, I prefer to put the herb in my pipe," said Sherlock, filling his enormous meerschaum, using the waxed envelope as if it were a tobacco pouch.

"Careful, don't overdo the portion," warned Anna Candelária as she lit her cigarette.

Holmes took a few puffs.

"Except for the smell, I don't notice anything." He tried again. "It has no effect on me at all."

"You have to draw it in deep and hold the smoke in your lungs as long as you can," the woman instructed.

Obeying her instructions, Holmes quickly consumed the first pipeful.

"I'm going to smoke another; I'm still as tense as before," he stated, helping himself to the *cannabis* again.

"Easy, my dear. It always takes a little time."

Not believing her, the detective went on taking heavy puffs.

"It must be because of my size. My dosage has to be huge," joked Sherlock.

"Don't exaggerate; I've seen *cannabis* knock out larger men than you."

After the fourth pipeful, Holmes stopped suddenly.

"I'd never noticed how colorful this room is. Did you notice, Anna, what lovely colors? I've never seen such a vibrant yellow. And the wallpaper? The flowers are dancing! Look how they dance! They seem to be in relief! It gives me a tremendous urge to laugh. The flowers dancing! Such a whirl! What fun!" said Sherlock, more Portuguese than ever, overcome by an uncontrollable fit of laughter.

Anna Candelária was also laughing.

"I warned you, my dear, that you smoked too much."

Guffawing, they fell onto the bed. Holmes began to kiss her impatiently, simultaneously trying to divest himself of his clothes and the woman of her dress.

"My sweet palindrome," he murmured in her ear.

"What was that you called me?"

"Palindrome, don't you know what that is?"

"Not exactly."

"A word that when read from left to right or right to left always means the same thing, like you, Anna. . . . Sherlock ama Anna. . . . Sherlock loves Anna. . . . In Portuguese there are two palindromes, ama and Anna. . . . ama and Anna. . . . Anna and ama. . . ." repeated Holmes, in a delirium, as he kissed the woman's perfect breasts. He began to suck, one after the other, the erect nipples of Anna Candelária, who moaned with pleasure. He then returned to kissing her sensual lips, joining his tongue to hers. Suddenly, the detective raised himself on his arms and said, "Do you know what I feel like doing?"

"What? I want you to do everything you want with me, my impassioned Englishman. . . ." said Anna, quivering with desire.

"Eating something sweet."

"What?"

"I don't know why, but I have an irresistible urge for sweets."

"*I* know why, it's the *cannabis*. The cigarettes create a special appetite for sugar. When I smoke a lot, I stuff myself with coconut candy," explained Anna, buttoning her dress and rising. "Don't go away. I'm going to the hotel kitchen to steal some sweets and I'll be right back," she laughed, heading for the door.

Sherlock, his mouth dry, lay back on the pillows, enjoying the immense happiness that had overtaken his entire being. For the first time since he had arrived, he didn't miss the London fog. The enchantment of the tropics had claimed another victim.

The doorman was snoring with his face resting on the concierge's counter, the newspaper he was trying to read to ward off sleep fallen to the floor at his side. Carefully, making no sound, Anna Candelária crossed the lobby and entered the Albion's enormous pantry. In a larder next to the cupboard where the dishes were kept, she found what she was seeking: a plate of coconut sweetmeats. She sampled one and found it sublime. Her judgment was dubious, though, for whenever she smoked an Indian cigarette, anything sugary tasted delicious to her. She returned by the same route by which she had come, carrying the fruits of her theft. She entered the room, closing the door behind her, and approached the bed, to find Sherlock Holmes in a deep sleep, a beatific smile on his lips. Not having the courage to wake him, she sat on the edge of the bed and ate all the candy by herself. Then she lightly kissed the detective's brow and carefully tiptoed out.

~

A piercing scream woke Holmes from the deep sleep in which he was dreaming that a naked mulatto woman with large breasts and long, firm thighs was dancing for him. She had Anna Candelária's marvelous body, but, curiously, the face was that of his mother. The detective forced that strange image from his mind. He touched the bedcover beside him and saw he was alone. The cries grew louder and louder, and he quickly sprang from the bed, searching for the revolver that he kept in the dresser. He noted that the bellows were coming from Watson's room and opened the door that separated his quarters from the doctor's. Watson, screaming incessantly, was strangling his pillow.

"Die, you blackguard! The barbarian has yet to be born who can attack me from behind!"

Relieved, Sherlock saw that it was a nightmare. Leaning over, he shook the doctor vigorously by violently jostling the pillow.

"Wake up, Watson, for God's sake, wake up!"

Dr. Watson opened his eyes. For a moment he appeared to be awake, but he quickly began grappling with Sherlock.

"So there are two of you now! Come on then, one's no match for a soldier of Her Majesty! Long live the queen!" he roared, delirious.

Holmes slapped him in the face.

"It's I, Watson. Stop it before you wake the entire hotel."

Slowly, the doctor emerged from his fantasy.

"Good heavens! I thought I was in India being attacked by a Ghazi warrior."

"Luckily, my dear Watson, it was merely a dream."

"It's this heretic food. From now on I'll stick to the cream crackers I brought from London," he declared.

"Let's try to get a little asleep. We had a rather hectic night," said Holmes, thinking of Anna Candelária.

"In any case, I'm sorry I didn't bring my old army Colt," complained the doctor when he saw his companion's revolver.

"Don't worry before it's necessary, Watson. Remember, what must happen, will happen," the detective stated philosophically, withdrawing toward his own bedroom.

The doctor pulled up the covers, agreeing with the detective.

"You're right, Holmes. As the old Scottish proverb says, the only birds that die the night before are the turkey and the pig."

Holmes closed the door, attributing the confused saying to his friend's frightful nightmare.

# 14

In 1693, distressed by the impiety and abandon into which newborn orphans were cast, perishing in the alleyways from cold and hunger, Governor Antonio Paes de Sande sent a letter to King Pedro II of Portugal asking that measures be taken, as the Holy House of Mercy could not shelter them all, for lack of sufficient income. The Senate had shown no interest in the rearing of these poor innocents. As Portugal had amassed immense riches thanks to the gold mines just discovered in Brazil, the king, feeling benevolent, ordered that the unprotected be fed from the goods of the Council, and that the necessary taxes should be imposed for the carrying out of this pious task.

The Senate began to employ the excess from certain taxes in the rearing of the small unfortunates who were thrown onto the mercy of the streets, where in some cases they were even devoured by dogs. There were, however, no fixed resources for this work.

The abandonment and misery of these tiny orphans having moved the heart of a certain Romão de Mattos Duarte, he decided in January 1738 to donate thirty-two thousand cruzados to the Holy House of Mercy for the rearing of cast-off children. The Wheel of Foundlings was established.

The Wheel was so called because at the side entrance of the building was a large wooden door over which could be seen an opening covered by a rotating cylinder, also of wood, with two shelves where unwanted babies were deposited. The cylinder turned easily at a slight push, and the foundling disappeared through the opening and into the house. A bell connected to the rotating apparatus informed the Sisters of Charity, who would gather up the abandoned babies, most often at night.

The Wheel of Foundlings began on Misericórdia Square and was later on Santa Thereza Street, but since 1860 had carried out its functions in a two-story building at 66 Evaristo da Veiga, which had earlier housed the School of Medicine.

The new Wheel of Foundlings had been inaugurated in July of that year in the presence of the royal family. The lobby was lined in marble, and on one side was the secretariat for payment of outside nannies, nurses who worked for the Holy House; on the other, the Wheel Room. Next to the Wheel was always stationed a Sister of Charity to receive the abandoned children. By the central staircase stood statues of St. Vincent de Paul and Charity. On the first floor were the refectory, the recreation room, the ironing room, the kitchen, the laundry tubs, and the garden. On the second, the administration room, the mother superior's office, chapel, dispensary, reading room, sewing room, the sleeping quarters of the Sisters of Charity, a room with forty cradles, and the foundlings' dormitory, with forty-two beds. Oil paintings of Pedro I and Empress Leopoldina and of Dom Pedro II and Empress Teresa Cristina graced the walls. The foundling girls who lived there were taught to read, write, and count, as well as grammar, sacred history, needlework, and ironing. Those who later married received a dowry offered by the sisterhood. Every year, Princess Isabel sent the Wheel of Foundlings trunks containing clothing made by her own hand, an act that revealed the immense goodness of her heart.

To demonstrate that the Wheel of Foundlings did not forget its benefactors, there was also a painting of its founder, the generous Romão de Mattos Duarte. However, what most moved visitors was the portrait in the cradle room, of a hydrocephalic child who had been put into the Wheel by an unknown woman in July of 1882 and had died two months later. Before he died, he was baptized with the name Mateus. Mateus was the symbol for all who worked at the Wheel.

What no one knew was that Mateus's mother had been working at the Wheel for over three years. Her name was Carolina de Lourdes, and she was the daughter of Josué Calixto, a highly regarded funeral agent with an establishment on Itapiru Street, immediately next to the São Francisco de Paula cemetery. Carolina had believed the false promises of Ariel Lemos, a youth who had come from Curitiba to study the secrets of embalming with Calixto. Ariel had seduced the pretty girl of seventeen and then fled to the interior of the state of Paraná, after which nothing more was ever heard of him. Josué Calixto, a widower and a severe, unbending man who was an assiduous reader of the Old Testament, expelled his daughter from the house. If not for the intervention of a spinster aunt in Niterói, Carolina would surely have had to take up the exceedingly arduous easy life of the prostitute.

As soon as the boy was born, Carolina, horrified, attributed the child's deformity to her own wickedness. A week later, breaking her lying-in, she left the unfortunate fruit of her sin at the Wheel; then she was reconciled with her father, who had pardoned her after obliging her to observe a long penance. Nonetheless, remorse began to steal the beautiful Carolina's sleep. She would lie awake nights, thinking of the poor sick little boy she had deposited on the cold wood of the Wheel. In the darkness of her room she imagined seeing the child's large, dull eyes looking unblinkingly at her. One day, no longer able to bear the guilt, she went to the Wheel of Foundlings. Great was her shock at discovering that her son had died and been transformed into the institution's child symbol. Without making her identity known, she decided she must do something in aid of the foundlings who, like her son, were thrown onto the mercy of the charity of others. With her father's consent, she began serving the Wheel as an outside nanny, receiving no compensation for the work. "The greatest payment is the comfort I afford to my 'little ones,' " she liked to say, referring to the small unfortunates. Everyone thought it strange to see that extraordinarily beautiful young woman, still almost a girl, dedicating herself to that hard task so patiently. She was greatly beloved at the Wheel. Carolina had no fixed hours and would offer to keep vigil at the Wheel when one of the sisters fell ill; the next day she would remain until late caring for the needy.

On that rainy night, Carolina de Lourdes left the Wheel of Foundlings after eleven o'clock. She had not been home for two days, and her father, worried about her, insisted that she rest a little, before she succumbed to pure exhaustion. He was to fetch her in his coach at the end of the evening, but the intense rainfall had made it impossible for the calash to get through. The sisters urged Carolina to sleep there, but the young woman rejected the possibility. She said that her father was nearly as abandoned as one of her "little ones," and began walking, in the storm, down Evaristo da Veiga Street.

～

A flash of lightning illuminates momentarily the figure in black who waits under a tree, on Chácara da Ajuda Road. Carolina de Lourdes heads toward Visconde de Maranguape Street. He sets out quickly after the young woman. The thunderclaps and the lightning cutting through the heavy drops of water give the street a gloomy appearance. Carolina increases her pace and turns to the right on her way to Nova dos Arcos Street. He follows rapidly behind her, taking care that his long steps touch the ground in the same rhythm as the girl's, thus concealing the noise he makes. With each stride he reduces the distance that separates them. Whenever the young woman stops, scanning the road in search of a tilbury, he remains motionless behind her, in a sinister improvised choreography. For a moment, both are framed by the arches of the aqueduct bridge, like two dancers lost on a gigantic stage. Not a soul is in sight. She passes Lavradio and continues down Resende. When he arrives at the same spot, he has an idea: he moves rapidly toward Riachuelo, breaking into a run. His feet scarcely touch the wet pavement. The cape gives him the appearance of an enormous vulture soaring through the rain. The two are now proceeding in parallel—Carolina, on Resende Street, and he, on Riachuelo: the defenseless sparrow and the bird of prey. He wants to encounter her from the front. He knows the woman has no way out; the next crossing isn't until Inválidos Street. He turns to the right and flies toward the other intersection. Panting, pressed against the wall of the last house on the block, he glimpses his victim. He hides the dagger under his cape, like a bullfighter's muleta, and waits.

Carolina de Lourdes only has time to raise her hands, attempting futilely to protect herself. The blade cuts through her palms and penetrates her lung. He yanks out the knife and strikes the girl again, one, two, five, fifteen times. Carolina is already dead on the ground when he kneels, opens her belly to the breastbone, tears out the girl's still warm liver, and rubs it ravenously on his own face. He licks, then breathes into the viscous organ. He feels no repulsion; to the contrary, the sweetish smell of blood makes him experience a violent spasm of pleasure. He feels drained. It will not be this time that he tastes the meat of sin. He prefers to wait, for he knows that the greatest delicacy is served only at the end of the banquet. Almost gently, he replaces the dripping bowel in the abject fissure. Then, in a gesture which has become mechanical from routine, he slices a flap of flesh from the girl's right side, stores it in his pocket, and takes out the violin tied to his waist. He plucks out another string, the A or *la*, the third one on the instrument, and executes the macabre ritual of placing it on the girl's pubis. Then he walks away, fingering a pizzicato on the last remaining string.

In the street, the rain washes away the blood of the poor girl lying on the sidewalk, her arms open in a cross, her hands pierced like the wounds of Christ.

~

Sherlock Holmes awoke with a dry mouth. His head felt empty, as if his skull were a hollow cavity hitherto occupied by an exceptional brain. It was once again the excess of *cannabis*. He had taken advantage of the previous evening's storm to spend the day in his room, reasoning about the case as he would do in Baker Street, but his thoughts were constantly interrupted by images of Anna Candelária in his arms. In London, Holmes would assuredly have resorted to cocaine to awaken his powers of concentration, but he saw on the table the package of Indian cigarettes that Anna had left behind in his bedroom and he had again preferred to fill his pipe with the herb. He had sat in front of the window watching the rain fall, then had picked up his violin and, under the effect of the smoke, had managed to extract some very strange sounds from the instrument, improvising melodies that recalled the native songs played by Mukumbe in the baroness of Avaré's house. He didn't remember how long he had remained there, smoking and playing— he hadn't even appeared for dinner at the hotel restaurant but had asked for food to be sent to his room. He had gone to bed early and had vivid dreams. Now, he awoke with a kind of aftereffect unlike anything he had ever known.

Dr. Watson opened the door with a jovial smile. To Holmes's surprise, he was in an excellent humor.

"Good day, my friend, I think it's time to hop out of bed," announced Watson, smiling and placing a curious hat on his head.

Holmes blinked several times, trying to bring his sight into focus. There was something bizarre about Dr. Watson that the detective's torpor would not permit him to identify. Holmes rubbed his eyes and finally managed to see: Watson was wearing the hat and sandals of a backwoods cowboy. Sherlock Holmes almost fell out of bed.

"Great Zeus, man, what is that?"

"I'm merely following your advice. Didn't you say I should get used to the habits of the country? These are accessories typical of the land. Why? Don't you like it?"

"May I know where the deuce you bought them?"

"Yesterday, while you were spending the day locked in, your friend Paula Nei took me for a turn about the city. They have everything in the streets, a veritable Persian market. A street vendor was offering these items and Nei convinced me to buy them. They come from the northeast region. I must say that the sandals are quite comfortable," said Watson jovially, wriggling his exposed anklebone.

"That may be, but they have a very strong smell," replied Holmes.

"That's exactly what I liked. They're made of cowhide; the odor reminds me of the Turkish tobacco I used to smoke in Ankara."

"And the hat?"

"A perfect replacement for my bowler. Paula Nei was enchanted," stated the doctor vainly.

Holmes did not wish to dash cold water on his friend's enthusiasm, but he knew full well that this was one of the bo-

hemian's pranks. The conversation between the two was interrupted by Inojozas, who came in bearing a folded sheet of
paper.

"If I may, Mr. Holmes, I—"

The detective interrupted the concierge.

"No need to say anything. I presume you suffer from the illness known as Saint Vitus's dance and that yesterday you had
an argument with your wife. Besides that, you are bringing me
a note from Miss Anna Candelária and had to grapple a short
time ago with a Gypsy whose earrings are not made of gold,"
stated Holmes casually, pulling his robe over his shoulders.

Watson, accustomed to Sherlock's mental exercises, showed
no reaction, but Inojozas, agape, was astonished by that extraordinary deduction.

"How did you arrive at those conclusions, Mr. Holmes?"
demanded the concierge.

"Elementary, my dear Inojozas. Saint Vitus's dance, a disease known in academic circles as Syndenham's chorea, pro-
vokes uncontrollable tremors in its sufferers, which explains
the water stains on your lapel, caused by a spilled glass of
water. The argument with your wife is easily explained by the
absence of a wedding ring on your finger, where the mark is
still visible; I also can see that the note you bring was penned
by someone with feminine handwriting, ergo, from Miss Anna
Candelária, from whom I am expecting news. The explanation
of the hand-to-hand struggle with the Gypsy is even more obvious. What better place to grab a Gypsy in a fight than by his
earring, leaving him completely defenseless? As for the proof
that his earrings were made of some metal other than gold, it
lies in the greenish stains of verdigris that I was able to observe
on your hands," announced Sherlock Holmes. He fetched his

clothes, his toilet set, and quit the bedroom in triumph, heading toward the bathroom and announcing, "I'll be back in an instant."

Inojozas sat down, astounded, across from Watson. The doctor attempted to reassure him.

"No need for surprise, old man; Holmes's deductive powers have astonished the best minds at Scotland Yard and sent many a criminal to jail. As for your Saint Vitus's dance, I can tell you as a doctor that opium pills have yielded excellent results in the treatment of the illness."

"Thank you, Dr. Watson, but I can assure you I suffer from no disease. My clothes are wet because it's still raining. Besides that, I'm unmarried; what I had on my finger was not a wedding ring but just a ring, which I took off because it was too tight. This paper here is not a note from that Miss Anna Candelária but a letter of my own that I was going to put in the mail, and it's been many years since I've seen a Gypsy. The stains on my hand are from ink, because I got them dirty while writing the letter," explained Inojozas.

"Details, my dear fellow, mere details. Let's not allow the results of the brilliant reasoning that we just witnessed to be tarnished by vulgar trifles. To what do we owe the honor of your visit to our quarters?" asked Watson, changing the subject.

"I came to tell you that Inspector Mello Pimenta telephoned," said Inojozas, standing up.

"Tell me, Mr. Inojozas, how do you say 'telephone' in Portuguese?"

"*Telefone.*"

"Then we have a telephone in the hotel?" asked Holmes, returning to the room in an immaculate white suit. "I have not yet become acquainted with that example of modernity."

"Of course, Mr. Holmes, and there are already over sixteen hundred subscribers. The only problem is that the maintenance of the lines is somewhat careless. We hope that in time this problem will be solved. The Secretary of Public Works has promised a solution soon," said the *hôtelier* with pride.

"And what about the note from my friend?"

Inojozas explained, abashedly, showing Holmes the envelope.

"I'm very sorry, Mr. Holmes, but this is just a letter I have to post."

"You mean I erred in one of my deductions? No matter. In any case, hitting the mark three out of four times is still a reasonable performance," commented the detective, as he finished knotting his tie.

Inojozas and Watson refrained from comment. Sherlock continued, "And what does our good Pimenta want with me?"

"It seems there was another crime last night. The inspector is waiting for the two of you at the scene."

"Just as I feared. Another girl murdered. Come, Watson, we mustn't lose any time," said Holmes.

Inojozas accompanied them to the hotel door and told one of the coachmen to take Holmes and Watson to the corner of Resende and Inválidos. The concierge of the Albion was perplexed and frightened. Despite the agreeable atmosphere of that rainy morning, a cold sweat was running down his temples. What no one could guess was that Sherlock Holmes, with all his deduction, had been right about something he had not seen. The detective had said that the writing on the envelope was feminine. Could it be that the flourishes of his writing had let escape the secret that, from earliest childhood, he had kept so well hidden? Inojozas prayed silently to Saint Onesimus, his patron saint, for his terrible secret never to be revealed. For

now, only Reginaldo, the young pantryman who had been living with him for five years, the love of his life, knew of the
*hôtelier*'s sexual preferences.

## 15

T he last of a fine rain was still falling over the city as the
tilbury carrying Sherlock Holmes and Dr. Watson made
its way down Novas dos Arcos Street. Holmes marveled at the
magnitude of the construction. The double arc formed by the
forty-two arches supporting the aqueduct's bridge did indeed
present a majestic appearance, recalling the ancient constructions of imperial Rome to those passing by. The aqueduct,
completed in 1750, had been built by governor Gomes Freire
de Andrade in colonial times. Dazzled, Holmes asked the
coachman what the work was. The driver, accustomed to
showing Rio de Janeiro to foreigners, explained.

"It's an aqueduct that brings water from Desterro Hill to
Santo Antônio Hill. Nevertheless, in spite of all the modern-
izations, the supply's still awful. The aqueduct can't meet the
demand."

"There's a shortage of water in Rio?" said the detective,
surprised.

"Every time you turn around. Good thing we've got the
fountains. It's all the fault of the people in power; they're a

bunch of thieves. Some time ago they even passed a special tax to solve the problem once and for all."

"And did it do so?" asked Holmes.

"Ha! Listen to this: to avoid the taxes going astray, they kept all the money for water service in a huge box with three locks."

"An excellent idea," commented Holmes.

"Apparently. Just think about it: one key was in the hands of the Senate, another with the governor, and the third with the Jesuit prior. Would you believe that, even so, the money disappeared? It's like I tell you, they're nothing but a band of pirates," he grumbled indignantly.

Soon afterward, the coachman pulled on the reins and stopped the car at the scene of the crime. Passersby had covered Carolina de Lourdes's remains with sheets of newspaper. Someone had lighted candles around the body, but the light rain had quickly extinguished the flames, save one candle that continued to flicker stubbornly close by the girl's head. The "bats," as the policemen were known, formed a cordon to prevent the approach of the morbidly curious. Suddenly, the distant sound of carriage bells and horses' hooves was heard. Everyone looked in the direction of the noise. Coming from Relação Street and turning onto Inválidos was the Black Maria. Completely sealed, the wagon stopped beside the murdered girl, and from the coachman's box leapt two "ghouls." With the practice and coldness acquired from years of experience, they opened the rear of the wagon, took out a thick canvas cloth, and wrapped Carolina in it. Holding the body by the feet and head, they threw the cadaver into the Black Maria. Before getting back into the vehicle, one of the "ghouls" retraced his steps and spat with deadly aim, extinguishing the last candle that shone tenaciously at the edge of the sidewalk.

In less than five minutes they had vanished down Resende Street.

Mello Pimenta and Saraiva, who had already examined the victim, came over to the two Englishmen. Pimenta made the introductions.

"Good morning, Mr. Holmes, Dr. Watson. This is our coroner, Professor Saraiva."

Holmes translated for his friend.

"A colleague of yours, Watson, the coroner, a fascinating speciality. Forensic medicine is the only area that knows everything. Unfortunately, it always comes too late."

Mello explained quickly what had happened the night before, and Holmes asked, "Is the girl's identity known?"

"Yes. Her name is Carolina de Lourdes Calixto. She was from the Wheel."

"I understand. Another prostitute," stated Sherlock Holmes, thinking that "wheel" was slang denoting the street of fallen women.

"No, Mr. Holmes, the Wheel is a charitable institution that takes in the abandoned newborn. The girl was the daughter of a funeral agent named Josué Calixto and worked at the place as a nanny, a volunteer."

"Who found the body?"

"Coincidentally, one of the Sisters of Charity of the Holy House of Mercy. The Wheel of Foundlings is very near there, on Evaristo da Veiga. I was already there asking a few questions."

"Did you find out if the lass by any chance had enemies?"

"Just the opposite; she was much loved. There's a great feeling of indignation and sadness on everyone's part."

"Did anyone happen to notice whether she was followed when she left?"

"No one knows. It was raining heavily, but even so, she insisted on going home."

"How irksome. We're right back where we started," lamented Holmes, pressing his fingers against his brow, which was beginning to throb.

Mello Pimenta apologized.

"I didn't want to bother you so early this morning, but, as it was a matter of the 'sirialquíler,' I thought it would interest you to closely accompany the investigation."

"You did exactly the right thing, inspector. I presume you've searched the area thoroughly for further clues."

"Of course, but the clues are the same: a flap of skin cut from the victim's side and this," said Mello Pimenta, showing Sherlock the violin string.

"At least it seems to me that there is no longer any doubt that the 'serial killer' and the violin thief are the same person. What worries me most is that there is still one string remaining on the instrument. Did you detect any footprints on the ground?"

"If there were any, the rain washed them away."

"Do you mind if I make a brief examination of the scene?" asked Sherlock Holmes, pensive.

"By all means, Mr. Holmes. You would be doing me a favor."

The detective took his magnifying glass from his pocket and went to the sidewalk darkened by bloodstains. When he kneeled to see the area more closely, he felt his head whirl and the lens almost fell from his grasp. He had to support himself against the wall in order not to fall down. Mello Pimenta, Saraiva, and Watson ran to his assistance.

"What was it, old man?" asked Watson, concerned.

"Nothing, just a bit of vertigo," answered Holmes, recovering. He then translated for Pimenta and Saraiva. "I felt dizzy. I think yesterday I overdid the herb a friend gave me. Indian cigarettes; I don't know if you're familiar with them. Excellent, to be sure, just that I smoked too much."

"Ah, I see that Mr. Sherlock Holmes has tried our *pango*," said the experienced Saraiva.

"*Pango?*" asked Sherlock.

"Exactly. That's what the Negroes call *cannabis*. There was even a lovely bed of it behind the kitchen at His Majesty's palace in São Cristóvão."

Mello Pimenta, worried about the detective's sudden indisposition, took him by the arm to lead him away.

"Mr. Holmes, I can assure you there's nothing here to interest us. It would be better for you and Dr. Watson to return to the hotel while I go to the morgue with Saraiva to watch the autopsy."

"Out of the question. Dr. Watson and I insist on watching the necropsy. After all, eight eyes are better than four."

"Not eight, seven."

"How so?"

"Saraiva is blind in one eye," explained Mello Pimenta, revealing an unknown detail of the professor's anatomy.

"A souvenir from the Paraguayan War," Dr. Saraiva explained stiffly.

"I didn't know you were a war hero," said Holmes, touched. "Was it a hand-to-hand fight?"

"No, an infection. I scratched my eye with a dirty hand," the coroner explained candidly.

"In any case, I'd like to go with you. This dizziness is transitory," the detective assured him.

Saraiva, who understood the aftereffects of drugs as few men did, gave him a prescription.

"If you'll permit me, Mr. Holmes, the best medicine for this morning-after sensation is a good dose of *cachaça*."

"*Cachaça?* What the devil is that?"

"It's a type of rum made from sugarcane. A very smooth drink, delicious. One dose will be enough for your complete recovery. In fact, I'll go with you. I'm feeling a bit poorly myself this morning."

"Saraiva, I don't know if it's a good idea to give Holmes *cachaça* at this hour," injected Mello Pimenta.

"Nonsense, my dear Mello Pimenta. I'm sure this venerable remedy will make our English friend into a new man," the doctor assured him.

The four men went to a bar at the corner of Riachuelo Street. Saraiva, with his enviable alcoholic experience, ordered two servings of the best rum in the house and downed the contents of his glass in a single swallow. When Dr. Watson saw the transparent liquid, which gave off a very strong smell of alcohol, he inquired what the drink was.

"Nothing to worry about, Watson, just a rum made from sugarcane. Professor Saraiva assures me that it has excellent curative properties," translated Holmes for his friend.

"I don't know, Holmes. From the smell, it looks to me like something quite strong. Maybe it'd be better not to drink it neat," he advised.

"What should I do then—add some water?"

"I think some fruit juice would be better. Orange or lime. They're excellent specifics. We even know of their undisputed properties in combating scurvy."

Sherlock turned to the owner of the bar.

"My friend here is suggesting that I put a bit of orange juice or lime in the drink. Have you by any chance got either of these fruits?"

"I have limes," answered the proprietor, intrigued, his eyes never leaving the hat and the Northeasterner's sandals that the doctor was still wearing.

Watson added, "Maybe it would also be good to throw in some ice and sugar, Holmes, to compensate for the heat produced by the alcohol."

Sherlock Holmes transmitted the doctor's demands. The bar owner went to the end of the counter and told his employee to bring the materials requested. Watson cut the lime into four parts and placed two pieces in the glass along with the sugar. He then proceeded to crush the slices with a spoon, saying, "To be on the safe side, it's best to put the segments in whole and squeeze."

When he finished the operation, he added a few pieces of ice and handed the curious potion to the detective.

"All right, Holmes, now I think you can drink it without danger."

From the end of the bar, the employee and the proprietor looked on in fascination. The young barman asked, "Boss, what language are they speakin'?"

"Hanged if I know. To me it's Latin or the devil's own tongue."

"And what's that concoction they're mixin' up?"

"I don't know, something invented by that *caipira* there," he said, pointing to Watson's cowboy hat and using the Brazilian term for a hick.

"Which hick, the big one?" asked the young man, indicating Sherlock Holmes, who was dressed all in white.

"No, the big *caipira* is just drinking it. The one who made it is the little hick, the *caipirinha*," replied the owner. Thus was baptized the exotic mixture that is Brazil's national drink.

~

The official morgue at Moura Square succeeded in being even more gloomy than the morgue of the Third Order. The floor was of dark cement and the *craquelé* of the white tiles on the walls, worn by time, did little to make its appearance more pleasant.

Ironically, besides the vapors of disinfectant, the place had also the smell of life. This was because its servants' quarters faced the rear of the huge kitchen of the Hospital of the Holy House, and the odors of food that emerged from the chimney, which stood over a hundred feet high and had been built with more than thirty-six thousand English fire bricks, hovered permanently over the Deposit of Cadavers. Many a visitor proved unable to withstand this odoriferous blend.

For almost an hour, Saraiva had been examining the open body of Carolina de Lourdes. Mello Pimenta and Dr. Watson watched the autopsy from a distance, but Sherlock Holmes, leaning over the stone table, followed attentively each of the coroner's movements. At certain moments his observations surprised even Saraiva.

"May I ask, Mr. Holmes, how you acquired such knowledge of this field?"

"As a detective, I find these matters fundamental, so I studied anatomy and paleontology with Sir Richard Owen, of the British Museum. Further, I have always been quite interested in the works of Leonardo da Vinci. Leonardo was fascinated by the *figura strumentale dell 'omo*, as you know."

"Of course," replied Saraiva, who didn't know.

Holmes gazed intently at the young woman's gaping entrails.

"Professor, there's one thing that I find strange. . . ."

"What, Mr. Holmes?"

"I don't know. I have the impression that the internal organs have been repositioned in the cavity. As if the murderer had first pulled them out and then put them back in place."

The pathologist leaned over the body.

"Man alive! You're right!" he said in amazement.

Saraiva stuck his hand into the exposed cavity, pushed aside the stomach, and extracted the liver. Holmes took out his magnifying glass and began to examine it in detail. He called Mello Pimenta.

"Look here, inspector, there are clear signs of fingernails and microscopic lines, invisible to the naked eye, in the tissue, as if the assassin had run it along a rough surface. From the deep impressions of the fingers and the fine grooves, it's possible he—" Sherlock hesitated. "No, it would be too horrible!"

"Say it, Mr. Holmes, please!"

"I know it's horrifying, but I'm almost certain the monster rubbed the liver on his own face."

Everyone but Watson, who didn't understand what was being said, was puzzled. The detective continued.

"At night, the beard has already started to grow, and these tiny striations must have been caused by the facial hairs. In a frenzy, the madman brushed the poor girl's viscera against his face," he concluded soberly.

Mello Pimenta agreed, horrified.

"There's no longer any doubt; we're truly dealing with a maniac. The director of the asylum made an appointment for us for next week. I'm going to send a message saying we will go see him this very afternoon."

Holmes was still examining the finger marks left on the flesh.

"A pity that Jean Vucetich's studies are still inconclusive."

"Pardoning my immense ignorance, Mr. Holmes, could you tell me who that is?" asked Mello Pimenta.

"An Argentine policeman from Buenos Aires who is developing a system of identification by means of the fingers. He calls the process 'comparative dactyloscopy.' According to Vucetich and some European anthropologists, there are no two human beings with the same patterns of lines on the skin of their extremities. If you examine your fingers using a glass, you'll see the traces of these lines. Sadly, for the present, none of that has any utility for us," informed Holmes, returning the girl's liver to Professor Saraiva.

At that exact moment, the conversation was cut short by a howl of pain coming from the entrance.

"Anathema! Anathema!"

At the door stood the tormented figure of Josué Calixto, the funeral agent and father of the unfortunate girl. Tall, dressed entirely in black, and wearing a top hat, Calixto was the very caricature of his profession. Deep rings creased eyes transformed into twin pools of blood from uncontrollable sobbing. Stepping forward, he asked in desperation, "My daughter, where is my daughter?"

Saraiva, who was holding the girl's liver, stealthily handed it to Holmes, while pointing to the autopsy table. As he was between Calixto and the table, the detective concealed the organ behind his back and moved out of his path. The funeral agent threw himself frantically onto his daughter's cadaver.

"I was the one who killed her, it's all my fault! Oh God, what a cruel punishment! My darling daughter, I'll never see you alive again!" screamed Josué Calixto, his pain making him state the obvious.

Unseen by the funeral agent, Holmes tossed the liver accurately to Mello Pimenta and went to the disconsolate father.

"May I ask why you feel responsible for this horrible crime?"

Josué recounted his daughter's long *via crucis* and how his intransigence had led the girl to the Wheel of Foundlings.

"If I had been more understanding, none of this would have happened. Oh God! Why didn't You take me instead of Carolina?" lamented the poor man, consumed by pain. Pimenta approached the spot where Calixto stood. En route, he left the liver again in Saraiva's hands.

"Mr. Calixto, I'm Inspector Mello Pimenta. I know this is a very difficult moment, but even so, I have to ask you a few questions."

"Please, inspector. Anything that can help discover this horrible murderer," replied the funeral agent between sobs.

"Do you know if your daughter had made any new friendships?"

"No, the poor thing was totally dedicated to the orphans."

"Did you observe anyone, recently, lurking near your house?"

"Also no. We live in a very quiet neighborhood. Any unusual movement would have drawn my attention."

"If you should remember anything that might be of interest to me, I'm at the third station house," advised Pimenta.

While the inspector was asking these questions, Holmes, standing apart, was closely analyzing the torn clothing of Carolina de Lourdes, piled in a corner. He saw, lost in the folds of the skirt, a long horsehair that had escaped notice in earlier examinations. Without anyone seeing, he rolled it in his fingers and put it in his pocket, while Josué Calixto, drying his tears, was saying, "Now, if I may, I'd like to have a few moments alone with my daughter. Who is the pathologist in charge?"

Saraiva, in a maneuver worthy of an acrobat, quickly tossed the liver to Dr. Watson and stepped toward Calixto.

"It's I, Saraiva, at your service."

"I know your name very well, professor. As we are almost in the same field, I would like to ask a huge favor of you."

"Of course, Mr. Calixto."

"I see that the monster savagely dilacerated my daughter. If you have finished your examination, I would like to use my every talent to restore to the unfortunate girl the appearance she had in life. I don't want her to be seen like this, nor would I like a wake with a sealed casket."

"Of course; it's the least we can do," answered Saraiva, shaking the hand of the girl's father. "My sympathies."

One by one, Holmes, Pimenta, and the coroner silently took their leave of the poor man. When his turn arrived, Watson, who had hidden the extirpated organ under his coat, took the liver from his pocket, cleaned it with his handkerchief, and handed it to Josué Calixto, stating compassionately in his best Shakespearean English: "I believe this belongs to you."

He put away the handkerchief and left the room of the dead with the gravity that the moment demanded.

## 16

The Dom Pedro II Asylum for the care of the demented, in the Praia Vermelha district, was an imposing structure in French neoclassical style. It occupied an area of 115,588 square feet, with the portico revetted with masonry and a stairway with ten steps leading to the entrance. Four stone columns with Doric capitals supported a marble balustrade. Between them could be seen three doors, and on the second floor were four more Ionic columns capped by a pediment bearing the imperial arms carved in marble. Three windows appeared in the middle of the columns, repeating the symmetry of the floor below. Along the sides of the building were twenty parapet windows on the first floor and twenty more on the second. All the windows were equipped with heavy iron bars. An attic adorned with statues and marble vases concealed the roof of the building. The plants and flowers in the vases helped mitigate the prisonlike appearance suggested by the bars.

Standing at the stairway to the asylum, Inspector Mello Pimenta waited for Sherlock Holmes. The sun had reappeared after two days of rain, lending cheer to the radiant morning. For the moment, there was little movement in the streets. The detective was late. A rented tilbury stopped near the entrance, but it was an old sailor who descended from its interior. He was wearing a threadbare blue jacket over a jersey with black and white horizontal stripes. His baggy trousers, slightly too short, held up by a belt with a square metal buckle, revealed his stockings, also striped, and his heavy wooden shoes. He had a black patch over his right eye and a hook in place of his left hand.

Limping, the strange figure approached Pimenta and suddenly whispered in the inspector's ear, with a strong Portuguese accent.

"Where is the treasure map?"

"Mr. Holmes?! But what kind of outfit is that?" asked Mello Pimenta, startled.

"Merely a disguise, my friend. I thought it would be better not to attract too much attention at this stage of the investigation," Holmes explained.

"Well, we can go in. The director of the asylum is waiting for us," said Pimenta, still not quite believing Sherlock's costume.

The hook and eye patch gave the Englishman a frightening mien. In addition, Holmes had on a false nose and a white wig under his mariner's cap. The inspector didn't know how he would explain to the doctor responsible for the hospital the presence at his side of an old Portuguese tar. They walked down a long corridor and came to the clinician's administrative area. An assistant led them to the director's office.

Dr. Hélio Pedregal Noronha was the chief alienist of the Dom Pedro II Asylum. Somberly dressed, he was not wearing the characteristic white smock. He cultivated a well-trimmed goatee and balanced a pince-nez on his nose. The walls of the room were covered with bookcases filled with medical textbooks. On his worktable was a small bronze statue of a skull with an owl perched on it. Pedregal Noronha could not take his eyes off the curious figure of Sherlock Holmes. He motioned for Mello Pimenta and the detective to take a seat in front of him.

"Frankly, inspector, I don't think I truly understand the rea-

son for your visit. I assumed it had to do with your investigations, but now I see it has to do with an internment," said the
alienist, pointing to Sherlock Holmes.

Holmes answered before Pimenta was obliged to explain.

"The doctor is mistaken. I am neither demented nor insane.
Allow me to introduce myself: Sherlock Holmes, at your service. These clothes are merely one of the thousand disguises I
use when I wish to escape notice."

"I understand," answered Noronha, who in reality didn't
understand a thing.

Mello Pimenta spoke up.

"I brought Mr. Holmes with me; he has been of inestimable
help."

"And what can I do for you?" asked the doctor, conspicu-
ously consulting the watch in his vest pocket.

"First, I would like to make it clear that whatever we say
here is strictly confidential," stated Pimenta.

"You may rest easy, inspector. Confidentiality is part of my
profession."

Mello Pimenta leaned back in the chair and told the doctor
everything he knew about the case. When he finished, Holmes
added, "The latest murder has led us to the certainty that there
is a lunatic on the loose who is carrying out these crimes."

"I would prefer that you use the term *aberrant* in speaking
of the afflicted. Ever since Philippe Pinel defended a more
humane treatment of the mentally ill, in his *Traité médico-
philosophique sur l'alienation mentale*, we have avoided certain
pejorative expressions," commented Pedregal Noronha in a
superior tone, despite never having read the book.

Mello Pimenta was indignant.

"I don't see what there can be that is *humane* in such a

monster. He tore out the poor girl's liver and rubbed his face in it."

"I can assure you that in all the years I have dedicated myself to the health of the soul I have witnessed worse things. Even so, I have never stopped considering my patients human, in their own way," retorted the alienist.

"What do you mean by worse things?" inquired Sherlock.

"Coprophagy, for example—sick people who eat their own feces. I once had here a woman with attacks of hysteria who attempted to commit suicide by ingesting great quantities of her own excrement."

"Is it possible for an individual to have completely normal behavior and at the same time practice these aberrations?" inquired Mello Pimenta.

"Naturally; it's even part of the pathology. One can have social contact with a deranged person for years without witnessing one of his attacks. The human brain is still an unknown and a challenge," asseverated Pedregal Noronha.

"Have you ever examined anyone with a disorder similar to that of our assassin?" continued Mello Pimenta.

"Right now we have here a man who suffers from a strange form of cerebral pathology. He possesses great intelligence and culture, but when he goes into a crisis he tears out and devours pieces of the flesh of whoever is within his reach. Ironically, before insanity overcame him, he was one of our most prominent alienists."

"What is the madman's name?" asked Sherlock Holmes.

"Dr. Aderbal Câmara. He suffers from acute cannibalism."

"May we speak with him?"

"I can't see how it will help you, but if you insist, I'll ask my assistant to accompany you. He's kept in the ward for the vio-

lent. Just yesterday he attacked one of the orderlies." Pedregal
Noronha stood up and went to the door. "Now, if you'll excuse me, it's time for my visitation rounds with our guests."

Antônio Belmonte, the medical intern who led Mello Pimenta and Sherlock Holmes through the damp galleries of the
asylum, had a curious cacoëthes. Every three steps, he would
stop and shine his boots on the back of his trousers leg. Finally, after traversing what seemed to the visitors a tortuous
labyrinth, they stopped before a massive wooden door that led
to a poorly lighted corridor. Belmonte opened it with one of
the keys on the ring he took from his pocket.

"He's in the last cell on the left. It's better if you go by
yourselves from here on. The loonies get real stirred up when
they see me."

"I thought that word was forbidden in this institution," said
Holmes.

"Dr. Noronha doesn't like us to use it, but to me loony is
loony. Be careful not to get too close to the cells. All of them
here are *dangerous* loonies."

"How do we call you when we're done?" asked Mello Pimenta uneasily.

"Call me Belmonte, which is what they all call me," replied
the intern, laughing aloud at his own joke. "There's a bell
hanging on the inside wall. Ring it and I'll come to get you."
He closed the bars and left, compulsively cleaning his shoes.

Sherlock Holmes and Mello Pimenta penetrated the gloomy
corridor. On one side was the row of cells; on the other, a
stone wall with a few gas jets that provided the precarious
light. There were no windows or other openings. Incoherent
words, mixed with screams, moans, and whispers, came from
the wretched madmen confined there. Holmes clearly heard a

hoarse masculine voice, dripping with lust, shout, "Sailor! Over this way, saaaailor!"

Even an inattentive observer would think immediately of zoos at coming upon the men caged in that prison. Heavy iron bars that ran from ceiling to floor separated the prisoner from the visitors. Inside, only a cot, a basin, a bowl, and a crude chair, where Dr. Aderbal Câmara sat. His face was covered by the infamous mask of Flanders.

Created by an obscure eighteenth-century Portuguese blacksmith at the order of certain overseers, the abominable object prevented Negro slaves with *banzô*, the deep and some-times fatal longing for Mother Africa, from eating dirt until they died. It was the sole, desperate form of suicide at the slaves' disposal. They preferred this monstrous death to cap-tivity. Those who worked in the mining of diamonds also wore the vile invention, which prevented their swallowing the stones and smuggling them outside the mining area. Even the most indifferent chroniclers felt revulsion at the description of the despicable instrument. Made of metal, the mask totally covered the face and was fastened to the lower part of the neck by two extensions locked shut. Small openings at the eyes and nose allowed the wearer to see and breathe but not to bring anything to his mouth. In some instances, it was also used in cases of drunkenness, for criminals, as punishment, and for the violently insane.

The ignominious apparatus was buckled to the man's head. His voice emerged muffled by the iron of the mask.

"Ah! Sherlock Holmes and Inspector Mello Pimenta! To what do I owe the honor?"

Both men were surprised at Dr. Aderbal Câmara's words.
"You know us, then?"

188 ~ JÔ SOARES

"Of course. I've been expecting you for some time. I've been following the investigations, but unfortunately they no longer let me read the papers. I ate the thumb of the orderly who brought me the *Journal of Commerce*. Delicious, I must say. No pun intended, but it was a real thumbs-up!"

"And why did you think we would come to see you?" asked Mello Pimenta.

"Pshaw, inspector. Only an imbecile would fail to perceive that the person you're looking for has something to do with me. An interesting personality. It wouldn't surprise me in the least if he began devouring his victims."

Holmes and Pimenta exchanged silent glances.

"From what I see, our bloody friend has run ahead of my prediction," smiled Dr. Aderbal.

After a hesitation, Mello Pimenta finally confided.

"No, but we have reason to believe that he rubbed the liver of one of his victims on his own face."

"What a waste! You can see right away that he's a beginner. He doesn't know what he's missing," lamented the madman.

"Do you really believe that?" asked Mello Pimenta, horrified.

"They say that tigers in India go crazy after they taste human flesh. The same thing happens with us. There is no victual more delicious," Dr. Aderbal assured them.

"Let's proceed to what matters," interrupted Holmes, for whom the discussion of anthropophagic gastronomy held not the slightest interest. "What we would like to know is if you, as doctor and . . . patient, knowing, shall we say, both sides of the coin, could tell us anything that might help us find the 'serial killer.'"

"'Serial killer' . . . I read the expression in the papers and found it quite original. . . . Nevertheless, Mr. Holmes, I don't see why I should help you. What have I got to gain?"

"Nothing, except the satisfaction of knowing you're aiding in the elimination of a terrible menace to society."

"I hate society, Mr. Holmes. It was society that locked me up in this dungeon, that condemns me to wear this dreadful iron mask whenever an irresistible urge compels me to taste the flesh of my fellow man. I can't even gnaw my fingernails, woe is me. A tamed sphinx: even if you don't solve my riddle, I will not devour you."

Mello Pimenta almost felt sorry for the wretched incarcerated madman.

"Well, Dr. Aderbal, it seems we have nothing further to do here. Pardon us for taking up your time."

"Good-bye, doctor," said Holmes, courageously extending his hand through the bars.

Aderbal Câmara, moved and disconcerted by the detective's gesture, said to his visitors, "So your visit won't have been a waste, I'll tell you a little riddle":

> Amid the islands' splendor,
> A word quite lovely ought
> The purpose well to render,
> Paulo Barbosa thought.
>
> Deep down it matters not
> If the name comes from the Greek,
> The monarch cares a lot
> For this tongue that none now speak.

Dr. Câmara recited the words in an enigmatic monotone through the vents in the mask.

Mello Pimenta rapidly jotted down the mysterious poem, while Holmes expressed his gratitude.

"I'm very indebted to you, doctor. I hope to be able to fathom what lies behind these verses."

"Did you like them? As you see, if there's a bit of the doctor, the poet, and the madman in each of us, in me there's a lot," stated Dr. Aderbal Câmara, alienist, bard, and maniac.

On his way out, Sherlock Holmes turned and asked, "Just one thing more, Dr. Aderbal."

"Certainly."

"How did you discover it was I, despite my disguise?"

"Look, my dear Mr. Holmes, I'm crazy, but I'm not an idiot," explained Aderbal the cannibal, loosing a terrifying howl of laughter.

# 17

Inspector Mello Pimenta had invited Sherlock Holmes to lunch at his house on Pinheiro Street. Dona Paciência, caught by surprise, was doing her best struggling in the kitchen with the *Brazilian Cookbook*, looking for a recipe.

"Why didn't you let me know you were bringing Mr. Holmes? I barely have time to prepare something decent," she complained from the kitchen as she hurriedly leafed through the book.

"Don't worry about me, Dona Paciência. I'm a table guest of very frugal habits," said Sherlock Holmes politely, to calm her.

Seated around the table, the two men attempted to decipher Dr. Aderbal's mysterious verses. Mello Pimenta opened his *pour-mémoire* and slowly read aloud:

> Amid the islands' splendor,
> A word quite lovely ought
> The purpose well to render,
> Paulo Barbosa thought.

> Deep down it matters not
> If the name comes from the Greek,
> The monarch cares a lot
> For this tongue that none now speak.

"Leaving aside the horrid literary quality, I see no meaning at all in the poem," confessed Sherlock.

"'The monarch cares a lot for this tongue that none now speak.' Everyone knows that Dom Pedro speaks Greek, Latin, and Provençal," Pimenta informed the detective.

"Provençal? He speaks Provençal?" the Englishman said, startled.

"Yes."

"With whom?"

"Nobody knows."

"My dear Pimenta, it will be difficult for me to help you with this undertaking. It's obvious that there is a reference to the emperor. However, I haven't the slightest idea who this Paulo Barbosa might be," said Holmes, lighting his pipe.

"Nor I, Mr. Holmes. Who can Paulo Barbosa be?"

"You don't remember, Hildebrando?" said Paciência, coming to set the table and calling the inspector by his Christian name.

"Remember what?"

"Paulo Barbosa was Dom Pedro's majordomo," answered Paciência, returning to the kitchen.

"When was that?" asked Pimenta.

Dona Paciência shouted from the kitchen, as she went on preparing the lunch.

"How disgraceful, Hildebrando. Mr. Holmes will think you're a very ill-informed politician. Paulo Barbosa was the one who gave the name Petrópolis to the emperor's city."

"Now I remember," lied Mello Pimenta.

"In fact, it's a famous case of historical flattery that we studied in school. When they were looking for a name for the place, he said, 'I remembered Petersburg, the city of Peter. I resorted to Greek and found the city with that name in the archipelago. And because it was Emperor Dom Pedro, I thought the name would go well,'" said Dona Paciência.

Sherlock Holmes stated excitedly, "I think your wife has solved the puzzle: 'Amid the islands' splendor' refers to the archipelago. 'A word quite lovely' is the name that Paulo Barbosa gave to the emperor's city, inspired by the Greek: *Petro* from Pedro and *pólis* from city."

"The cannibal is telling us that the criminal is from Petrópolis," opined Mello Pimenta.

Dona Paciência interrupted once again, speaking from beside the stove.

"I think you're mistaken, dear. To me, he seems to be hinting that the murderer belongs to the court, or frequents it."

The inspector grew irritated.

"Could Madame Know-it-all perhaps tell me why Dr. Aderbal didn't refer directly to the imperial palace?"

"For several reasons. First, because it would be a very direct piece of information and he insists on presenting the clue as a riddle; second, because, by speaking just of the palace, the suspects would be restricted to the members of the court; and finally, because this weekend José White is going to organize a benefit recital in honor of Princess Isabel at the Crystal Palace, in Petrópolis. The emperor has also invited Sarah Bernhardt, and she has postponed her performances in order to attend. She was enchanted when they told her that Petrópolis was a Brazilian miniature of the cities of Switzerland," said Dona Paciência effusively.

"And how do you know all this?"

"I read it in Múcio Prado's 'Mundanities,' in the *Journal of Commerce*," confided Dona Paciência, entering the room with the lunch tray.

Sherlock Holmes marveled at the keenness of her reasoning. "Madame, I must compliment you on your extraordinary intelligence and powers of deduction."

"Thank you, Mr. Holmes. I hope that my culinary talents are also to your liking."

"What did you make us for lunch?" asked Mello Pimenta, still piqued.

"Pig's liver cooked *à la nature*," his wife informed them proudly, lifting the lid of the serving dish to display the shiny piece of almost raw meat, so similar in odor and appearance to the entrails of the murdered girl.

Blanching, Sherlock Holmes and Mello Pimenta dashed headlong for the bathroom, leaving Dona Paciência to weep silently with the tray in her hand.

~

In 1821, Emperor Dom Pedro I purchased the Córrego Seco plantation, atop Estrela Hill, eight hundred meters above the sea, with the intention of building his summer residence there.

Destiny and the management of business affairs dictated the mortgaging of the lands, and the project was postponed until 1843, when the then-majordomo of the imperial household, Paulo Barbosa—it was the regency of Dom Pedro II—succeeded in paying off the mortgage. Barbosa leased the plantation to the German engineer Júlio Koeler but reserved a good part of the property for the construction of the palace. Thus the son realized his father's dream.

The journey to Petrópolis was a mere four hours. Leaving from the Prainha port in Rio de Janeiro and taking a boat to Mauá, one then proceeded by train to the foot of the mountains. A few years earlier, travelers were obliged to traverse the last eight miles from the foothills in carriages or coaches; but the final stage of the Príncipe Grão-Pará railway had recently been inaugurated, carrying passengers all the way to the city.

Sherlock Holmes and Mello Pimenta were drinking warmed-over coffee at Galego's Bar, at the foot of the mountains, a compulsory stop for the train. Dr. Watson, who was accompanying them, had declined the invitation to drink the thin infusion and was standing a short distance away, amidst the vegetation and rocks, leaning on a thick mountaineer's staff and observing the countryside. Holmes had informed the emperor that he would attend the concert, pursuing a lead about the assassin. He had cautiously omitted mention of the origin of the clue. The detective had also called Anna Candelária, who, unlike Sarah Bernhardt, had to take part in weekend performances. He thought again of the beautiful woman who had come so unexpectedly into his life. Since the latest murder, he had not been able to see her for very long; he had been with Anna only briefly, in chance meetings at the theater door. Either she had to rehearse a new scene in the revue or he was with Mello Pimenta in pursuit of the investigation. He missed the young mulatto woman. Never before had he experienced that sensation of longing, at once sweet and painful, that the Brazilians call *saudades*.

A howl of pain interrupted his reverie. Holmes and Pimenta looked in the direction of the shout and saw Watson, who was bellowing in terror, pointing to the ground.

"A snake! A snake bit me!"

Advancing, Sherlock saw a coral snake slithering through the grass toward an opening in the rocks. He yanked the staff from Watson's hand and, in a fast and agile motion, delivered a mortal blow to the serpent's head. Watson sat down on a rock, moaning and holding his leg while Mello Pimenta came running to his side.

"My God! That's all we needed! We must find help immediately!"

"I think it's too late for that, inspector. The doctor was bitten by a coral snake," said Sherlock, consulting his watch. He knelt and picked up the snake, ringed with red, black, and yellow. He took the magnifying glass from his pocket and examined it carefully. "I don't know how this happened. Corals are docile snakes; it's very rare to be bitten by one." He turned to Watson. "By Zeus, man! What did you do for this animal to attack you?"

"I don't know. I think I must have unwittingly stepped on its tail," lamented the doctor.

Holmes ran the glass over the reptile's body, counting the colored rings.

"You're a lucky man, Watson. This coral isn't poisonous." He then translated for Mello Pimenta in the finest Lisbon Portuguese: "This ophidian possesses no venom."

Relieved, Pimenta commented, "I wasn't aware you knew about snakes, Mr. Holmes."

"I learnt all about them when I dedicated myself to exotic poisons in Macao, with the Portuguese master Professor Nicolau Travessa. Even the poisonous coral, the *Micrurus corallus,* seldom attacks man. Which is fortunate, as its venom is extremely lethal."

"I saw you examine the snake in detail, even counting the number of rings on its skin. Was that how you knew it wasn't a poisonous coral?"

Sherlock Holmes explained.

"No, inspector, I simply applied the method perfected by Travessa, in Goa, when a Hindoo was bitten by a serpent. I waited the exact time that coral poison needs to take effect. As Watson was still alive after that time, I deduced that the snake wasn't poisonous."

Mello Pimenta looked at the doctor, who was massaging the area of the bite.

"Do you plan to tell him about the system you used?"

"I see no reason to bother him with minor details," declared the detective, tossing the dead snake into the distance and wiping his hands on a kerchief.

"I must say I envy your ability to deal with these animals. I confess a terror of snakes, spiders, and lizards," revealed Mello Pimenta.

Holmes recalled an incident that had occurred many years before, on a hunt in India.

"Imagine, inspector, I was hunting tigers in the middle of the jungle, in the Punjab region, with a friend named Wilfred Marmeduke, when he was bitten by a *naja* in a very delicate spot—how can I put it—right on the end of his penis."

"Why precisely there?!" asked the horrified Mello Pimenta.

"Marmeduke had decided to yield to an urgent physiological necessity, and by chance the stream fell on the head of the sleeping serpent."

"Terrible!"

"I saw it would be to no avail to transport him, as Wilfred was writhing in frightful pain. I mounted my horse and sped to the nearest village, intending to seek out the only doctor there, but the man was in the middle of surgery. So I asked him how I should proceed."

"What did the doctor say?" asked Mello Pimenta anxiously.

"He said there was only one way to avoid the death of my dear friend, for whom I nurtured the greatest affection. He ordered me to make an incision with a knife, at the location of the bite, and, with my mouth, suck out all the venom."

"Fantastic, Mr. Holmes. And that's how you saved his life?"

"No, inspector. He died," replied Sherlock Holmes, his gaze fixed on the horizon.

Despite its tragic outcome, the incident had become an anonymous anecdote perpetuated in the clubs of London.

The locomotive whistled, alerting the passengers that it was time for the train to continue on its journey. The three men headed for the first-class car and embarked for Petrópolis.

～

The recital organized by the violinist José White had turned into the social event of the year. The proceeds were destined to Princess Isabel's charitable works in favor of emancipation of the slaves, and the setting could not have been more appropriate. Built to serve as a greenhouse, the pavilion of the Crystal Palace had been an initiative of her husband, the Count

D'Eu, president of the Petrópolis Agricultural and Horticul-
tural Association. The majestic iron-and-glass construction,
made to order in France in the workshops of Saint-Saveur-les-
Arras, had a dazzling appearance, especially at night, when the
illumination emphasized its lightness and transparency. The
musicians' platform and chairs for the audience had been
placed among the plants, and immense candleholders completed the *décor*. The room was packed. In addition to the royal
family and the court, obviously, the cream of Rio de Janeiro
society had lent its prestige to the event. Sarah Bernhardt and
her son, Maurice, took their places beside several intellectuals
and bohemians who had also come up the mountain. The
baroness of Avaré, Maria Luísa Catarina de Albuquerque,
who kept her distance from Dom Pedro whenever he was accompanied by the empress and their children, was sitting with
the marquis of Salles. On the platform, a Pleyel grand pianoforte dominated the space. Sherlock Holmes, Mello Pimenta, and Dr. Watson remained standing at the rear of the
pavilion. They scrutinized the room with care.

"So, Mr. Sherlock, have you any idea of who our man is?"
asked Pimenta.

"Not yet, inspector. But something tells me he's nearby.
Perhaps he will commit his next crime right here."

"In the midst of this crowd?"

"After the recital."

"I don't know, Mr. Holmes. I'm beginning to think this trip
was a waste of time."

"At least we'll have the advantage of hearing the music,"
the detective said, enthusiastically.

In an instant, all conversation ceased in the Crystal Palace.
The Cuban José White and the Portuguese Artur Napoleão

came onstage to heated applause. Napoleão sat at the pianoforte, as White brought the violin to his shoulder and started the concert. The program began with sonatas by Vivaldi, Bach, Handel, and Mozart. The exquisite technique and talent of the two musicians quickly enthralled the listeners. Ladies closed their fans so that the rustling wouldn't debase the purity of the music.

After the sonatas, joined by Julius Weber on the viola and Manuel Zeferino on the violoncello, they played Beethoven's Quartet in E Flat, opus 16. Sarah Bernhardt was moved. She had never expected to find in the tropics execution on that level. The extraordinary quality of the interpretation was matched only by the vibrant reception accorded it by the spectators.

José White called the violinist Adelelmo do Nascimento, for whom he nurtured great admiration, to join the group and together they performed Brahms's Quartet in F Major, opus 34. The audience was delirious with emotion. When they finished, the Cuban wiped his brow with a delicate linen handkerchief, raised his hands to ask for silence, and said in a mixture of Spanish and Portuguese: "Ladies and gentlemen. I know that tonight we have with us *el señor* Sherlock Holmes, who as everyone knows is a phenomenal English detective. But what few know is his ability as a *violinista*. I would like to ask *el señor* Holmes to give us the honor and the pleasure of playing with us."

Dom Pedro II was the first to rise to his feet applauding, followed by Sarah Bernhardt, who exclaimed, "*Bravo!* Monsieur Holmes! Monsieur Holmes!"

The emperor echoed her call from the other side.

"Sherlock Holmes! Sherlock Holmes!"

Immediately copying the monarch, the entire audience at the Crystal Palace shouted his name.

"Sherlock Holmes! Sherlock Holmes!"

Feigning modesty, the detective made a gesture as if to refuse, but Pimenta and Watson pushed him toward the platform. The detective climbed the improvised proscenium, mildly embarrassed, saluting the musicians one by one. Finally, he approached José White, who handed him his instrument.

"Thank you, Mr. White; it's not always that we have the opportunity to play a true Stradivarius," he said, winking surreptitiously at his fellow violinist.

Uncomfortably, the Cuban pretended not to understand the allusion to the exchange of violins. Holmes turned to Artur Napoleão.

"If you please, maestro, something lively that you know by heart, as we don't have the scores here: Schumann's Quintet, opus 44."

He slowly tucked the violin under his chin, raised the bow in a theatrical gesture, and unwaveringly attacked the nostalgic melody.

In reality, Sherlock Holmes could play with any orchestra in the world. He possessed talent, technique, and aplomb. Further, his figure reminded one of those pallid romantic violinists who made young damsels sigh. The audience was delighted with the unexpected attraction, not knowing that it would soon be receiving yet another surprise: as soon as Holmes began the third movement, in which the players have the opportunity to display their virtuosity at its fullest, the marquis of Salles leapt onto the stage, grabbed the instrument from Adelelmo, the second violinist, and, standing there, initiated an unexpected duel with the detective. Sherlock Holmes rose and immediately joined the contest. The pair moved about the platform, face to face, executing the melody with frantic rhythm. At the pianoforte, Artur Napoleão could barely keep up with the frenzied pace of the violins. Flying across the strings, the bows seemed more like foils in the hands of consummate fencers. As soon as Holmes completed the notes of a phrase, De Salles would respond. They continued in this frenetic fashion until the end of the movement. Then, together, the pair attacked and finished off the fourth and final section of the work.

Faced with that spectacular exhibition, the select audience at the Crystal Palace lost its composure. Despite the presence of Dom Pedro, Empress Teresa Cristina, and Princesses Leopoldina and Isabel, the listeners rose to their feet and exploded in applause and shouts: "*Bravo! Bravo! Viva* Holmes! *Viva* De Salles!"

On the stage, José White and Artur Napoleão congratulated the duelists on their sensational performance. De Salles and Holmes descended from the stage, each praising the other.

"Congratulations, my friend."

"I didn't know you played the violin, marquis, and in such brilliant fashion. It was difficult to keep up with you."

Sarah Bernhardt made her way through the throng of people elbowing each other in their effort to greet the players.

"*Mémorable!* I want to be the first to kiss the heroes. Impossible to say which one was better. If they were sabres, you would both be dead!"

Mello Pimenta came up to the detective.

"Congratulations, Mr. Holmes. Just hearing you made the trip worthwhile. A pity I can't say the same for our investigation."

"I don't know, inspector. I had the sensation that the killer was very close to us."

"Do you suspect someone?"

"An intuition, just a— I don't know how to say it in Portuguese. In English we say 'hunch': just a hunch."

"Curious, I had a hunch also, but in our profession it's evidence that counts. Unfortunately, except for the mystery of the flaps of skin and the strings, we have no other clues."

"We have one," said Sherlock, taking from his pocket the horsehair he had removed from the folds of Carolina de Lourdes's skirt, at the morgue.

"What is that?"

"A hair from an English thoroughbred horse."

"And what does it mean?" Mello Pimenta asked.

"It means that soon we shall be going to the races," answered Holmes enigmatically.

The marquis of Salles approached, surrounded by the gang and Maria Luísa, the beautiful baroness of Avaré, who stepped forward.

"After a performance like tonight's, I lament a little less the theft of my Stradivarius. I would never be able to play it like that."

Solera de Lara, always the *literato*, exclaimed, "Extraordinary! A fusion of Paganini and D'Artagnan!" cried the bookseller.

Chiquinha Gonzaga, who already considered the detective part of the group, added enthusiastically, "Mr. Holmes, when you wish to participate in one of our revues, don't be shy. The number you performed tonight with the marquis is worthy of any theater."

Albertinho Fazelli took from a leather pouch several small

metal glasses and two bottles of Dom Pérignon '74, the greatest vintage of the century.

"I always come prepared," he explained, opening the champagne.

The group began an animated celebration of the success of the event, in a party that would last until early morning in the bar of the Hotel MacDowal. Chiquinha Gonzaga sat at the piano and heartened everyone with her repertory of polkas, from "The Attractive Woman" to "Radiant."

Amid the euphoria, Sherlock Holmes regretted only that Anna Candelária was not present to witness his thunderous success, that unforgettable night at the Crystal Palace.

# 18

*Sitting cross-legged on the waxed floor of his room, he fortifies himself by lacerating his back with a lash of seven thick leather strips, made from the belts with which his father used to punish him when he was a boy. Despite the welts already marking his flesh, he feels no pain. It even produces a sensation of pleasure to flog his body in this manner. The self-flagellation is necessary, for the moment of the final confrontation is coming. Despite the flaps of skin and the strings, he has not been discovered and now he is certain that nothing will stand in the way of the outcome so anxiously awaited. He was at her side again, at the Crystal Palace.*

*The last woman. The last and the first. The one who unchained in him the primordial need to extinguish the lust that rages inside his body. He smiles as he thinks of her: so powerful and so fragile, so distant and so close. She cloaked herself in the fame of infamy. Several times he had lightly brushed his hands against the woman's indecorous dress, without anyone present noticing that at each touch his entire being quivered with disgust. He thinks about Sodom and Gomorrah. He thinks about angels. Not the guardians of the soul and the bearers of good tidings, but those the Lord sends to earth to carry out His most terrible designs. The messengers of plague, God's executioners. He also desires to suck out her soul through her mouth, like an avenging angel. A pity not to have been able to annihilate her in the middle of the Crystal Palace, in the midst of the rabble pressing around her. Petrópolis would be the perfect mausoleum for the great whore. Petrópolis, a city putrefied by the court. Petrópolis, Putrípolis, Putrópolis. A tomb worthy of the greatest of all whores. He feels his knees sliding lightly. He lowers his eyes and sees that the blood provoked by the incessant lashing of the whip against his back has formed a viscous pool, causing him to slip on the warm planks of the floorboards.*

~

The São Cristóvão Derby Club had been inaugurated almost a year earlier, but the Prado Fluminense, at the Jockey Club in São Francisco Xavier, was still the preferred choice of bettors. Even the most hardened losers could not fail to appreciate the beauty of the place. Going to the races had become a *belle promenade*.

The stables housed thoroughbreds from England, France, the Argentine, and São Paulo competing in almost sixty races per year and creating more than five hundred betting pools, considerable activity even for a city of four hundred thousand inhabitants like Rio de Janeiro.

It was the day of the Grand Prize, and the emperor would be there. For the first time, the Jockey Club Grand Prize was offering five thousand *réis* to the winner and a thousand *réis* to the second-place finisher. The morning newspapers announced the substantial sum on their first pages:

A PILE OF MONEY!

1st—5000 *réis*

2nd—1000 *réis*

In the advertisements, the usual notices:

- PERSONS NOT WEARING SHOES WILL NOT BE ADMITTED
- ANY DOG FOUND ON THE PREMISES WILL BE KILLED
- THE RACES WILL END AT SIX O'CLOCK WITH THE ANGELUS-BELLS

Rio society paraded through the *pelouse* at the beginning of that sunny afternoon in early July. The gentlemen, in their Prince Albert coats and top hats, binoculars dangling from their shoulders, were attentively studying the recently launched magazine *The Jockey,* in search of inspiration. The ladies, young and older, their vast skirts held off the ground by panniers, their large straw hats covered with flowers or feathers and ribbons, strutted along the grass. They walked in small groups, before and after each race, more preoccupied with their appearance than with the animals' pedigrees. Many a love affair, licit and illicit, began there, as an innocent colloquy.

The owners of the stud farms, enormous cigars in their mouths, strolled through the paddock, giving instructions to the uniformed jockeys, always in a low, conspiratorial voice to keep valuable tips from falling on the ears of adventurous speculators. In keeping with European practices, the Jockey Club followed the regulations of English racecourses: "a best of heats." Machado de Assis was wont to say that Brazilian races were the equal of any at Epsom Downs.

Circulating among the racing enthusiasts who gathered around the wagering slates was Fernando Limeira, Sorrel. Limeira was not a gambler, but the track afforded him an exemplary opportunity to apply one of his simplest and most ingenious swindles. Before the race, he would approach a bettor and whisper in his ear: "I've learned, confidentially, from the trainer that the winner is going to be number such-and-such. I don't want anything from you in advance, but when the animal wins, which is a sure thing, you'll give me 35 percent of the winnings." If there were five horses in the running, Limeira would repeat this stratagem with five bettors, supplying a different horse's name to each. At the end of the race he would return to the winner and collect for his valuable "tip."

The Grand Prize was about to be run, with ten animals competing. Sorrel had already convinced nine credulous bettors with his "confidential information." He lacked only one dupe to whom to pass the name of the final horse. It was difficult. He had already offered his assistance to two Portuguese and three plantation owners from the interior, and all had turned a deaf ear. Nine of ten was a reasonable assurance of having the winner, but Fernando Limeira detested risk. He was becoming apprehensive; he must find a "customer" before the judge waved his colored flag to start the race. It was then that he saw Salomão Calif, accompanied by his family. The Arab was an inveterate gambler and used the pretext of taking his fat wife and their twin children for a visit to the downs in order to wager enormous sums of money. Sorrel approached the tailor and tugged his sleeve.

"Salomão, how good to see you!"

"Why good? I can't find anything good today," grumbled Salomão Calif, in an ill humor because he had yet to pick a winner.

"Because I have some information from the stable on this race. Scarlet Thunder will win, number one. I found it out from the trainer himself," whispered Limeira.

"What?! I was examining the forecasts and nobody but Panache is going to win this race, number four. I'm betting my last cent on him."

Panache, owned by the president of the Jockey Club, Luiz Gaudie Ley, was without doubt the favorite in the race. He should lead the Grand Prize from start to finish. Fernando Limeira disguised his anxiety, as he had already "sold" number four to an habitué, an old lady in the members' stands. "Don't talk nonsense. Scarlet Thunder is the winner. I don't want you to pay me; you know I don't charge my friends. Make your bet, and when you collect, then you can give me something from the winnings," proposed Sorrel, looking in distress at the animals approaching the starting place.

"I'm betting on Panache and not giving you anything," said the Arab stubbornly, tossing wrapped pieces of candy to the twins, dressed identically, who were playing on the grass.

In near desperation, Limeira played his last card.

"Salomão, you're my friend and I can't let you lose your money without one final word. I'll tell you the truth. Panache really should win the race easily. Even the jockeys were secretly planning to bet on him."

"And?"

Limeira lowered his voice even further.

"Except that the animal woke up funny this morning, and for no reason refused to eat its feed. As you well know, when an animal doesn't eat, it's because he's sick. So the trainer and his friends decided to gull the owner. They agreed to rig the race. He'll let the animal run even so, as the favorite, and bet high on Scarlet Thunder, since Panache was the only horse that could beat him."

The tailor became interested.

"How did you discover all this?"

"One of Panache's stablemen is keeping company with my parents' cook," improvised Sorrel.

It was what was needed to convince Salomão Calif; the Arab ran to the wagering area and placed everything he had on number one. Fernando Limeira walked away in satisfaction, to watch the race from a distance. If the horse won, he would return to collect his "commission"; otherwise, he had no wish to be near any of his "clients."

While the encounter between Limeira and Calif was taking place on the *pelouse,* in the royal box Dom Pedro II, surrounded by counts and barons, the marquis of Salles, who pretended to be escorting the baroness of Avaré, and the fawning viscount of Ibituaçu, was recounting to Sherlock Holmes and Dr. Watson the marvelous curative powers of the waters of Araxá.

"I tell you, Araxá doesn't take second place to Wiesbaden or Vichy. Whenever I can, I spend a couple of weeks there; it does my rheumatism tremendous good. You two should visit the city. I'm sure that Dr. Watson, as a man of medicine, would be impressed by the waters there."

"Perhaps, at some future opportunity," replied Watson politely, wriggling out of the uncomfortable journey.

Standing some distance away, Miguel Solera de Lara and Guimarães Passos were observing the young coquettes decked out in the latest finery from Paris.

"So, Miguel, you're a bachelor and considered a good catch, why don't you take an interest? Just look at those stunners," said Guimarães playfully.

"To be candid, my friend Passos, I find these pathetic exhibitions of feminine vanity ridiculous," confessed the bookseller, stifling a yawn.

The baroness of Avaré was enthusiastically reading to the marquis of Salles passages from the critique that had been published in the *Journal of Commerce* about the soirée in Petrópolis.

". . . they were born to concertantes, as both possess an extraordinary *sangfroid*. It is a pity that, because one is a detective and the other a nobleman, they do not pursue this career, for an uninterrupted succession of triumphs would await them. . . ."

Holmes, happily examining the animals trotting around the track, said to the emperor, "I wasn't aware that Your Majesty enjoyed the races. As you know, it is an ancient tradition of the English royal family. There was even a coarse prank played on our King George, who loved horses."

Dom Pedro, his gaze fixed on Sherlock, shot back laconically, "Filho da Puta."

The monarch's entourage froze, astonished by the imperial swearword, which means son of a whore.

"Exactly, Filho da Puta," replied Sherlock Holmes calmly.

The emperor burst out in laughter, followed by Holmes.

Dom Pedro explained to the perplexed nobles surrounding them.

"Filho da Puta was the name of a thoroughbred that belonged to King George IV. It was so christened by the Portuguese ambassador, a playful man who was a good friend of his."

Sherlock Holmes added, "The prank would have been without consequences, as the king possessed dozens of colts; but it happened that the blessed horse turned into a champion. It won the St. Leger, in Doncaster, and various engravings were produced celebrating its victory."

"Fortunately, only those who know our language perceive the irreverent Portuguese's jest," added the emperor to the small audience, which now was laughing as well, relieved.

The viscount of Ibituaçu, a hopeless sycophant, did not miss the opportunity for flattery.

"Only a monarch of the highest breeding could recount that *double-sens* with such subtlety."

Suddenly, a tumult was heard, and all eyes turned to the entrance. Sarah Bernhardt had just arrived. She was accompanied by Philippe Garnier, who, as rumor had it, besides playing Armand Duval in *Camille* was also her lover. The Divine One was wearing a marvelous blue dress with full skirts and a large flowered hat tied to her chin by a ribbon of the same color. She seemed like a gigantic butterfly fluttering toward Dom Pedro.

"Forgive me for the delay, Your Majesty. I had to make my way through a group of young people who were demonstrating their opposition to slavery. They were carrying placards and singing, turning the protest into a party."

"I hope you were not inconvenienced, madame," said the emperor, mildly put out.

"Just the opposite. They were gay and jovial. I became so excited that I almost joined the group. Philippe tried to intervene, because he was still worried about last night, but of course there was no cause."

"What happened last night?" asked Sherlock Holmes.

"Nothing, merely an unfounded fear on the part of my young friend. He was convinced we were being followed when we left the theater."

"Did you see who it was?" asked the detective.

"No, it was rather dark and he stayed at a distance. It was probably just an admirer. I'm used to that sort of adoration at a remove, but Philippe is overly zealous when it comes to my person," said la Bernhardt, smiling and caressing the actor's cheek.

"Even so, when I saw that mob screaming at the gates to the racecourse, I became apprehensive," said Garnier in his own defense.

"*Chéri,* I wouldn't call these young men, striving in behalf of such a noble cause, a 'mob.' In fact, Your Majesty, be sure to congratulate your daughter for me; I have learned that she's one of the champions of abolition."

The emperor quickly changed the subject.

"The Grand Prize is about to begin. Does Madame Bernhardt plan to place a wager?"

"I would love to, but I really don't know which one to bet on. All the horses look so marvelous," stated Sarah Bernhardt.

Sherlock Holmes offered his assistance.

"If you'll permit me, I can make a suggestion. I attended the showing of the animals, and Scarlet Thunder looked the best to me."

Sarah examined the list of horses.

"I think my dear Holmes is choosing this animal only because it has an English name. As a Frenchwoman, I'm going to stick with Panache," she replied, and opening her small purse she asked Philippe Garnier to place the wager. Sherlock Holmes and Dr. Watson refrained from betting; the others, out of gallantry, followed Sarah's hunch.

Moments later, the horses were running rapidly down the track. A thoroughbred from the Argentine, Rayo de Luna, took the lead, quickly distancing himself from the other animals. The public roared, cheering on its favorites, yelling their names: "Go, Biscaia!" "Run, Saltarelle!" "On, Regalia!" "Now, Bonita!"

The animals rounded the first turn, and little by little Rayo de Luna began to show signs of tiring. Three colts emerged from the pack and came forward to do battle with him: Scarlet Thunder, Bonita, and, running on the outside, Panache. They completed the final turn and entered the home stretch, thundering toward the finish. Bonita and Scarlet Thunder were galloping together, one almost glued to the other, alternating in the lead. The jockeys whipped their sweating flanks with their small crops. The crowd howled in continuous exhortation. Salomão Calif, seeing his horse in that nose-to-nose battle, began shouting like a man possessed, revealing the Arab accent that sometimes surfaced in moments of nervousness: *"Bass him! Go, gurse you, bass him!"*

So entranced were the gentlemen that they didn't notice the explosive advance of Panache, burning up the outside, hugging the wooden fence that adorned the track. Sarah Bernhardt's choice rapidly sped into the lead and still had the wind to distance itself several lengths from its two adversaries as it reached the finish line victoriously.

The euphoric turfman Dr. Luiz Gaudie Ley was already at the paddock, awaiting his glorious victor. As president of the

Jockey Club and owner, he was doubly happy: at bestowing the prize and at receiving it. In the imperial gallery, all were congratulating Sarah on her intuition. The actress goaded the detective.

"You see, my dear Holmes? At least at the downs the French arrived ahead of the English."

"Congratulations, madame. A pity that Napoleon's generals did not have the same good fortune," the detective retorted.

*"Touché,"* replied the Divine One, laughing.

Sherlock Holmes turned to the emperor.

"With your permission, I must say good-bye to Your Majesty. We are on our way out. It was a charming afternoon; I thank you immensely."

Watson and Sherlock kissed Sarah's hand and said good-bye to everyone. As they descended the steps of the gallery, Holmes turned and asked, "Before we return to the hotel, there is one small thing I should like to inquire. How is it possible to see the stables?"

The marquis of Salles offered to accompany them.

"I have free access to the stalls."

They crossed the grass in the direction of the stalls. Inspector Mello Pimenta was waiting for them at the entrance to the paddock.

"Marquis de Salles, what a surprise. I didn't expect to see you here."

"It's been years since I missed a Grand Prize, inspector. As a matter of fact, I have a horse entered in the Southern Cross, in September."

Sherlock Holmes attempted to free himself of De Salles.

"Thank you, marquis. I presume the inspector will take charge of us from here."

Pimenta addressed the detective.

"So, Mr. Holmes, are you finally going to tell me the reason for this mysterious meeting here at the downs?"

"Come, inspector," said Sherlock, crossing the paddock and heading toward the stalls. Mello Pimenta, showing his documents, came close behind, along with Watson. Spurred by curiosity, the marquis followed the group.

As soon as they entered the first stall, Holmes took out his glass and began running it over the wide leather protectors used to prevent the animals from injuring themselves upon entering their cubicles. He ran his hand along them, and his fingertips came away greasy.

"Just as I suspected. . . ."

"Suspected what, Mr. Holmes?" asked Mello Pimenta, excited by this singular research.

Holmes did not reply. Instead, he went to the horse resting in the bay and, with an abrupt yank, pulled one of the hairs from its tail. The colt, taken by surprise, loosed a violent kick, knocking the detective to the ground. Luckily, Holmes was only grazed and the blow was without greater consequences, but the damage had been done. Nervously, the animal began to whinny. One of the stablemen came running, before Mello Pimenta could interfere.

"Hey! What are you doing here?" he shouted, kicking at the Englishman.

Holmes got up agilely, avoiding the punch the man launched at his chin. He raised his guard and positioned himself in a pugilist's stance. He had been a superb boxer since his school days. He threw a quick left jab, but to his surprise the man whirled away and, supporting himself with his hands on the ground, executed a pirouette, clipping Holmes with both feet. While the Englishman tried to regain his balance, the stableman, almost lying on his back, turned in a wide circle, tripping him again, and Holmes fell a second time. Watson and De Salles were about to interfere, but Mello Pimenta stepped forward and interrupted the fray.

"That's enough! Police! Inspector Mello Pimenta; we're here on an official mission."

"I'm sorry, inspector. I thought it was the 'rig gang.' They're always here tormenting us," the worker apologized, referring to the band that lived from cheating on bets.

"Are you hurt, Mr. Holmes?" De Salles helped Sherlock to his feet.

"Do you wish to lodge a complaint about this attack?" asked Pimenta.

The detective straightened his wrinkled clothes.

"By no means. The young man had right on his side; we were the interlopers."

Worried, Watson continued to probe his friend's body in search of a possible fracture. Holmes, recovered from his surprise, was curious.

"I should just like to know what form of combat that is. I've never seen such agility with the legs."

As the stableman was still downcast, Mello Pimenta explained.

"*Capoeira.*"

"*Capoeira?*"

"A method of fighting invented by the Negroes of Angola. I'm amazed that the man would have made use of it before my eyes. He knows very well that *capoeira* is dangerous. We're even trying to outlaw it," the inspector concluded in a severe tone.

Sherlock argued in the fellow's behalf.

"I think in this case we should overlook it. After all, the man was risking his life."

"Risking his life?" said Pimenta dubiously.

"You have to understand, inspector, that my boxing blows are fatal. I have what we call a 'forbidden fist,'" he informed, flexing his fingers.

"Well, we'll let it pass, this time. Off with you before I call the Black Maria," said Mello Pimenta, shooing away the frightened worker.

Holmes returned to the stall, where the colt was once again calm. He caressed the animal's silky withers.

"At least I found what I was looking for. Once again, my deductions were correct."

"May I be informed of what you're talking about?" asked Mello Pimenta impatiently.

Holmes took from his vest pocket a rolled-up hair and, placing it beside the one he had pulled from the horse, revealed his findings in detail.

"When we were at the morgue, I found a horsehair in the clothing of the murdered girl. I saw immediately it was from a thoroughbred."

"How so?" inquired the inspector.

"The grooms normally put a special brilliantine on the mane and tail of the animals to keep them shiny. Notice how both fibers are covered with the same material."

De Salles and Mello Pimenta examined the hairs. Watson, who didn't understand a word of what was being said, waited patiently for a translation. Sherlock Holmes continued.

"It's Mr. Brewster Pomade, especially made on German Street. If you observe closely, you'll see traces of that ointment on all the protectors in the stall, caused by the horses rubbing themselves against the bay."

"Therefore——?" asked Mello Pimenta still not understanding Holmes's reasoning.

"Therefore, the murderer we're looking for either has regular dealings with, or is the owner of, racing thoroughbreds," stated the detective.

The inspector was left openmouthed by the Englishman's impeccable conclusion.

"Mr. Holmes, I think we've taken an important step in our investigations."

"I seriously doubt it," said the marquis of Salles, running the hairs through his fingers.

"How can you doubt it? Mr. Holmes's reasoning is flawless."

"Almost. By feel, one can tell that the essences impregnating the hairs are different. One of them really is soaked in pomade, but the other, the one found on the dead girl's skirts, bears another substance, rougher and less shiny."

"And what would that be?" asked Holmes.

"Resin. The resin that's used on violin bows. As you know, the instrument's bows are made of horsehair, and the horsehair is always coated with resin. The one you found on the victim's clothes was from the violin bow used by the assassin," concluded De Salles, returning the hairs to Sherlock.

Holmes knew when he had been vanquished. Even so, he was not a man to give up easily.

"Congratulations, marquis, you are absolutely right. Of course, I saw that at once and was merely testing your powers of deduction." He tossed aside the two horsehairs.

"Can we go?" asked Dr. Watson, tired of listening without comprehending.

The four men headed for the exit, Sherlock Holmes in the lead, showing total disdain for the trifling error that had brought him to the races. As they passed through the *pelouse*, they were surprised to see Salomão Calif chasing desperately after Fernando Limeira, Sorrel. The distraught Arab, hot on his heels, torn betting slips in hand, was shouting, "So Panache wouldn't eat his feed! Scoundrel! Liar! He ate his and the other horses', too!" And he cursed, out of control: *"Filho da puta! Filho da puta!"*

His bellows were so loud they reached the imperial gallery. Observing the emperor's discomfort faced with such scurrility, the viscount of Ibituaçu, eternal flatterer, dissembled by commenting servilely, "Look, Majesty, someone else also knows the story about the English horse. . . ."

# 19

In this year of 1886, the Public Promenade was quite different from when it had opened its gates more than a century before.

At that time there was in the environs of the Convent of Holy Succor a lake that poisoned the city. The viceroy Luiz de Vasconcellos ordered it drained, thus destroying a pernicious focus of infection. Not satisfied, he decided to transform the hitherto useless and pestilent land into a garden. Thus was born the Public Promenade.

The gardens quickly became the favorite spot of the city's

inhabitants, who would go there for recreation and to appreciate the soft breeze, the sweet aroma of the groves, and the war-
bling of the birds.

At night, on the stone benches beneath the trees, could be
heard the moaning of the guitar, the rhythmic sound of a voice
singing love songs:

> All the songs I know,
> The wind has swept away.
> One alone, that speaks my love
> Is in my heart to stay.
>
> I'm going away, away.
> No, no, no, I'm not.
> Even if my breast departs,
> My heart can't leave this spot.

Facing the gate was a street the people had dubbed "Beautiful Nights," for on moonlit nights courting couples would pass
that way. After some years the poetic name was changed to
Marrecas, after the fountain built there.

Surrounding the promenade along its entire circumference
was a wall that ended in an enormous terrace beside the sea.
The iron gates at the entrance were decorated with a large
medallion of gilded bronze with the Portuguese coat of arms
on one side and likenesses of Dona Maria I and Pedro III on
the other. Under the portraits, in bas-relief, was the inscription: "Maria I et Petro III—Brasiliae Regibus 1783."

The promenade, divided into ten streets lined with trees,
led to a lake located in the center of the garden. The lake
ended in a waterfall, upon whose stones and bushes perched

bronze herons with dripping beaks. In the middle of the falls rose an iron coconut palm painted in natural colors, and at its base two entwined alligators spouted water from their mouths, producing a gentle and melodious murmur. Behind the fountain was a small statue of a boy with a turtle in his hand, pouring water into a stone barrel. The boy was nude and carried a pennon with the words: "Even at play I am of use." It was the Fountain of Love.

Down the pathways, adorned with vases and marble busts, that led from the gates to the immense terrace overlooking the ocean, could be seen stone tables and chairs under belvederes and jasmine shrubs from India.

There still existed, to the right, the old café, of Greek architecture, beside the stand where in good weather a band would perform German music. The bohemian students gave it the highly pornographic nickname that persists to this day: the "Mother's Ass" Café. In the presence of ladies, they referred to it as the M. A. Café or Modern Athens.

In '86, the promenade had undergone major modifications. Rain had ruined the coconut tree at the waterfall. However, it was not time alone that had labored to spoil the effects of the promenade: through indifference and lack of care, the viceroy's successors had failed to preserve the ornamentation executed with such effort and good will. The birds that decorated the falls disappeared, and when King Dom João VI, fleeing from the Napoleonic wars, transferred Portugal to Brazil, the sculpted lampposts were removed to illuminate the palace. As one newspaper said, "The neglect of public administration leads public institutions to a degrading death more quickly than the damage inflicted by the years and the toll of weather."

The garden was still beautiful. The area of more than

thirty-seven thousand square feet, gas lit, had been redesigned with a modern perspective. No more the old regularity in planting; the calculated symmetry of gardeners of bygone times had given way to graceful curving lines, in an elegant and at the same time relaxed imitation of nature. Metal fences had replaced the wall, and through them could be glimpsed garden beds of grass of varying sizes, now covered with flowers. Above the greensward, solitary bushes alternated with groups of trees, forming small copses.

Immediately at the entrance, a sign next to the sentry stations warned the uncivil:

ENTRANCE TO THE PROMENADE IS FORBIDDEN TO HARMFUL ANIMALS OF ANY TYPE, TO INEBRIATED AND CRAZY PERSONS, THOSE BAREFOOT, INDE-CENTLY DRESSED, OR ARMED, AND TO SLAVES, EVEN IF PROPERLY DRESSED, EXCEPT FOR NURSEMAIDS ACCOMPANYING CHILDREN.

ACCESS IS ALSO FORBIDDEN TO MINORS UNDER TEN YEARS OF AGE IF NOT ACCOMPANIED BY A RESPONSI-BLE PERSON TO PREVENT THEIR ENGAGING IN MIS-DEEDS OR ENTERING PLACES DANGEROUS FOR THOSE OF THEIR AGE.

THE PUBLIC WILL REFRAIN FROM REMOVING ANY-THING FROM THE PROMENADE AND FROM ANY ACTION THAT MIGHT DAMAGE THE PLANTS AND DEC-ORATION IN THE GARDEN.

It was through this edenic locale that Sherlock Holmes and Anna Candelária were strolling. The full moon stood out in a sky filled with stars. The two were finally seeing each other

again after several unsuccessful attempts. Taking advantage of
Anna's free day from the theater, Holmes had invited her for
dinner at the Maison Dorée, on Carioca Square, and afterward
had offered to see her to her home. As she lived on Marrecas
Street, when they arrived at her door, Anna suggested they
take advantage of the mild evening for a walk in the promenade. Sherlock was ecstatic, as radiant as an adolescent. He
had discovered a new emotion, and they walked the entire time
hand in hand, something he had never before experienced. For
the first time in his adult life he felt the touch of a woman for a
long period. The soft, warm palm of the girl's hand evoked in
him almost feverish sensations. No longer was he Sherlock
Holmes; he was only an extension of Anna Candelária, as if
those entwined hands were more than the chance encounter of
two extremities. He wanted to remain like that forever, fused
with her. It did him good to forget for these brief moments the
violin, the strings, the crimes, and the flaps of skin. The young
woman was speaking to him in her sweet voice of the wonders
of the locale.

"From my window I can see the entire park. Sometimes, on
Sundays, I stand there for hours looking at the people who
come here to spend the day. It's interesting to observe without
being observed. Some families bring picnic baskets, some
spend the whole time scolding their children, but, since I met
you, what I like most is listening to the sentimental songs of
the guitar players." Not taking her eyes off Holmes, Anna
sang in a low voice:

> One day you may grow tired of me
> And someday you and I may part
> But I pray you let no other

Replace my love in your heart.
What will I do with this longing
At that moment I so dread?
That's why all my tears
Are waiting to be shed.

Holmes, embarrassed, didn't know what to say. His romantic knowledge was limited to a visit to Keats's tomb, in Rome, and to a staging of *Romeo and Juliet* at Christ Church College, at Oxford, in which he had played the role of Mercutio. Juliet had been interpreted by a fat, freckled fellow. If not for the influence of the *cannabis*, he would never pronounce an amorous phrase. The truth is that he lacked experience in intimacy with the weaker sex. How could he have learned to converse with women when he had no sisters and, since his days at boarding school until Caius College, at Cambridge, he had been constantly surrounded by male companions? The most intense feminine contact he'd had was with his housekeeper, Mrs. Hudson. Luckily, Holmes was a man of many resources. He might not understand lyricism, but he was an expert in botany. When Anna Candelária finished singing, he murmured tenderly in her ear, pointing to the landscape.

"Many think these asymmetrical gardens were invented in England...."

"What's that, dear one?"

Sherlock cleared his throat and repeated, even more affectionately than before.

"I said: Many think these asymmetrical gardens are an English invention...."

"And?"

"But they're not, my love. They were first used in China,

during the reign of Long-Teching, and were transported to Europe by the English. Less-informed people think it's an English invention, O passion of my life. . . ."

"I know," said Anna Candelária, intrigued, pulling the detective down on a stone bench under a luxuriant *jequitibá* tree.

"That's right, my love, in Europe it was the architect William Kent who established the first landscape garden, like this one here, in Stowe House. Despite the apparent disorder, the combination of plants is scientific, beloved Anna. . . . The irregular forms led the writer Horace Walpole to write that to Kent 'all nature was a garden.' Isn't that beautiful, my dearest?" concluded Sherlock gallantly, as if he had just recited a love poem.

Speechless at first, Anna Candelária laughed. "You know what's beautiful? It's that I'm dying to give you a kiss!" exclaimed the girl, quickly placing her lips on Holmes's.

The Englishman responded to the caress with surprising ardor. He didn't know he had so much desire inside him. He began to caress her breast with one hand, outside her blouse, while attempting at the same time to find a path beneath the beautiful mulatto woman's ample skirts. Suddenly, with a daring hitherto uncommon in such matters, he found himself panting and asking, "My love, why don't we go to your house?"

"I would very much like to, but I rent a room and the housekeeper is extremely strict," explained Anna Candelária, almost breathlessly.

"Can we go to my hotel?" asked Sherlock, kissing her while lying atop her on the bench.

"It's too far. . . . Don't stop! Don't stop!" whispered Anna, clutching the Englishman ever tighter to her body.

Deliriously, he felt the hot, moist thighs under the heavy dress. The girl's nervous hand ranged over the detective's sex. Even in the midst of their passion, his analytical mind could only reflect on this startling phenomenon: he had never imagined that his member could attain such proportions or become as rigid as this. He nibbled on her fleshy lips and she responded by exploring his mouth with her tongue. They lost any notion of time and space. They no longer knew where they were. They cared little that it was the Public Promenade; the lovers' heightened instincts transformed the vast garden into a bedroom. They tried to rip off their garments to better feel the heat of their bodies and were about to attain climax right there, on that improvised bed of stone, when they were brusquely interrupted by a functionary from the Urban Police Corps.

"Police! You're under arrest!"

The couple arranged themselves as best they could. Anna Candelária was frightened, but Holmes regained his composure.

"Calm yourself, constable. I assure you that we were doing nothing worthy of reproof. We were merely conversing," he stated, stuffing his shirttails into his trousers and furtively attempting to button his fly.

Despite being short, the policeman was irascible.

"You Portuguese are very cheeky. What were you thinking? You have to respect the law. This isn't a colony anymore!" he roared, confused by Holmes's accent.

"You are mistaken. I'm English and my name is Sherlock Holmes."

"I don't care who you are. I only know that I caught you red-handed in an act against public morality and proper behavior. This is the Public Promenade, citizen, not Mother Joana's house!" declared the policeman, using a slang term for a brothel.

Holmes, who was unfamiliar with the expression, retorted, "The young lady's name is Anna, not Joana, and kindly leave her mother out of this."

"Enough talk. We're all going to the station house."

"Not all of us. The girl has nothing to do with what happened. If anything worthy of censure took place, she was merely the victim of my senseless abandon," confessed Sherlock, placing himself protectively in front of Anna Candelária.

The policeman thought of protesting, but as he was alone, and noting Holmes's resolute attitude and above all his size, he opted for a conciliatory solution.

"All right, but if necessary she'll have to testify later."

The detective said good-bye to Anna, who was still trembling, with a British handshake. The girl left rapidly in the direction of her house, before the "dog-killer" changed his mind.

He turned to the policeman.

"Shall we go?"

The policeman took him by the arm and they headed for the station house. Given the difference in height between them, if not for the elegant uniform of the Urban Police Corps it would have been difficult to say who was arresting whom.

Sherlock Holmes had come within an ace of losing his ineffable virginity under the boughs of a leafy *jequitibá* tree in the idyllic Public Promenade.

~

Captain Pina Couto of the fifth district of the Imperial Military Police was in an indescribably bad mood. He had good reason. First, he hated incidents during his night shift; second, he could not tolerate the fame that was beginning to bring the name of Mello Pimenta to greater and greater prominence. And the one responsible for most of that notoriety was none other than the tall, erect Englishman standing before him. The policeman who had brought him in over an hour earlier had explained the circumstances in which Sherlock Holmes had been arrested, but Pina Couto knew full well that, notwithstanding the immense pleasure it would give him, he could not book him. After all, Holmes was a personal guest of the emperor and was engaged in unraveling the heinous crimes of the "Flap Hunter," as the papers were calling him. Much against his will, he recognized that he could not indict Holmes for offenses against public morality and proper behavior. Besides which, when Inspector Mello Pimenta learned of the incident, he would free his "partner" from any imbroglio. Even so, he would teach the detective a lesson. Before Pimenta could interfere, he would keep him in the lockup until morning, along with the veteran prisoners, the rabble of the calaboose. He was no prude, but neither was he about to allow a foreigner, with no excuse, to transform the city's gardens into a forest of satyrs.

"What you have done is very serious, Mr. Holmes, very serious. I can't understand why you didn't at least hire a coupé to drive around the park," said the captain, referring to the elegant rental carriages decorated with mirrors, damask, and silver trim—veritable ambulatory beds—which were advertised daily in the newspapers.

"I have already told you that I have no explanations to offer. Please be so good as to call Inspector Mello Pimenta."

"I have no way to reach him at this hour. I'm very sorry, but you'll have to spend the night in the 'jug.'"

"*Preposterous!*" exclaimed Sherlock in English, not finding the equivalent word in Portuguese.

"I don't know how it is in your country. Here the law is the same for everyone," asserted Pina Couto cynically.

"I assure you that you will regret this imprudent act."

"Pardon my saying so, Mr. Holmes, but it seems to me the imprudent act was yours. . . ."

Pina Couto called the guards and ordered them to take the detective to the jail located in the rear of the station house. Inside the same cubicle, five gigantic criminals waited to greet him with the tender reception reserved for neophyte prisoners. Holmes stiffened when he saw the lawbreakers behind the bars.

"I demand at least a separate cell!"

"The captain said it's right here," one of the guards informed him.

The prisoners rudely called to attract his attention.

"What's the matter, pretty boy, don't you like us?"

"Don't be afraid, all you'll get from us is hugs and kisses. . . ."

They laughed and made obscene gestures in his direction. Sherlock tried to break loose from his jailers, and another guard came to their aid. They went on dragging the detective, who resisted, demanding that they release him. The closer they got to the bars, the more the prisoners bellowed in an infernal din.

"That's right! We want that little beauty just for us!"

At the moment the jailer was about to open the iron door, an order froze him in his tracks.

"Release that man!"

Inspector Mello Pimenta came running down the corridor, accompanied by Pina Couto.

"Are you all right, Mr. Holmes?"

Holmes shook loose the guards who were still holding his arms and walked toward him.

"A sight for sore eyes, inspector. How did you discover where I was?"

"Miss Anna Candelária managed to find me through the station house. I realized at once that you could only be in the fourth, fifth, or sixth district. I was lucky enough to come here first. In fact, all of us were lucky—myself, you, and especially this idiot Pina Couto. I don't even want to think what I'd have done if anything had happened to you," said Pimenta, glaring fiercely at the captain.

"I'm sorry, inspector. It was all just a misunderstanding. When you arrived, I was already on my way to free Mr. Holmes," apologized Pina Couto shamelessly.

Mello Pimenta did not deign to answer. He turned, with Sherlock at his side, and both headed for the exit, while the prisoners in the cell lamented facetiously.

"Come back soon, sweetheart!"

"Oh, what a pity! What a shame!"

"To think we almost had us a fresh Portagee. . . ."

# 20

Finally, after almost two months in Rio de Janeiro, Sarah Bernhardt was saying her farewell to the Brazilian public in the São Pedro de Alcântara Theater. For this finale to a memorable season, she had chosen Racine's *Phèdre*, playing the title role. She had already been to São Paulo, on a brief *tournée*, at the São José Theater, where she had performed in *Fédora, Frou-Frou, Adrienne Lecouvreur*, and, of course, *Camille*. At the theater, the actress had been saluted several times by students of the school of law on São Francisco Square. In their excitement, they had thrown their capes to the ground and shouted in a language they thought to be that of Victor Hugo: *"Pisez! Pisez! Pour favour, pisez sur nos capotes, madame!"* they repeated, not knowing that in French *capotes* meant not "capes" but "condoms." Elegantly, the Divine One had revealed the harmless error and declared to the newspapers before returning to Rio: *"La jeunesse intelligente et génereuse de Saint Paul ne sait cacher ce qu'elle sent."*

It was raining again in the city, which would in no way dim the luster of the event. The last ticket had been sold four days earlier.

Despite the tribulations of the previous evening, Sherlock Holmes would not have missed tonight for anything in the world. He and Dr. Watson would attend the performance from the imperial box. Personally, he felt that Racine could not hold a candle to Shakespeare, but seeing the great Sarah Bernhardt overcame any disagreement. He was finishing his toilet while Watson waited impatiently.

"Let's go, Holmes. It won't do to get there after the emperor."

The detective placed his pipe and a packet of *cannabis* in his pocket. Since he had known Anna Candelária, he had traded the noxious habit of cocaine for the gentle effect of the herb. He took a last approving look in the mirror and left with Watson for the entrance to the Albion.

The rain made it more difficult to find a rental coach. Watson was looking anxiously at his watch, when, in a headlong gallop a calash pulled by two white horses stopped abruptly at the door of the hotel. Out leapt a gigantic Negro, whip in hand, and advanced toward Sherlock Holmes. It was Mukumbe, factotum of the baroness of Avaré. He addressed the detective in an English more than correct.

"Good evening, Mr. Holmes, Dr. Watson. I am happy that you have not yet left."

"What is it, Mukumbe? We're already late. We can't miss the start of the play."

"I am very sorry, sir, but I fear that the two of you are not going to be able to go to the theater tonight."

"Why not?"

Mukumbe came closer to Watson and Sherlock and asked in a low voice.

"Have you heard of *candomblé*?"

"Of what?"

"*Candomblé*. It's the religion of the Yorubas, my people."

Distressed, Watson answered as he checked the time again.

"Never heard of it, and at the moment we have no time to

discuss spiritual matters. The curtain goes up in a few minutes."

He attempted to walk away, taking Holmes with him, but Mukumbe grasped him firmly by the arm.

"The matter is serious, Mr. Holmes. My *babalorixá*, King Obá Shité III, ordered me to take the two of you to his *ilê*. It has something to do with the murders."

"Before anything else, what are *babalorixá* and *ilê*? "

"*Babalorixá* is the high priest and *ilê* is the temple where he's waiting for you."

"And what do you have to do with this?" inquired Holmes, still confused.

"I am *ogã axogum* of King Obá Shité III."

"I still don't understand."

Mukumbe explained hurriedly.

"*Ogã* is the master of sacrifices, who has the cutting hand. We don't have much time, Mr. Holmes. King Obá Shité has received important information from the *orixás* about the monster who has been killing the girls."

Watson was getting irritated.

"Well, tell King Obá Shité that the emperor is expecting us."

He was about to hail a passing victoria when Holmes stopped him.

"My dear Watson, our friend is right. If this matter has to do with the crimes, unfortunately we will not have the chance to applaud Sarah Bernhardt today." He pushed the doctor toward the calash, climbing in after him. Mukumbe leapt into the coachman's box and lashed the animals, who sped off down the damp cobblestones of Fresca Street.

〜

The *ilê* of the *babalorixá* Iorubá Nagô, King Obá Shité, was
at the foot of Gamboa Hill. There, the purest ritual of the
Yoruba religion was practiced. When they turned onto Saúde
Street, Holmes and Watson had already heard in the distance
the beat of drums announcing the rites. It was the day of departure of a "boat," when the priests and priestesses officially
took into their bodies their *orixás,* or spirit guides, for the first
time. The mysterious chanting of the novitiates imbued the
night with a disconcerting tellurian mysticism. Mukumbe
brought the horses to a halt at the entrance to the *ilê.* The three
men crossed the worship site where the initiates, after emerging from the small waiting room, were dancing, attired in the
rich apparel of Xangô, Ogum, Iansã, Nanã, Iemanjá, Oxum,
Oxóssi, and Oxumarê. They continued to the *aperê,* the throne
on which the *babalorixá* King Obá Shité III sat imposingly.

The *ogãs* intoned the final chants, or invocations, of the
Xirê, in homage to Oxalá, bringing the ceremony to a close.
Without a word, King Obá rose and ordered the visitors to accompany him to the *peji,* or sanctuary, a small room to one
side, where, on a table covered by a cloth of white lace, was a
set of whelk shells. The *babalorixá* gestured for them to take
their places around the table and began to spread the shells in
front of him.

"First, I have to see who your guardian *orixá* is, my son," he
explained, alluding to the saints who, according to the Yoruba
religion, govern and protect the life of every person. He
picked up the shells and, in a sweeping gesture, threw them on
the table in front of him, confiding to Sherlock: "You are a son
of Xangô." He picked up a colored string of brown and white

beads and placed it around Holmes's neck. "You must always wear this necklace, my son. Never forget: Xangô is your father. Xangô is your protector."

Then the *babalorixá* gathered up the shells to begin the consultation. He again threw the mixture of shells, stones, and coins, but this time the oracle's tokens fell in a disorderly fashion, as if unable to come together. Concerned, King Obá Shité revealed, "I do not understand. The *orixás* summoned you here, but they refuse to manifest themselves further. I am very sorry, my son. There seems to be some current blocking the flow."

Watson, who didn't understand what was happening, stood up indignantly.

"Mukumbe, tell this gentleman that I'll never subject myself to this witchcraft!" He turned to leave, but before he got to the door his body began to shake, and suddenly the intrepid Dr. Watson, former surgeon of the Fifth Northumberland Fusiliers, was stooped over like an old man, twirling about the room in the traditional posture of the *orixá* Omolu. He whirled around three times and fell prostrate on the floor.

"What's happening?" asked Holmes, startled.

"Nothing serious. Dr. Watson has received the saint for the first time," explained Mukumbe.

"Now he must have his hair cut and his head shaved," declared Obá Shité.

Holmes attempted to collect himself.

"I know that you have the best of intentions, but I can assure you we have no time to practice any kind of initiation ceremony." The detective began shaking his friend violently. "Watson! Watson! Come on, get up, man!"

Mukumbe tried to reassure the detective.

"Stay calm, Mr. Holmes. This is a sign that Dr. Watson is a very sensitive man. He has captured the fluids of the *ilê*. As he was untrained, any entity could enter him. Luckily, it was his guardian *orixá*. It could be worse; it could be—"

Mukumbe was interrupted by a hoarse guffaw coming from Watson's throat.

"—a *pomba-gira*," Mukumbe said, terrified.

"What's that?" asked Holmes, growing more frightened.

The *babalorixá* Obá Shité explained, taking charge of the situation.

"It is a devil-*orixá* in female form, a demon with the behavior of a courtesan. It usually only comes into women or into— is that fellow *adé*?"

"What's that?"

"Effeminate," Mukumbe translated, embarrassed.

"No, he's English."

"Then the *pomba-gira* must have got confused," concluded Obá Shité, shrugging.

Standing up, Watson approached Holmes seductively, hands on hips.

"What an *olorundidum Oibó*," he sighed, breathing heavily on his friend's neck.

Sherlock Holmes's embarrassment was palpable. Mukumbe came to his aid.

"He's saying that you're a nice-smelling white man."

Watson began to scream like a common strumpet.

"What? I want *oti*! I want *itaba*, you shits! And you can light th' *inãs*!" he demanded in Portuguese and Yoruba, without the slightest accent.

Holmes was more alarmed than ever.

"It's unbelievable! Watson never spoke either of those languages!"

"It's not he, it's the *pomba-gira* asking for rum, a cigar, and candles," explained Mukumbe.

The *babalorixá* quickly attended to the request. Watson emptied the bottle of cheap rum in a single swig and took several puffs on the cigar.

"So yuh wan' know whooza zirikila?'"

Holmes deciphered the near gibberish.

"Exactly. We need to know who the 'serial killer' is."

*Pomba-gira*/Watson gave another mocking laugh.

"Ha! Ha! Ha! Ha! But yuh already know th' zirikila. Yuh been with 'im. He wuz right nex' to yuh. Yuh ain't found 'im 'cause yuh've smoked too much *itabojira* in yur pipe. . . ."

Sherlock needed no translation to deduce that the reference was to *cannabis.*

"If it wasn't for the *itabojira*, yuhda already found out why th' zirikila leaves the string and takes th' flap! Ha! Ha! Ha! Ha!" *Pomba-gira*/Watson laughed again and continued: "Th' zirikila is a *okorin* with *owô odara* and he's gonna *kufá* another *obirin* with th' *obété*."

Mukumbe again acted as interpreter.

"She says the 'serial killer' is a man with much money and that he is going to kill another woman with the dagger."

"And why does he do this?"

Watson gulped another bottle of rum and burst into laughter.

"Why? 'Cause th' zirikila is *kolorí*," he declared, and no one had to tell Holmes that *kolorí* was "demented."

*Pomba-gira*/Watson again placed his hands on his hips and bellowed, "Well? I want *menga*! I want *ejé*! If I don' get it, I won' leave!"

"What is it now?"

"She's asking for blood. She wants the sacrifice of a bird before she leaves the body."

"Ridiculous! Watson was always a vegetarian!"

Mukumbe tried again to explain the phenomenon, while the *babalorixá* went in search of the necessary items.

"Mr. Holmes, it was not Dr. Watson but the *pomba-gira* who made the request. Your friend is merely the vehicle for its manifestation."

"Couldn't I ask the name of the murderer?"

"It would do no good. When she asks to leave the body, it means she'll refuse to say anything further. Now, if you'll excuse me, as *ogã axogum* it's my duty to make the offering." Mukumbe took the knife and the chicken from Obá Shité's hands and, holding the bird over the doctor's head, cut its throat.

*Pomba-gira*/Watson laughed and smeared himself with the animal's blood. He rubbed his face in a frightening grimace, and, guffawing, said insanely, "Oluparun! Oluparun!" which in the Yoruba language means "The Destroyer."

With the same rapidity with which the possession had begun, the reverse occurred: Watson dropped like an old coat tossed on the ground, then rose, only slightly dizzy.

"Well then, can we go? It's obvious that nothing out of the ordinary is going to happen tonight."

Sherlock Holmes could hardly believe what he had witnessed.

"Watson, don't you remember anything?"

"I remember perfectly well. We were in this room and that African in a costume fiddled with some shells. Outside of that, nothing happened. I regret having missed the wonderful Sarah Bernhardt because of this lad's hasty enthusiasm."

Holmes desperately tried to awaken his memory.

"Come on, man! Tell me the name of the 'serial killer'!"

The doctor replied coolly: "My dear fellow, I think the tropical sun has cooked your brains. Why the devil do you think I know the identity of that abominable assassin?"

Holmes tried to tell him what had happened.

"But, Watson—"

Paying no attention to him, a haughty Dr. Watson hurried toward the exit.

"Good evening, gentlemen," he said curtly, pulling his hat onto his hair, which was soaked with chicken blood.

## 21

Despite the early morning hour, a gay and noisy band had come to bid Sarah Bernhardt farewell. If three thousand people had greeted her when she arrived, at least twice that number now crowded the Pharoux quay.

The evening before, the farewell performance of *Phèdre* had exceeded all expectations. At the end, the actor Vasques declaimed verses of his authorship written especially for the occasion, the refrain of which repeated in each stanza: "... your name, Sarah Bernhardt!"

The audience couldn't contain itself, throwing hats, umbrellas, and frock coats onto the stage. The French delegation had invaded the stage, carrying an enormous *corbeille* with the colors of France, made of roses, camellias, hydrangeas, and myosotis.

Braving the bad weather, innumerable admirers, with a thundering ovation, had accompanied the carriage that took the Divine One to the Grande Hotel after the show. Cries of "*Viva Sarah Bernhardt!*" and passages of the *Marseillaise* had echoed through the streets until early morning.

Exhausted and moved, wishing to avoid displays at the moment of sailing, Sarah had arrived very early at the *Britannia*, the Pacific Steam Navigation Company steamer that would take her to Buenos Aires. The effort had been in vain. Her admirers would not stop calling her name affectionately as long as she did not appear on the deck. The loving public waved blue, white, and red handkerchiefs.

Among those gathered to pay this final homage to the great actress were Sherlock Holmes, Artur Azevedo, Miguel Solera de Lara, Guimarães Passos, the marquis of Salles, and, of course, Paula Nei, who had been the first to greet her on board, a month and a half earlier, on the *Cotopaxi*.

Dr. Watson had remained at the hotel, attempting to eliminate the last traces of coagulated chicken blood from his scalp. The good doctor still refused to believe the unusual experience that had occurred at Obá Shité's *ilê*. He attributed the incident to a joke in poor taste, stubbornly claiming that someone had put the blood in his hat.

The Heller company had appeared with its entire cast. Anna Candelária confessed to Holmes, "I'm sad."

"Why?"

"This departure reminds me that one day, sooner or later, you're going to leave us. . . ."

Sherlock felt something clutch at his heart. In a peculiar way he had become very fond of this country so filled with contradictions. He touched the *Xangô* necklace that Obá Shité had given him. Furthermore, he knew that, when the moment came, he would deeply regret leaving Anna Candelária. He had an idea.

"Why don't you come with me to London?"

Anna Candelária looked at him for a moment, as if weighing the possibility.

"I don't know, I think it would be difficult. . . . My place, my life have always been here."

Before the detective could insist, he heard his name called in the midst of the tumult.

"Mr. Holmes!"

It was Inspector Mello Pimenta approaching, clearing a path. He was agitated, and carrying an envelope.

"Good morning, inspector. So you've come to see Madame Bernhardt off, too?"

"Actually, I came to find you. I have news," he said, waving the paper.

"What happened?"

"I received a letter from the murderer at the station," he said softly into Sherlock's ear.

Holmes tried to grab the missive from Pimenta's hands.

"No, Mr. Holmes. There are too many people here. In addition, we're going to have further assistance. Obviously, you've never heard of Nina Milet."

"I can't say that I have."

"Who is Nina Milet?" asked Guimarães Passos, insinuating himself into the discussion.

"A young criminalist and pathologist from Bahia who's doing his doctorate here in Rio. He has been of great help to us in several investigations and has become interested in our case. He wants to help us trace the profile of the assassin."

The marquis of Salles, who had joined the group, injected, "An excellent idea. We can meet for lunch at the Lacombe. I'll get the gang together. I think we can all contribute something."

Mello Pimenta was about to say he disapproved of the idea; after all, it was a police matter. But Sherlock thought it a valid suggestion. Given the impasse in which they found themselves, any collaboration, even coming from amateurs, was welcome.

"Then we'll all meet at the Lacombe? I'll see to taking Mr. Holmes," offered Guimarães Passos.

The detective turned to resume his conversation with Anna Candelária, but the girl had drifted away silently, returning to the Heller cast, which had already begun leaving the dock. Holmes tried to call her, but his voice was drowned out by the joyous hubbub of the crowd.

The *Britannia*'s plaintive whistle sounded, giving the impression that the transatlantic ship lamented the hour of parting. Several small launches were still alongside the steamer as it began to pull away. Thrice, the passengers of the small vessels raised cries of *"Viva!"* to the living myth. Finally, they threw their blue, white, and red handkerchiefs into the sea, forming an immense colored carpet in the ship's wake. As the vessel sailed into the distance, Sarah Bernhardt, moved, was waving and holding the Brazilian flag.

~

The Lacombe restaurant was in a two-story house on São José Street. Its menu comprised the most varied of dishes: cashew soup, small birds fried with bananas, tiny oyster pies, squash flowers, taro stalks, turtle eggs, parrots and parakeets roasted on a spit, breast of veal with shellfish, oxtail with lentils, roasted beef heart, stewed goose with fern leaves, venison, frog gravy with lizard, and tortoise ragout. Even so, the truly special dish at Lacombe was snake. Afrânio, the chef, took great pride in every detail of his recipe.

"Snake offers very delicious meat, second not even to the best fish, with which it has similarities. Those who have eaten snake meat prefer it to anything else. The greatest advantage, however, of the use of this meat is its efficacy in curing illnesses of the heart, syphilis, and above all, leprosy, which, if in its initial stages, disappears completely with the ingestion of snake meat. It goes without saying that one must set aside the horror the animal inspires, and even more so the prejudice that its meat is poisonous: it is quite well known that the venom is found only in small sacs located under the fangs. In any case, if the venom is consumed, it does no harm whatever; it is toxic and even lethal only in contact with the blood. It is therefore necessary, before preparing snake meat, to cut off the reptile's head, remove its skin, and then open and clean it. The snake is next divided into pieces, simmered with two spoonfuls of fat and a diced onion; it is then sprinkled with a spoonful of flour, and a cup of water, salt, parsley, peppers, and a bit of grated nutmeg. Allow it to cook close to the flame until done, having added to the sauce two egg yolks stirred into a glass of wine. The meat of viviparous snakes is preferable to that of the oviparous variety, and among the viviparous snakes, the rattlesnake is the most delicate and tasty."

With the exception of Albertinho Fazelli, who ate anything, no one in the gang had ever dared try the appetizing morsel.

The truth is that they went to Lacombe not for the food but for the relaxed atmosphere. The other customers were unconcerned with the noise that the group usually made. They had pushed two large tables together to accommodate everyone. Seated at the head was the guest of honor, Dr. Edmundo Nina Milet. A serious young man of twenty-four with dark, deep-set eyes, a large mustache, and a wide forehead, Nina Milet reminded some of Rui Barbosa; others thought the resemblance lay only in the fact that both were from Bahia. Milet was a pathologist and criminalist as well as a sociologist and ethnographer. He studied the African race and its Brazilian descendants with special attention. Inspector Mello Pimenta began reading the letter he had received from the murderer.

Dear inspector, at the moment you read these ill-written lines I shall be preparing myself to execute much more clearly defined lines in the body of another harlot. What must I do for you to discover me? Must I write my name in full on the whores' carcasses? I thought the Englishman was cleverer than you and would read my clues, but apparently he is so stupid that he should hide his donkey ears under that ridiculous hat he wears. I hope you two are enjoying yourselves as much as I am. Do something soon, for I'm hungry, very hungry, and I still have one violin string remaining. Speaking of remaining, I remain yours truly.

"It's signed 'Oluparun.' "

"Oluparun? What does that mean?" asked Chiquinha Gonzaga.

Nina Milet translated the word that Sherlock Holmes had heard at King Obá's *ilê*.

"It's Nagô Yoruba. It means 'The Destroyer,' 'The Exterminator.'"

"Then the murderer is a Negro," declared Alberto Fazelli, precipitate as always.

José do Patrocínio entered the restaurant at exactly that moment.

"I see I've come at a good time. You speak of someone of my race and immediately assume he's a criminal. Apparently, besides struggling for abolition, we're also going to have to fight for our innocence."

Guimarães Passos related what had happened, introduced Patrocínio to Nina Milet, and added, "You'll have to forgive our Albertinho. You know very well how hasty he is."

Inspector Mello Pimenta continued, as the missive passed from hand to hand.

"In reality this note doesn't tell us much. Only that the man wishes to be discovered."

"He's obviously an educated man, but I note that he was careful to write in a scrawl in order not to be recognized by his calligraphy," stated Holmes, examining the letter. "Did it come by post?"

"No, it was left with a policeman at the station house, by a messenger boy. The boy disappeared as soon as he handed over the envelope."

"He's probably a mulatto," said Nina Milet.

José do Patrocínio grew vexed.

"How can you make such a baseless statement?"

"There is nothing baseless about what I said. It's purely scientific. Read the *Essai sur l'inégalité des races humaines*, by Gobineau, an intimate friend of our emperor. As Negroes belong to an inferior race, the mixture of races leads to the creation of degenerate beings, many of whom are born with a propensity toward mental aberrations and criminal strains."

"Those are the kinds of absurdities that hold back the abolition movement. You should be ashamed of what you just said," retorted an indignant José do Patrocínio, who was already acquainted with such speculations of social Darwinism.

Nina Milet was unshaken.

"My dear man, I know whereof I speak. Studies of phrenology and craniology do not lie. Look at Lombroso, for example: if we followed his theories, we could catch the criminal before he committed the act."

"How?" asked Chiquinha Gonzaga, intrigued.

"By classifying the population by means of phrenology. We know that individuals with criminal tendencies suffer from facial and cranial asymmetry. They have the occipital region predominating over the facial, strong superciliary arches, and prognathous jaws." He paused. "And, like the majority of mulattoes, they possess thick lips and wide noses."

Holmes remembered Anna Candelária and decided to interrupt this nonsense.

"I know these theories well, Dr. Nina, but it seems to me a little hasty to attribute to Negroes and mulattoes the existence of crime. If this were so, London and Paris would be the most peaceful cities in Europe."

Nina Milet proceeded, almost pedantic in his affected way of speaking.

"Mr. Holmes, the mixing of races is no longer a privilege of the New World. Furthermore, I am merely quoting *L'uomo delinquente*. In the same fashion, Lombroso also assures us that individuals with these harmful impulses have a tendency toward epilepsy and other psychological disturbances, such as

246 ~ JÔ SOARES

numbing of the sense of touch, a dulling of the senses of smell and taste, and vision and hearing that alternate between weak and acute. Not to mention the sociological elements, like tattoos on the body, and physiological ones, like ambidexterity."

Holmes turned to Mello Pimenta.

"Then you had better arrest me, inspector. Since childhood I've done everything with both hands."

Everyone laughed at the riposte, which served to alleviate the tension provoked by the criminalist's inopportune remarks.

The inspector tried to be more objective.

"This is getting us nowhere. Let's examine one point at a time. First: what does the removal of a flap of skin mean?"

"A sick form of fetishism by someone who feels a burning thirst for affection," responded the marquis of Salles, paraphrasing the romantic novelist José de Alencar.

"What about the violin strings?"

"They might be just a joke in bad taste," said Alberto Fazelli, who was not endowed with great imagination.

Sherlock Holmes intervened.

"Impossible. He himself insists they are clues left deliberately."

"Why does he only kill women?" asked Chiquinha Gonzaga.

"Because they're weaker," ventured Alberto Fazelli.

"Not all of them," Chiquinha assured him.

"Because he hates them," suggested Paula Nei.

"That makes sense. But does he hate all women?" asked Guimarães Passos.

"Perhaps to him woman is the symbol of the perverted customs that dominate our times," stated Solera de Lara.

"Maybe he's afraid of them," added Chiquinha Gonzaga.

"It's possible. He fears something that they arouse in him," ventured Holmes.

"Or that they don't succeed in arousing," said Agostini, who till then had remained silent, drawing in his sketchbook.

He turned the pad and showed the drawing of a violinist dressed in black. Instead of the bow, he held an enormous pair of calipers for measuring skulls. He wore a necklace made of flaps of skin, and he was dancing on a pile of naked dead women from whose almost hairless vaginas sprouted violin strings coiled like watch springs. His tiny, flaccid member hung outside his trousers. He was such a frightening figure that everyone present stared as if hypnotized. Gradually, they perceived that the monster had the features of Nina Milet. It was the artist's silent protest against the absurd theories espoused by the doctor.

The only thing positive about the lunch was the dessert specially made by Afrânio: the Delight of the Afflicted, a sweet made with chocolate and ambergris, avidly consumed by all, for, according to the chef, it was excellent for restoring the power lost to sexual excess.

## 22

*H*e is alone in the chapel beside his mother's open coffin. Ironically, after long years of feigning illnesses, the crazy old woman had succumbed in a few days to a devastating fever, from smallpox. He feels neither pain nor pity. A sensation of freedom invades his soul as he observes the wasted body in the casket. The Negro slaves had been right, on those nights of black magic at his father's plantation, when in terror they called him, still a child, Oluparun. Like the exterminating angel, he too is the Destroyer. He is one of the seven angels who guard the seven seals of the Apocalypse. He is the shroud of the Great Whore. The Great Whore came to pollute the kings of the earth and thus was able to pervert the emperor of the tropics. Enough. The inhabitants of the earth are no longer intoxicated by her concupiscence. He knows that Oluparun must cut down the woman whose name is blasphemy, the woman always adorned with gold and precious stones and pearls and carrying in her impure hands the cup of execration and the filth of her libertinage. The time has come to slay the Great Whore of this backwoods Babylon. The woman who awoke in him the beast of lust. Now, he and Oluparun and the Beast and the Angel have merged into a single creature. He is the Beast who will become drunk with the blood of the mother of all the whores and abominations of the earth. He is anxious for the moment of writing a single word on her brow: mystery. The Beast hates the Whore and will leave her desolate and naked and will eat her flesh and consume her in the fire, because the Angel has put it into his mind to execute the

*designs of Oluparun. Only then will he cease to be the Beast. The
Angel will love the Beast that was but is no more.*

⌢

That cool mid-July night, the baroness of Avaré, Maria Luísa
Catarina de Albuquerque, finishes reading *Splendeurs et misères des courtisanes*, by Balzac, comfortably ensconced in the intimate study of her mansion in Cosme Velho. As she is not
expecting guests, she is wearing a silk *peignoir* over her delicate
organdy nightgown. From time to time she serves herself a
*marron glacé* or a sip of champagne. The breeze turns a page of
the book. Maria Luísa finds this strange, for she is certain she
closed the door to the balcony behind her. She looks over her
shoulder, and he is there, standing on the terrace. She upbraids
him in surprise.

"You? I almost died of fright! Since when do you come here
like this, at this hour and without being announced?"

He says nothing. He advances slowly into the room toward
Maria Luísa. The baroness doesn't know what to say, seeing
him come closer, somber and wordless. She recognizes that
sometimes the loss of a loved one can provoke curious reac-
tions in people.

"They told me your mother died. I was distressed. I know
how much you loved her."

He does not reply. She stands up and begins to draw away
almost imperceptibly. He continues to approach, step by step,
his hands crossed behind his back. The baroness notices there
is something unusual in his behavior. She tries to jest.

"Don't you know it's unseemly to visit young widows at
night?"

Slowly, he uncrosses his hands to reveal the violin with its single string. He glides the bow over the instrument, drawing out the sad, monotonous sound. Maria Luísa recognizes the Stradivarius and, suddenly, horrifyingly, understands everything. She runs for the exit in search of help.

"Mukumbe! Mukumbe!"

She opens the doors of the study and her scream freezes in the air: atop the balustrade of the stairs leading to the foyer is a silver tray holding Mukumbe's head. His lifeless eyes seem to stare at her in a plea for forgiveness.

He drags her by her hair to the study, the long dagger in his hand. Maria Luísa struggles, fighting for her life, but her efforts are futile before that preternatural strength. She begs, grasping his legs.

"Why?! Why?!"

Her appeals are silenced by the dagger that, with a concise blow, pierces her mouth and penetrates her brain.

He kneels beside her, livid, tears open her breast with the knife, rips out her still warm heart, and devours the bloody organ. He moans in orgasm and his trousers are stained with semen during this macabre banquet.

Maria Luísa Catarina de Albuquerque lies dead at the feet of Miguel Solera de Lara.

He remains there panting beside the profaned body. Without haste, he cuts away a flap of skin and, not forgetting the indecorous gesture, buries the last remaining string of the violin, the D string, or *re*, amid the curly pubic down.

There is still one detail to complete the morbid ceremony. He wets his fingers in the blood spouting from the open mouth and writes the word *mystery* on her forehead. Then he rises and, leaping from the terrace, is engulfed by the sheltering night of Cosme Velho.

Poor baroness of Avaré, the gay courtesan of the palace. Her greatest sin was to awaken, innocently, the pernicious lust of Oluparun.

∼

For Pimenta and Holmes, who were drinking coffee at a table in the bar of the Hotel Albion, there could be no doubt: from the start of the crimes, the murderer had set his sights on the baroness. He had placed himself at risk by executing the victim in her own house. This was proved by the bloodbath that marked his passage. In addition to Mukumbe, he had quickly killed three slaves and two housemaids in order to catch Maria Luísa unawares. And she alone had merited the enigmatic inscription.

"Do you have any idea what it means, Mr. Holmes?"

"If I'm not mistaken, it's a reference to Apocalypse, in Saint John. There is a passage in which the prophet describes the 'Great Whore' with the word *mystery* on her forehead."

"I'm very sorry the madman so misjudged the baroness," said Mello Pimenta, turning his spoon slowly in the small cup.

They were deeply depressed. They had spent the morning carefully examining the mansion in Cosme Velho, without finding anything to aid their investigations. Pimenta had picked up the violin string, with an uncomfortable feeling of relief. Something told him, perhaps mistakenly, that, if nothing else, the cycle of horrible crimes connected with that damned fiddle had come to an end. He had accompanied Sherlock to the Albion in the early part of this afternoon, and neither of them had spirit or appetite to order lunch after seeing the arena of horrors into which the baroness's lovely mansion had been transformed. Silently, they were drinking small sips of coffee when the concierge Inojozas rushed excitedly into the bar. His hair, usually neatly combed, was tousled, and he had not even bothered to apply his mustache wax.

"Mr. Holmes, something terrible has happened. I don't know how to tell you!"

"What is it?"

"In all my years as manager, this has never happened!"

"Out with it, man, say what it was!"

"Your rooms have been broken into."

"How?"

"The chambermaid just told me. When she went to tidy up the rooms, she found the window broken."

Sherlock Holmes and Mello Pimenta, with Inojozas leading the way, headed for the stairs. They leapt the steps two at a time and ran to the apartment. A maid, trembling, her face ashen, was waiting for them at the entrance. Holmes quickly opened the door and went into the room. At first glance, nothing seemed in disorder, except for the double windows that had been forced open and were hanging loosely on their hinges. Suddenly, Mello Pimenta spoke in a grave tone, pointing to the bed.

"Mr. Holmes, look."

On the bed, resting against the pillows, was the Swan Song, the Stradivarius violin stolen two months earlier from the deceased baroness of Avaré. Without its strings, the instrument seemed obscenely naked. There was a short note pinned to the bow, written in a careful and refined hand. Only one word, in English: *good-bye*.

~

Try as he might, Sherlock Holmes could find no further reason for remaining in the city. Beyond doubt he had adapted himself to the indolent rhythm of Rio de Janeiro. He went to sleep late and awoke late, and no day went by without his filling his pipe with *cannabis*. He had definitively forsworn cocaine for the herb. Nor had he dispensed with sugarcane rum—always, of course, with ice, sugar, and lime. However, Dr. Watson's insistence that they return to Baker Street was growing ever more vehement. That was why, with Watson at his side, one day soon after the tragic denouement, he stood with the violin under his arm awaiting His Majesty the emperor, in a small visiting room in the imperial palace at Boa Vista.

The doors opened and Dom Pedro II entered to receive them. Visibly distressed, he looked even older than his portraits. He addressed the visitors in English, in a grave and saddened voice.

"Mr. Holmes, Dr. Watson, I regret that your visit has taken place in such baleful circumstances. I would like to invite you to amuse yourselves for a time in Petrópolis, but, at the moment, the duties of state oblige me to remain at the palace."

"It is very kind of Your Majesty, but we must leave on the next ship. I have come to thank you for your generous hospitality and to return the Swan Song, which was finally located, under sorrowful circumstances," said Holmes, holding out the instrument.

The emperor delicately pushed away the violin.

"Forgive me, Mr. Holmes. The Swan Song would bring back painful memories of my gentle friend. Merely looking at it rends my heart," he explained, surreptitiously drying what Sherlock imagined must be a tear.

"I understand, Majesty. But what should I do? After all, it is a Stradivarius."

"You know that, officially, this violin never existed. To all effects, the Swan Song belongs to José White, who has just left for an excursion in Europe. I ask you to keep the instrument."

Sherlock Holmes was confused by the offer.

"I don't know if I can accept a gift of such value, despite the bloody history connected to it."

The emperor insisted.

"Of course you can; it will be our secret, a remembrance of your time in the tropics."

As Sherlock still hesitated, Dom Pedro continued.

"In Rome, Mr. Holmes, when Caesar returned victorious from battle and the multitude acclaimed him in the parades of triumph, according him the honors of a divinity, he would have a slave beside him whispering into his ear, 'Thou art bald, old, and hast a big belly . . .' His purpose was to remind himself that he was merely human. Humility is the mother of all virtues. Keep the Swan Song as a trophy of the difficult case that you were unable to solve."

Touched, Holmes accepted the violin.

"I am very grateful to you, Your Majesty. One thing continues to intrigue me: the clues that the assassin insisted on leaving. He even addressed the matter in the letter he sent us, but I cannot fathom what they mean."

"Don't torture yourself, Mr. Holmes. Probably, cutting off flaps of skin and leaving the strings where he left them were the tortuous and unconnected lucubrations of a twisted mind," philosophized Dom Pedro II.

"Possibly. The only comfort left us is to know that we've come to the end of the crimes of the mad 'violinist.'"

"Can we be certain?" asked the emperor.

"So it seems to me. There are no more strings, and the violin was returned, so I assume the fury of the monster has been sated," concluded Sherlock dejectedly.

The monarch attempted to raise his spirits.

"Good heavens! Another brilliant deduction, Mr. Holmes. I don't know how you do it."

Before Sherlock could reply, Watson, silent till then, broke in, responding to the sovereign with audacious intimacy, leaving the detective and the emperor stupefied.

"Elementary, my dear Pedro. . . ."

## 23

Anna Candelária had chosen an original place to meet Sherlock Holmes: the Egyptian Room of the National Imperial Museum, which possessed an important collection of authentic mummies from the time of the pharaohs. The first had arrived in 1826, with an Italian antiquarian, Nicolau Fiengo, and the functionaries at the customs office, confused by that singular cargo, didn't know how to categorize the precious baggage. At first indignant, they thought that the funereal objects constituted a lack of respect for the customs authorities, but after much conferring among themselves and consulting of texts and dusty tomes, they finally allowed the mummies into the country, classifying them as "items of dried meat." Upon learning of their arrival, Dom Pedro I waxed enthusiastic and bought them for the recently founded Royal Museum. Later, the museum had been enriched by another important acquisition: in 1876, after a visit by Dom Pedro II to

Egypt, King Ismail presented him with the tomb and the body of the priestess Sha-Amun-Em-Su, from the sanctuary of the god Amun. The priestess had been mummified with arms and legs free, a process that emerged in the final dynasties. There were only three others like her in the entire world. To house her to greater effect, a kind of reliquary had been built next to the main hall. According to legend, a curious curse went with the mummy: sensitive young women, even when not having their period, would begin to menstruate as they approached the girl-priestess Sha-Amun-Em-Su.

Sherlock Holmes caught sight of Anna Candelária in the middle of the hall, beside the bronze statuette of the archpriest Menkhperre. Her dark skin contrasted with the immaculate white of her linen dress. He came up silently behind her and murmured.

"Dear girl, I must tell you that I am fond enough of the Egyptian collection in the British Museum, but I can't understand why you wanted to see me in this indecorous mausoleum."

Smiling, Anna led him by the hand.

"Forgive me, my love, but when I wish to reflect on something important, this is where I come. As you can see, it is as silent as a church, and there is almost never anyone around. Besides that, it clears my thoughts to think about life at the side of those so long dead."

"And about what were you thinking?"

"About your invitation to go to London with you," confided Anna Candelária, lowering her eyes.

Holmes felt his pulse race.

"I hope the mummies have been good counselors."

"I think you're going to hate them and me."

Sherlock tried to contain his emotions.

"You mean you're not going?"

"Try to understand, darling. In London I would be like a fish out of water. How long would our love endure in a strange land?"

"But wasn't this a strange land for me?" argued Holmes.

"It's different. You're a man, you speak our language. Today, if not for the accent, with the habits you've acquired so easily, you'd be taken for a Brazilian."

"Anna, in London you'd be my wife, you'd be Anna Candelária Scott Holmes," the detective declared proudly.

"I have my profession. I'm too independent to be just a wife."

"You could work. The English theater is among the best there is."

"Don't be silly. I don't speak a word of English."

"You'd learn in an instant. And there's something you don't know. I was an actor. I worked with the Sasanoff Shakespearean Company, under the name of William Escott," Holmes confided.

"Is that true?" asked Anna dubiously.

"By all that is most sacred. I have many friends in English repertory companies," declared Sherlock.

"It wouldn't do any good. I'm just starting, and my career is nothing great, but they've promised me a good role in *Zé Caipora*, which the actor Machado is going to begin rehearsing at the Príncipe Imperial Theater," explained the delicate mulatto girl, not realizing the absurdity of comparing the stages of the West End to the boards of the Rossio.

Sherlock Holmes saw that he had lost Anna Candelária forever. He thought of abandoning everything and remaining by her side, but he could foresee that, sooner or later, fate would wrench him back to England. He was devastated. Passion, intransigent, was coursing through his entire soul. He wanted that young woman as he had never desired anything in his life. He had dreamed of living at her side, of hearing her, touching her, sipping her lips, breathing her breath. Still, he knew he must resign himself to Anna Candelária's unshakable determination. The two walked, arm in arm, into the burial chamber of Sha-Amun-Em-Su.

"I leave tomorrow. Will you come to my sailing?" asked Holmes, his voice almost inaudible from emotion.

"No, my love. I prefer to say good-bye now. I don't know if I would have the strength to see you at the quay."

"Then this is good-bye?"

Anna embraced him and said in a low, languid voice, "I don't want you to go away without feeling you inside me at least once. . . ."

"Here?" exclaimed Sherlock, perplexed.

"Why not? We're alone. The guards are elderly men, old soldiers mutilated in the Paraguayan War. They sit at the entrance and never stir from there," she said, trembling in excitement.

Leaning against the priestess's sarcophagus, Anna accommodated herself to him. She kissed him avidly, becoming intoxicated with the heat of his lips. Holmes responded to her kiss with even greater force. A pleasant sensation, warm and damp, enveloped his loins. He pushed away, to divest himself of the clothing that encumbered him. It was then that he saw the reason for that dewy warmth. A large circle of blood was imprinting itself on the whiteness of Anna Candelária's dress. Once again the curse of Sha-Amun-Em-Su had come to pass.

Sherlock Holmes drew back, embarrassed. Although a

savage desire had taken over his body, to make love under those conditions was unthinkable for a loyal subject of Queen Victoria.

He patted his loved one's face and withdrew with the knowledge that he would take back to London his invincible virginity.

~

Only Inspector Mello Pimenta and Julio Augusto Pereira, the marquis of Salles, had come to the embarkation of Holmes and Watson for England. Unlike the gaiety surrounding the farewell of Sarah Bernhardt, the atmosphere was one of melancholy. They were on board the *Kaikoura*, which in a few moments would set sail for Liverpool. Sherlock Holmes was again wearing his heavy English clothing. On his head was the customary hat, and his long checkered cape covered his frock coat. At his side, on the railing, was the violin case. He expressed his gratitude for the kindness of his Brazilian friends.

"Don't forget, when you come to London, there will always be room at 221 B Baker Street."

"Thank you, Mr. Holmes," stammered Mello Pimenta, touched. He knew he would miss this affable and impetuous Englishman.

"And when you return to Brazil, I insist you stay at my house," De Salles offered.

"I am grateful for your kindness, marquis, but I fear that's unlikely."

As they were speaking, a man dressed in black was rapidly mounting the ship's gangway. Four slaves were bringing aboard several trunks with his baggage. Mello Pimenta recognized him immediately.

"Look! Isn't that Miguel Solera de Lara?"

De Salles called his name.

"Miguel! Over here!"

The bookseller approached.

"Good morning, gentlemen. Mr. Holmes, Dr. Watson, does this mean we'll be traveling together? What a happy coincidence."

"I didn't know you were going to England. Is it for a visit?" asked Sherlock.

"No, a move. I plan to live in London."

The marquis of Salles teased him.

"So, you take French leave even when going to England."

"You know very well this old aspiration of mine, and you've even mocked it," replied Miguel Solera.

"Did you always plan to live in England, Mr. Miguel?" asked Mello Pimenta, from curiosity.

"Always, inspector. If not for the illnesses of my poor *maman*, I would have left long since. Now that she is gone. . . ." Solera de Lara explained solemnly.

"My condolences, Mr. De Lara. I didn't know your mother had passed away," said the detective.

"Thank you, Mr. Holmes. Ironically, the nightmare that is the loss of my mother has been transformed into the realization of a dream: to open a small bookstore in London, to live a quiet life and dedicate myself to the study of the classics."

"If you need anything, I am entirely at your disposal. I should like to repay in some small measure the generous hospitality that I received in your country," stated Sherlock.

"I am very obliged to you, Mr. Holmes. Now, if I may, I have to take care of my bags," said Miguel Solera de Lara, taking his leave with a discreet bow.

The group watched as the melancholy figure in black disappeared in the direction of his quarters. Sherlock Holmes was moved to pity.

"Poor man. He's truly downhearted."

"He was completely devoted to his mother. Miguel is a good and gentle man," commented De Salles.

A steward came to say that the visitors must disembark. The *Kaikoura* was ready to weigh anchor. Mello Pimenta shook Watson's hand and embraced the detective, overcome by emotion.

"Good-bye, Mr. Holmes. It was an honor and a privilege to meet you. May your voyage be a good one." And before Sherlock could react, Pimenta planted a kiss on each of the Englishman's cheeks.

The marquis of Salles said good-bye to Watson, and, fully understanding the reasons of the heart, took Holmes by the arm.

"My good friend, a long journey is the best panacea for the pangs of love."

The detective smiled gratefully. Then he took a package from his coat and handed it to the marquis.

"It's what's left of the *cannabis*. Please, keep it. I could never again smoke it without reminding myself of Anna Candelária. To me, she will always be remembered as *the woman*," he confessed, raising the empty pipe to his lips.

The steamer slowly pulled away from port, as if the indolence of the tropics were clinging to its hull. From the deck, Sherlock Holmes pensively fixed his gaze on his two friends in the distance, who were waving from the Pharoux quay. He caressed his old violin case, which now secretly protected the Swan Song. He noticed that, at his side, Watson was making entries in a small notebook.

"What's that? Are you recording impressions of the journey?"

"No, Holmes. I'm finally taking the advice of Madame Sarah Bernhardt. I'm going to start writing about all your cases. The Frenchwoman is right; this lark should bring in a goodly number of pounds. What do you think? I already have a title: *The Adventures of Sherlock Holmes.*"

"I think it's excellent, Watson, but this story taking place on Brazilian soil is the only one you must never tell," said the detective, fingering under his shirt the colorful necklace of Xangô. Inexplicably, a hoarse cry sprang from his throat, in the unmistakable salutation of the *orixá*.

"Kawô-Kabiyèsilé! O great chieftain, permit us to gaze upon Your Royal Highness!"

## 24

*U nder the starry sky of a hot and cloudless night, the Kai-koura ploughs slowly through the ocean. Alone on the upper deck of the old vessel, he breathes the warm Atlantic air. He thinks with disdain of the foreigner who was unable to read the signs, so obvious, of his bloody trail. He smiles. He recognizes that he was playing with marked cards. In England, the notes of the scale are always designated by letters. To the stupid Englishman, the strings of the violin, an instrument he had never had the courage to*

*play in public, were G, D, A, and E. To Latins,* sol, re, la, *and* mi. *In his euphoria he spells to the winds, in the solitude of early morning:* mi *for Miguel,* sol *for Solera,* la *for Lara,* re *for Aphrodite's Retreat, the name of the bookstore, a stroke of genius. Aphrodite. The obtuse investigator hadn't even remembered Greek mythology. The barbaric Saxon didn't know that the daughter of Uranus, born on the foam of sperm from her father's severed genitalia, was venerated by whores and was the protectress of trollops. Aphrodite, enthroned in her concha. The imbecilic detective doesn't know they call the vagina* concha. *"Cunt," as in English itself. He laughs at the play on words. The* concha, *the* vulva, *where he left the strings, glistening with the sweat of panic, in those hairs of sin. All that is left is the flaps of skin. So obvious, the flaps. He guffaws again. Deep inside, he always knew the half-witted Englishman would never link them to him. Flaps. The flaps of a book. Book, bookseller. Miguel Solera de Lara. The poor idiot knew the language well, but he spoke like a Portuguese, for whom such flaps have a different name. He pulls a handkerchief from his pocket, opens it, and contemplates the dried skin that he excised from the four victims. He leans over the railing and tosses into the sea the last traces of his unpunished crime. Finally he feels at peace. He, the redeemed Beast; he, the dark Angel; he, Miguel Solera de Lara; he, the Oluparun. A disquieting thought disturbs his harmony: what if the Messalina hidden beneath some skirt should make the pacified Avatar in him come forth anew? He shrugs, not caring. It doesn't matter. He carries with him the ritual dagger from the pagan rites of his childhood. The cold blade kept next to his belly soothes his spirit. For the last time, he looks at the country-continent where he was born, now tiny in the distance, almost one enormous shadow. Good-bye, Brazil, good-bye, land of the sun. The fogs of Albion await him.*

## THE STAR

LONDON, SEPTEMBER 2, 1888

WHITECHAPEL—Never was a murder practised in such a ferociously brutal manner. The knife, probably long and sharp, penetrated the woman in the lower part of the abdomen and was then pulled upward, not once, but twice. The first cut turned at an angle to the right, cutting the groin and passing over the left hip; the second, however, rose in a straight line through the center of the body, reaching the sternum. Such actions can only have been the work of a madman.


## THE TIMES

LONDON, OCTOBER 4, 1888

To the Boss
Central News Office
London

Dear Boss:

I keep on hearing the police have caught me, but they won't fix me just yet. I have laughed a lot when they look so clever and talk about being on the right track. . . .

I am down on whores, and I shan't quit ripping them till I do get buckled. Grand work the last job was. I gave the lady no time to squeal. How can they catch me now. I love my work and want to start again.

You will soon hear of me with my funny little games.
The next job I do, I shall clip the ladies' ears off and
send to the police officers just for jolly. . . .

Yours truly

JACK, THE RIPPER
London, October 3, 1888

# BIBLIOGRAPHY

Azevedo, Moreira. *Mosaico brasileiro*. Rio de Janeiro: Garnier, n.d.

———. *O Rio de Janeiro*. Rio de Janeiro: Garnier, 1877.

Baring, William S. *Sherlock Holmes of Baker Street (A Life of the World's First Consulting Detective)*. New York: Gould-Clarkson N. Potter, 1962.

Bastos, Sousa. *Carteira do artista. Apontamentos para a história do teatro português e brasileiro*. Lisbon: José Bastos, 1898.

Beanis, H. and A. Bouchard. *Précis d'anatomie et de dissection*. Paris: J. B. Baillière et Fils, 1877.

Berger, Paulo. *Dicionário histórico das ruas do Rio de Janeiro. Centro*. Rio de Janeiro: Gráfica Olímpica, 1974.

Bernhardt, Sarah. *Memórias de Sarah Bernhardt. Minhas duas vidas*. Rio de Janeiro: José Olympio, 1949.

Besouchet, Lídia. *Pedro II e o século XIX*. Rio de Janeiro: Nova Fronteira, 1993.

Brochier, Jean-Jacques. *Sade*. Paris: Editions Universitaires, 1966.

Caldeira, Jorge. *Mauá: Empresário do Império*. São Paulo: Companhia das Letras, 1995.

Caldeira, Pedro Soares. *Questões de higiene e alimentação (Corte do Mangue-Degeneração sanitária)*. Rio de Janeiro: J. Villeneuve, 1889.

Calmon, Pedro. *História de d. Pedro II.* 5 vols. Rio de Janeiro: José Olympio, 1975.

————. *O rei filósofo.* São Paulo: Companhia Editora Nacional, 1938.

Caminhoá, J. M. *Estudos das águas minerais de Araxá.* Rio de Janeiro: Laemmert, 1890.

Carmil, Renato. *Anthropometria. Método para verificação de identidade pessoal. Relatório.* Rio de Janeiro: Tipografia do Jornal do Commercio, 1898.

Carqueja, Ulpiano Fuentes e. *O anedotista ou Leituras para rir.* Rio de Janeiro: Tipografia a Vapor dos Reis, 1883.

Cascudo, Luís da Câmara. *Conde D'Eu.* São Paulo: Companhia Editora Nacional, 1933.

Coaracy, Vivaldo. *Memórias da cidade do Rio de Janeiro.* Rio de Janeiro: José Olympio, 1955.

Couto de Magalhães, José Vieira. *O selvagem.* São Paulo/Rio de Janeiro: Magalhães, 1876.

*Cozinheiro nacional ou Colleção das melhores receitas das cozinhas brasileira e europeas.* Rio de Janeiro: Garnier, 1880.

Cruls, Gastão. *Aparência do Rio de Janeiro.* 2 vols. Rio de Janeiro: José Olympio, 1965.

Dempsey, David and Raymond P. Baldwin. *The Triumphs and Trials of Lotta Crabtree.* New York: William Morrow & Co., 1968.

Diniz, Edinha. *Chiquinha Gonzaga, uma história de vida.* São Paulo: Rosa dos Ventos, 1984.

Doyle, Arthur Conan. *The Complete Sherlock Holmes.* New York: Barnes & Noble, 1992.

Edmundo, Luís. *O Rio de Janeiro do meu tempo.* 3 vols. Rio de Janeiro: Imprensa Nacional, 1938.

————. *Recordações do Rio antigo.* Rio de Janeiro: Biblioteca do Exército, 1949.

Ferreira, Procópio. *O ator Vasques, o homem e sua obra.* São Paulo: n.p., 1939.

Fonseca Jr., Eduardo. *Dicionário yorubá (nagô) português.* Rio de Janeiro: Civilização Brasileira, 1988.

———. *Zumbi dos Palmares.* Rio de Janeiro: Yorubana do Brasil Sociedade Editora Didática Cultural, 1988.

Fonseca, Rubem. *O selvagem da ópera.* São Paulo: Companhia das Letras, 1994.

Freyre, Gilberto. "D. Pedro II, imperador cinzento de uma terra de sol tropical," *Perfil de Euclides e outros perfis.* Rio de Janeiro: Record, 1987.

———. *Ordem e progresso.* 6th ed., Rio de Janeiro: Record, 1993.

———. *Sobrados e mucambos.* 10th ed., Rio de Janeiro: Record, 1992.

Gold, Arthur and Robert Fizdale. *A divina Sarah.* São Paulo: Companhia das Letras, 1994.

Holanda, Sérgio Buarque de. *O Brasil monárquico.* 2d ed., Rio de Janeiro/São Paulo: Difel, 1977.

*O império do Brasil na exposição universal de 1873 em Vienna d'Austria.* Rio de Janeiro: Tipografia Nacional, 1873.

Jorge, Fernando. *Vida e poesia de Olavo Bilac.* São Paulo: T. A. Queiroz, 1992.

Lautréamont, Count de. *Les chants de Maldoror.* Paris: Gallimard, 1973.

Le Pileur, A. *Le corps humain.* Paris: Hachette, n.d.

Leite, Míriam Moreira. *A condição feminina no Rio de Janeiro do século XIX.* São Paulo: Hucitec, 1993.

Lima Oliveira. *O império brasileiro.* São Paulo: Melhoramentos, 1927.

Lyra, Heitor. *História de d. Pedro II.* 3 vols. São Paulo: Companhia Editoria Nacional, 1938–40.

Magalhães Jr., Raimundo. *Antologia de humorismo e sátira*. Rio de Janeiro: Civilização Brasileira, 1957.

————. *Artur Azevedo e sua época*. São Paulo: Martins, 1939.

Maurício, Augusto. *Algo do meu velho Rio*. Rio de Janeiro: Brasiliana, 1966.

Mauro, Frédéric. *O Brasil no tempo de d. Pedro II*. São Paulo: Companhia das Letras, 1991.

Meneses, Rodrigo Octavio de Langgaard. *Minhas memórias dos outros*. 3 vols. Rio de Janeiro: José Olympio, 1934–36.

Menezes, Raimundo de. *Aluísio Azevedo, uma vida de romance*. São Paulo: Martins, 1958.

Monteiro, Fernando. *A velha Rua Direita*. Rio de Janeiro: Banco do Brasil, 1965.

Mosse, Benjamin. *D. Pedro II, empereur du Brésil*. Paris: Fermin/Didot, 1889.

Needell, Jeffrey D. *Belle époque tropical*. São Paulo: Companhia das Letras, 1993.

Ottani, Juan Carlos. *Stradivario: Vida y obra del famoso constructor de violines*. Buenos Aires: Claridad, 1956.

Paiva, Salvyano Cavalcanti de. *Viva o rebolado!* Rio de Janeiro: Nova Fronteira, 1991.

Poe, Edgar Allan. *The Complete Tales and Poems of Edgar Allan Poe*. New York: Barnes & Noble, 1992.

Queirós, Eça de. *Uma campanha alegre (As farpas)*. Lisbon: Edição Livros do Brasil, 1890.

Quérillac, Anne and Pierre Trévières. *Manuel nouveau des usages mondains*. Paris: Delamain et Boutelleau, 1926.

Raeders, Georges P. H. *D. Pedro II e os sábios franceses*. Rio de Janeiro: Atlântica, n.d.

————. *O inimigo cordial do Brasil (O conde de Gobineau no Brasil)*. Rio de Janeiro: Paz e Terra, 1988.

Renault, Delso. *O Rio antigo nos anúncios de jornais*. Rio de Janeiro: José Olympio, 1969.

Rostand, Maurice. *Sarah Bernhardt*. Paris: Calmann-Lévy, 1950.

Ruy, Afonso. *Boêmios e seresteiros bahianos do passado*. Salvador: Livraria Progresso, 1954.

Sarmento, Alberto. *Os crimes célebres de São Paulo*. Campinas: Tipografia a Vapor do *Diário de Campinas*, 1886.

Schwarcz, Lilia Moritz. *O espetáculo das raças*. São Paulo: Companhia das Letras, 1993.

————. *Retrato em branco e negro*. São Paulo: Companhia das Letras, 1987.

Sharkey, Terence. *Years of Investigation*. New York: Dorset Press, 1987.

Silva, Lafayette. *História do teatro brasileiro*. Rio de Janeiro: Ministério da Educação, 1938.

Stidworthy, John. *Serpentes*. São Paulo: Melhoramentos, 1993.

Távora, Araken. *Pedro II e o seu mundo através da caricatura*. Rio de Janeiro: Documentário, 1976.

Veneziano, Neyde. *O teatro de revista no Brasil*. Campinas: Unicamp, 1991.

Verneuil, Louis. *La vie merveilleuse de Sarah Bernhardt*. Paris: Brentano's, 1942.

Vianna, Helio. *D. Pedro I e d. Pedro II. Acréscimos às suas biografias*. São Paulo: Companhia Editora Nacional, 1966.

Wolff, Frieda. *Pedro II e os judeus*. São Paulo: B'nai Brith, 1983.

Woon, Basil. *The Real Sarah Bernhardt (Whom Her Audiences Never Knew)*. New York: Boni and Liveright, 1924.

## ABOUT THE AUTHOR

Jô Soares is one of Brazil's best-known and most-loved cultural figures. His hugely successful career in television, theater, and film has been supplemented over recent years by his entry into the world of books and journalism with the publication of three works of nonfiction and numerous articles in Brazil. *A Samba for Sherlock* is his first novel.

## ABOUT THE TRANSLATOR

Clifford E. Landers is Professor of Political Science at Jersey City State College. His translations from Brazilian Portuguese include novels by Rubem Fonseca, Jorge Amado, Joao Ubaldo Ribeiro, Patricia Melo, Chico Buarque, and Marcos Rey, as well as shorter fiction by Lima Barreto, Rachel de Quelroz, and Osman Lins. He is currently translating the nineteenth-century romantic classic *Iracema*, by Jose de Alencar.